Up Close

*to Liz Porter —
for her encouragement and help*

Up Close

SHELAGH WEEKS

Published by Cinnamon Press
Meirion House
Glan yr afon
Tanygrisiau
Blaenau Ffestiniog
Gwynedd
LL41 3SU
www.cinnamonpress.com

British Library Cataloguing in Publication Data. A CIP
record for this book can be obtained from the British Library

All the characters in this book are fictitious and any
resemblance to actual persons, living or dead, is purely
coincidental.

Designed and typeset in Garamond by Cinnamon Press
Cover design by Mike Fortune-Wood from original artwork
'Woman Eating Cookies' by Pavalance Stelian; agency:
dreamstime.com. Printed and bound in Great Britain by
the MPG Books Group, Bodmin and King's Lynn

The publisher acknowledges the financial support of the
Welsh Books Council.

Prologue

Sucked into a warren of unmade roads, the battered car circled the lanes for hours, and it seemed to the family inside they would soon pass ghosts of themselves. They strained ahead to glimpse their own shadows—a man, a woman and three children careering down the country lanes.

'A crossroads! A crossroads!' Freya sang out, as if the bleak place could reveal secrets. She was seven and optimistic, immune to setback. She believed in magic, in happy endings. Owen, her father, wound the window down, letting the smell of earth and rank hedgerow rush in, filling the car. It was already five o'clock. Jan, his wife, peered out at the signpost that blocked their way, growing at an angle, weeds and grass tufting from its base.

'It's not on my map. There's no place like this anywhere.' She glanced back down at the O.S. map across her lap. The stiff, coded paper draped across her faded jeans, its intricate brown and yellow roads trailing into a debris of sandwiches at her feet. She shrugged. 'We're lost!' At last, she sounded sure of something. She took off the sunglasses that had been perched on her head and slung them onto the littered floor.

Owen could hear rustling beyond the thick line of hedge and trees and, in the far distance, gunshots. It was the sort of place where people disappeared or had accidents, where bodies were not found for weeks. The family had been travelling all day, a journey full of hold-ups, tail-backs, missed turnings and glimpsed accidents. And now the place names—Y Groes Ffordd, Fynydd Betws, Y Mynach—were all alien and indecipherable: none quite as tangled as the clutch of y's and d's etched on the grey post ahead.

'Perhaps we don't exist anymore,' suggested Freya, helpfully.

Owen glanced at his wife squinting at the tangled lines on the map, tracing them, lemming-like, into blue sea. He aimed the car at the most promising and used track. His two older children were asleep, sensibly absenting themselves.

'Abandon hope all ye who enter,' Owen muttered, heaving at the steering wheel so that wild hedgerow pressed in and twigs thwacked the laden roof rack. The fourteen year old woke up, nudged his older sister.

'We're there!' he insisted.

They bounced down a dirt road while Freya sang wispily and out of tune; a song no one recognised. After five minutes they reached a muddy dead end. Nettles rose as high as the car, a swarm of late afternoon midges circled under a tree. The sea glittered from a distance—cold bands of blue and green and grey. Owen rested his head on the steering wheel in theatrical despair before looking up and out to sea. About a mile away, surrounded by a ribbon of breaking waves, an island basked like a great, black whale. The image hung in his mind as he slowly reversed down the overgrown track: along the tunnel of dark hedgerow, past the lonely farm with its cowpats, barking chained dog and barn split open to the sky. All the way, while his family complained, he could see that crisp edge of white and the calm, stranded island.

Holiday

At the end of the world, they didn't so much feel that they had arrived, as that they'd been washed up. Pulling out knives and cafetière from the holdall, Jan said that everything was wrong: they should have been at the cottage hours earlier; they had no coins for the electricity meter; they were too far from the nearest town. She turned to Owen, pushing hair behind her ears in a hopeful, efficient gesture. She was probably assessing the mood of the three children, calculating how they would survive the next few weeks.

'I'll put the kettle on.' She handed him keys. 'You drive back to that garage we passed. See if they've got milk, eggs, bacon, pound coins—and cake. For a treat.'

Cake was her solution to most things. He sighed, not enough to cause an argument, just enough to register his martyrdom. They had been married sixteen years and each holiday was the same—bundles of irritation and strain tossed onto the unstable scales of marriage, so that by the end they would be barely speaking, and glad to return to routine and boredom. It was amazing they still bothered to take holidays at all. The children—Anna, Flinn and Freya—had become alchemists, mixing out of the simmerings of discontent a different potion: the smell of the sea, country walks, pink curled shells and smooth white stones, round and perfect.

'I know you said to pack the milk and eggs. I know it was me who said it wasn't necessary. But couldn't we just improvise: have black tea and tinned soup or something? It's the Middle Ages out there: earth, sheep and peasants.' But even as he spoke, he knew the answer. 'Don't blame me if I never make it back. I'm going out; I may be some time...'

Owen saluted and clambered over the hastily unloaded rucksacks, thrown into the hallway like an improvised barricade. Impossible, he thought, to know in advance what was superfluous, what essential. They had brought too much, and nothing that was truly useful. Wash bags were piled on suitcases, boxes of supermarket tins were stacked on top of DVDs, and a pile of art books and light novels were toppling at the bottom of the stairs. They had pitched their London life into the dingy hallway before country blackness closed in on them. And here their stuff looked incongruous, a clutter of stupid urban essentials. He went outside into the cold porch, listening to his family from a distance, hearing them as if they belonged to someone else. He'd like them if they were not his.

The porch was a tacked-on wooden structure, an owner's afterthought. There were rough wooden shelves full of geraniums, a large window facing out to sea, a door to the garden and a windowed door that led back into the house. Through the small window Owen watched Jan plug the kettle in. She looked so tired when off-guard: childlike, almost. He wanted to go back in and tell her everything was okay, it was just a stupid holiday that they had to get through—only that would not have been the truth. She was bent over, unpacking, and when she stood up banged her head on a cupboard crammed into the space over the worktop. Jan swore and kicked the old table hard, making the faded plastic flowers wobble in their vase. She glared at the noisy kettle, the gloss painted dresser and faded blue curtains. Perhaps it was good he'd escaped, before he was blamed for those things too. Out in the porch, he could hear the thud and creak of the upstairs floorboards as the children explored the tiny rooms. Like a ship, Owen thought, watching Jan rub her temple. We've been cast out to sea on a ship. And when he saw her go out of the kitchen door into the garden, he followed her out to tell her this. She was emptying the full, mouldy teapot left by previous tenants. The house and scrub of garden were perched on the end of the peninsula so that outside, it was even more like a ship.

'Haven't you gone yet?'

'I wanted to say something.'

'What?'

Owen climbed onto the white-painted stone wall and pointed out the shadowy spread of sea to left and right.

'It's strange we ended up here. My great grandfather must have known this place. I was named after him. He fished.'

'You've told me before. You told me yesterday. It's a long way down, Owen. Be careful. You pitching over the side is the last thing we need right now.'

'I'm not going to fall. But I was just thinking, if there were a tidal wave, we'd all be swept away.'

'Always the positive one.'

The children found them, each eager to tell first.

'There's no television,' announced Flinn, as if it were a bizarre joke.

'There must be,' Jan told him. 'There's always a television!' He shrugged and chewed on his nails.

'But there isn't,' said Anna, the oldest, insistent. She twisted her feathery hair around one finger, fixing on her mother, as if Jan could conjure out of the gloom a television set, a fairy cottage, a less austere setting. 'And no shower either.'

'We'll just have to compromise, make the best of things.'

But Owen could see that Jan felt the disappointment palpably, an indigestible lump of present and future complication. The rooms were cold and damp. The oven didn't seem to work. There would be nothing for their children to do.

'I'll try for that garage, try to get provisions. Do you want to come, Flinn?'

Owen's son looked at him as if he were mad.

'Back in that car? No thanks. Even this hole is better than that.'

Jan had found the cryptic advert on-line. The cottage was cheap, and she'd booked an impulse holiday because Owen's plans, as usual, had fallen through. He'd talked about them all going to a Villa in France, but by the time he got around to ringing the woman a second time, someone else had snatched up the place. There'd been a swimming pool, games room and en suite bedrooms. Jan and Owen had suspected this would be the last family holiday (Anna and Flinn said they'd prefer, in future, to stay home) so they'd talked about making the event a memorable one. It was the end of an era. But they kept telling each other it was barely any time since they'd been students together or since the children were tiny and they'd saved to buy their London home (which they managed when Owen's grandfather left him money). And when they got going on the subject, they said it was only yesterday they were children themselves, though Jan's memories of growing up were hazier than Owen's. He said his childhood was packed tight inside him, like layers of rock, and every so often certain bits rubbed their way back onto the surface. Whenever he smelt geraniums he knew what it was to be a talkative boy, straining for his father's attention. Why do I disappoint my father, he'd ask Jan: but Jan couldn't say. Her own mother was a blank; she'd died so young, Jan could no longer remember her.

Owen watched Jan staring glumly at the low stone walls, the sparse grass and bent trees. When she looked up, it was as if she travelled from a great distance.

'Thanks for going, Owen.' She smiled briefly at him before taking the teapot back up the path to the waiting house. Like ducklings the children followed, pressed tight in single file, hurrying from the wind and sea that battled at their backs: Freya, Flinn, Anna—youngest to oldest. Once they were inside he could still hear their voices, flung and tossed like disembodied spirits—Flinn low voiced and monosyllabic, Anna assertive and complaining, Freya whining, or was it plaintive? She was usually plaintive. Owen would have liked to take sanctuary in the draughty porch with its plants and wobbly row of coat-hooks. There was a comforting smell of dog there, even though they didn't own one anymore. Rusty had been sent back to the dog's home after he bit Freya. Owen still missed the walks, the purpose the animal gave to weekends. The wind was making a strange flapping sound. He imagined how Jan might find him, hours from now, frozen and cowering by the front door. Would she begin to love him if he were dead?

Owen sprinted for the car, parked down by the rusty field gate. He wanted to make the blood pump around his body, to feel vigorous again. He could hear, more strongly now, the sea pounding and clawing somewhere beneath the cliff, sucking waves up and dashing them down again, the rush and crash eating away the ground under his feet. If they returned in twenty years' time there would probably be no field, no low stone walls and possibly no cottage either. He gulped stream-water air that iced his smoker's lungs, then fumbled to close his jacket against the cold. In the distance were hills and the faint glimmer of streetlights—garish orange dots amidst a subdued and shadowy green; perhaps the isolated row of houses they had passed (twice) an hour earlier. He yanked open the car door, threw himself in. It still reeked of sick. Up on the chimney pot of the shadowy cottage, a proprietary gull eyed him.

Owen drove, windows shut tight, ignoring the smell. He flicked on Radio Four. Crackles and snatches of words erupted and faded. He fumbled for buttons, frowning, peering ahead down the dark, rutted road. He almost went into a hedge, braked hard and heaved the steering wheel left to take a tight bend he could not remember being there before. The world was scrambling, twisting in on itself. Was Jan punishing him by sending him out? She might have guessed how irretrievably he could spoil the holiday. As the car faced west, Welsh erupted from the radio, voices talking and laughing with confident impenetrability.

Nearly two months earlier Owen had escaped to Venice, taking a group of students on the yearly trip. He'd felt, as he did now, that the meaning of other languages lay just beyond his grasp. June sun had whitened the palazzos and, in the churches and galleries, he'd felt a strange, cleansing coolness.

11

Something important had come to him. He was not exactly sure what he had learned, but it was complex, to do with perspective and the sludge and layering of human existence. At the time, he'd tried to talk to a colleague, telling him he had a new theory about painting, about life, too. Owen thought they'd got it wrong, thinking that truth lay in the clarity you get from distance. By getting up really close to paintings, to life, you have to exist, as the painter does, in the slurs and knots, in the indeterminate. But Chris had already stopped listening. He was pouring wine and trying to make sense of the menu he and the other students studied as intently as any of the art they'd looked at that morning.

Owen later heard a student saying she thought he was having a mid-life crisis. He was never sure if he'd really heard the words, or whether the judgment was his own. He'd shuffled away, peering up at the tangled bodies crowded over the high ceiling, examining through a mirror the twisted and tortured flesh. He'd always thought of himself as a good teacher. He translated complexity, made a bridge to profundity via homely analogy. But it had come to him like a revelation, standing in front of *Massacre of the Innocents*, that he was a sham. His teaching and his life had been a simplification—an avoidance of muddied truth. He'd never been brave—either in classes, or in his private affairs. And that was what had started it.

Somewhere across the fields, Owen heard the eerie clunks and clangs of farm machinery. When he peered into darkness, expecting the headlights to reveal a tractor, there was nothing. Only high banks, a rough verge and the narrow lane. Owen's world was narrowed to the illuminated circles of the car's lights: kaleidoscope shifts of hedgerow or ragged ditches, a mouse scuttling to safety. The randomness was strangely consoling. The car, struggling with the terrain, growled up a steep hill, wheels crunching and skidding on a layer of gravel some farmer must have laid.

'Summer in Wales!' Owen muttered. 'I should have known.' He conjured winter—painted the scene with snow, saw a muffled world with a dead weight of silence. It was a clichéd, satisfying vision, which, if offered in a painting, he'd have rejected. Reaching the top of the hill, he glimpsed sea, a magical sheen of molten grey that spread to the darker sky. He scanned for something else, the smudge of an island, the glimpse of escape, but the car carried him on, surfing the crest of the hill, plunging down into overgrown lanes, past field gates, a crouched church and rushing streams that flowed over the road. He was rolled up in a rural, stagnant past. Only it occurred to him, as he changed gear yet again, that the future is not always kinder, especially when it lies in wait, slowly taking aim, fixing you in its sights.

Perhaps because he was wrapped in thought, Owen found the garage easily, instinctively, as if it was his local. The man spoke in Welsh as Owen emerged out of darkness into the sanctuary of neon light and the warm fug of paraffin fume.

'Pardon?' said Owen, in a voice that somehow gave away Englishness, class, his feelings about the Welsh language.

'I'll be closing just now,' repeated the man in a strange sounding English, jangling a bunch of keys and pointing to the sign on the door.

'Friday,' it read, 'Closed All Day.'

The garage man switched his eyes back to the small television—it was a game show, the married couple absurd to Owen, gesturing and gabbling in Welsh, nudging one another as they discovered that they had got it wrong, didn't know one another after all. Owen watched too. Outside he could hear the wind, the scatterings of rain. Suddenly, the people on the screen laughed in unison, probably at him.

He found the cakes next to the dog biscuits and barbecue fuel. He dithered carefully—rejected the chocolate gateau he fancied, in favour of fruitcake that he thought Jan might like.

'Do you have bread?' he called out.

'Aye,' said the man, pointing out a pile of processed white bread. Owen put the bread, then Danish bacon and factory eggs into his basket. The food had travelled as far as they had, and looked just as tired.

'The rain should stop soon,' said the man. He began turning off lights at the far end of the shop. Owen knew he'd forgotten something from Jan's list and stared hard at the horse pellets, hoping for inspiration. He felt like the character in a story he'd once read to the children—a rhyming shopping list, increasingly scrambled and tangled, causing the shopper to buy a rake, not a cake. Something to boil? Olive oil? It didn't work; he couldn't trace his way back to Jan's original injunction. But he could see her—long dark hair pushed behind her ears, stocky and challenging, lovely olive skin and something deliberate and dogged in her expression. He had once been fascinated by the sturdiness she seemed to possess; now her real self seemed fugitive and insubstantial, barely there.

At the counter he added cigarettes (three packets, for a siege).

'And some mints and do you have beer or lager, mate?'

The man gave him a tin that was warm from the paraffin stove.

'This is the one I drink. That's why I keep it close.' He grinned out at Owen. 'Holiday-makers, eh? You'll have a few good days, a few bad next week. I'm open most days, unless I'm off fishing.'

Back in the car, Owen plunged into the lonely night, swimming the country blackness, twisting through tunnels of darkness. He slowed by the bent, old church, coming to a gravelly halt. There was no one about, no sound except the rush of trees cleaving the night sky. It surprised him to find the oak door open. The lights revealed the usual pale brown of renovation.

On a cold wooden bench he sipped metallic beer and began to roll a joint, carefully ripping off a corner of the OS map to make a roach. He could not stop himself cataloguing:

14

carved roodscreen, Norman nave, twelfth century font, nineteenth century restoration. But surfing and interweaving these automatic, professional accountings (so safe) were other thoughts: family, work, holidays, mistakes. He propped the beer on a prayer book while he fumbled with cigarette papers. The saints and animals, the brass eagle holding up the biblical texts peered down, as he took a deep, consoling drag.

His audience in the dark windows, the crucified, the betrayers and the betrayed—the biblical stories he could name—began to mutter, to whistle and howl like the wind outside. It was uncanny in there, the wrong place to be. Owen slunk out of the great latched door and let it bang hard behind him. The dark yew spread its even darker shadow as he stood, back against the ancient wall, smoking and trying to phone London. The dangerous yew, he thought, that people thought they had tamed by setting church walls around it. Just like sex.

He tapped the digits into his phone. He had expected no one to be in. But he hadn't expected this part of Wales to be beyond any signal. Nothing. All he could hear was the wind and a lone dog barking. Over the weedy skunk he smoked— given to him by a student—he caught the rank smell of something else. He could not make it out. But leaving the place, he saw the low lying church was almost flooded, surrounded on all sides by over-spilling streams and dark ditches filled with the oily shine of stagnant water.

'It's awful!' said Jan as Owen slammed back through the door. He thought, at first, she meant the cake he was placing on the table. He swallowed the mint he was crunching.

'It's all they bloody had.'

But as she stood, fingering the tacky Formica on the wooden draining board, she gave a wave (that might have included him) toward the living room with its swirly orange carpet, horse brasses and glass coffee table. The complaint lay deeper.

'I didn't expect it to be this original!' she said bitterly, noticing at last the unappetising cake. 'There's nothing here: no dishwasher, a few coat hangers upstairs, the oven doesn't work and even the grandfather clock has stopped.'

'But you chose it because it was old...'

'Only because you messed up booking that villa. And you lied. Said you'd phoned her when...'

'I did fucking phone!' He rummaged in his jacket pocket for the map and realised it had fallen out. The children erupted down the stairs, slicing through the argument.

'Ugh! Dad!' said Anna 'That looks sick.' His daughter poked disdainfully at the cake, perhaps calculating calories.

Flinn picked it up, put his nose to the wrapper. 'Smells of beer,' he said.

'Get your face off it.' Owen grabbed the cake and banged it back down on the table. The stoned feeling was abandoning him. 'If you'd just driven two hundred miles, you'd be grateful for any cake to eat.'

'You didn't drive two hundred miles,' insisted Freya, in her lispy voice. She pushed her finger into the cellophane so that it made indentations. 'Mum drove too.'

'I'm going to unpack,' said Owen, dumping the plastic carrier bag on the table and banging his head on the low doorway as he went out.

'The beds are lumpy,' Jan shouted after him, 'and it's no smoking.'

'I don't smoke,' he called back down.

They ate a greasy, unsatisfying meal.

Freya pointed out the cobwebs draped over the low beams, the spiders everywhere. 'I don't want to go upstairs. I don't want this holiday. I want to go back.' She huddled on the leatherette settee while Jan ineffectually tried to make things nice: unpacked, tidied, scooped away the most offending ornaments. But however hard she tried to shut the floral curtains, they would not meet; an exposed band of blackness slashed into the room. Anna, her back

16

determinedly to the window; read aloud to Freya from a handwritten leaflet:

The holy well, set beneath the cliffs, can only be reached at low tide. BEWARE OF ATTEMPTING TO CLIMB DOWN WHEN THE TIDE IS TURNING. There have been numerous deaths along the coast from cliff walking. Legend has it that a priest's ghost still haunts the fields.

'Legend has it,' added Anna, 'that the priest waits for a London family to take him back in their luggage.'

Freya buried herself deeper under cushions.

It was nearly midnight. Owen was making the beds, shouting instructions no one could hear. Jan was vacuuming—stabbing the attachment up at the ceiling, sucking up spiders and centuries of dust. 'I'm hoovering up the ghosts as well,' she was assuring Freya, when the grandfather clock, which they all thought broken, whirred into action. Freya emerged from the cushion and counted.

'The spirits of the place are sending us a message: we are not to be vacuumed,' said Anna. She was flicking through a magazine of celebrity break-ups, true-life anorexia stories and tips on how to make your sex life more effective. Jan dumped the hoover behind the settee, said they should all go to bed.

'Before you're swallowed by time?' Anna blithely asked as she pushed aside her magazine and extracted Freya from the cushions. 'Come on scaredy-cat. Let's get you to bed.'

At about 3 a.m. Owen woke, wondering where he was. He was sweating, still in a dream. He could hear the priest's voice accusing him of treachery, other voices whispering in agreement. Gradually he identified the sloping roof, the shadows and the sound of a radio. He lay there a while, the face of the priest vivid and hard, hissing voices filling his head, like the rushing of trees. He was in this room because Freya was sleeping with Jan. Flinn snored a few feet away. Owen could have touched the boy's orangey straight hair growing in defiant tufts. His soft features were just taking the cast of manhood, but asleep he was still Flinn the silent,

Flinn the gentle. Flinn who did not read books. Flinn who preferred machines. Anna, in her curtained recess off the landing, safety pins pinning the heavy drapes to secure her privacy, was more like Owen than Flinn had ever been. It was her burbling radio talking to the darkness, to the loneliness that pressed in on them all.

Owen hauled himself out of the soft bed, aware of his lower back aching and of sweat turning cold under his T-shirt. He felt his way along the rough wall to the alcove and then crawled under the dusty, velvet curtains, intensely aware of the slope and smell of old floorboards. In the dark, listening to Anna's gentle breathing, he soft-groped for the radio he could hear but not see. He turned the knob the wrong way and a blast of drum and bass erupted like a sentinel's alarm. He flicked it quickly back, the noise still reverberating inside him. But no–one stirred, no-one else woke. He crawled his way back under the dusty curtain while Anna started to mumble, the words the tip of a dream that kept swinging her, this way and that, in the arms of the night.

Next day they decided to go to the beach. Huge clouds hung low and the wind flapped at the sheets hanging on the line, (Freya had spilt tea in bed) but the light had a pale intensity that boded well. They would take a picnic, Owen said, play ball, splash in the sea. Anna and Jan looked doubtful. By the time Jan had made sandwiches, packed the buckets and spades (weren't her children too old for that now, she wondered) by the time she'd rummaged for towels, books, windbreak, washed up the breakfast things in cold water and made the beds, she remembered again how she hated the seaside, hated family holidays. Flinn and Anna were arguing. Freya had disappeared. Owen, who was meant to be preparing that night's meal, was following butterflies down the high bank, cross-referencing them against the book his mother had given him for Christmas. She could hear him calling out improbable women's names, excited as a child.

'Vanessa Atlanta!' he yelled. 'Cynthia Cardui!'

Freya poked her head out from the disused pigsty and when she saw it was only her father calling, disappeared again.

They drove back inland and took the road that wound down to a span of beach. The lanes and banks were speckled with wild flowers. The sea glinted. In the distance, a flat island with skirts of white foam spread itself at the entrance to the bay.

'The sea!' said Freya, and then voicing what they all thought: 'Your island, dad!'

'Too small,' disclaimed Owen. He seemed relieved, Jan thought.

Tourists dawdled through the village, taking photos of bent houses. People were in the middle of the road, or leaning over the quaint, arched bridge.

'It's a twee film set,' said Anna.

'The sea, the sea,' sang out Freya, bouncing up and down on her seat until Anna held her down.

'Why didn't you bring my proper cricket set?' accused Flinn. He eyed the bats small children carried. 'I'm not playing cricket with a plastic thing.'

The village houses faced in on themselves, their backs to the wind and the ocean beyond, a defensive huddle of wagon-train lives circled against threat. Owen said he knew how they felt. The village stream, speckling its way past the simple houses and under the bridge where children sloshed in wellies, was unaware that around the next bend it would be sacrificed to the unforgiving Atlantic.

Jan watched Owen struggle with the windbreak. He'd wrestled it out of her hands when she couldn't make the poles stay upright, muttering something about the wrong angle. So she felt a mixture of satisfaction and sadness as he failed to make camp. Each time he forced it into the soft sand, the windbreak stood for a moment, then gently fell backwards. Other holidays, Owen had followed the puritan example set by his father. Windbreaks were for sissies. You burnt. You froze. You strode off for adventures down the

19

beach, scrambled up cliffs and found your way back via sand dunes or fields. You did not encumber yourself with poles, canvas and the trappings of the holidaymaker.

Jan hated these echoes from Owen's past. She caught glimpses of something forced and unhappy. Something antagonist to accommodation and to women. She didn't know when she'd first thought this, nor when things had gone wrong between them. But it felt like all the oxygen of their relationship had been steadily sucked out. And now that the children were bigger and she'd been given some gulps of time and space, it was all too late. She couldn't have borne another holiday where they all played inept football to keep warm, then went home once they were scorched by the sun. This year, she and Anna had demanded the windbreak. Anna had said she would not come if there was nowhere to change, Jan had said that she could not bear the cold—nor the sun. She wondered why she had never said this before.

Owen had found a rock and was hammering at the pole, saying he wished he'd not bothered with the windbreak, the circus-tent. He was furtively looking at the other camped families, tents and windbreaks erect, no doubt wondering how they did it. Jan, Anna, Freya and Flinn stood with bags and picnic things hanging from their arms. As the third effort keeled over, Flinn put down the picnic bag and took control. Assembling clusters of weathered rock to support the poles, he made a camp that everyone quickly huddled into.

It was cold on the beach. Fine sand blew in their faces. The wind whipped off the sea. Jan attempted a pencil sketch of the island, huddled under a towel. Owen, perhaps remembering those rare moments when his father had played with him—challenged Freya to a game of French cricket. He ran off to the sea, white legs flashing while Freya, also in shorts, dashed after.

Their voices, thinned by the wind, came back faint as they ran at the water's edge. Flinn watched enviously for a bit, then drifted off to sit on a wall and assess the tractors chugging up and down, dragging boats across the beach to the sea. Anna, squinting back at the little town and car park, announced, 'I'm going to the shops. See you.'

Jan could hear Owen shouting 'Well done!' with grim enthusiasm each time Freya hit the ball. Like an increasingly tired dog, he went padding across the wet sand in pursuit of the red dot she batted this way and that. Jan looked down at her picture, then up at the island. Shutting her eyes she could hear a pee-wit, pee-wit sound somewhere near the sea's edge. On her lips she tasted salt. Her face was already satisfyingly taut from wind and sea. When she opened her eyes and looked at her picture, she could see nothing, none of this reality—just a false and pretty surface. She screwed up the paper and shoved it in the picnic basket, then closed her eyes.

While Jan and Freya ate sandwiches boxed inside the windbreak, Owen went off to buy a paper.

'Checking my stocks and shares,' he told them. 'Think I'll invest in sun-making machines. They'd be a sell-out in Wales.'

Freya, licking the salty knees drawn up before her, stared blankly at her father.

'If you did have stocks and shares,' said Jan 'I'd have cashed them in and we'd all have gone to Venice with you.'

Owen stared for a moment.

'It rained.'

Owen had to queue to use the only phone-box and waited while someone with a Birmingham accent made arrangements to visit a grandchild. He thought he would keep his own voice low. He had just dialled when Anna rapped on the glass side.

'Who are you phoning?' she mouthed, as if he could not hear her perfectly well.

'Wahida,' he lied. 'See if the cat's okay.'

'Since when have you liked the cat?' she scoffed back, opening the door, as he cut off the call. 'I bet you're phoning work. You can't keep away from it.' And she fixed him with a searching and critical look.

Anna went to spend the money Owen had given her while he hid in the local church—a tiny, private sort of place, with a low Norman doorway tilted at an angle. From outside, it seemed as if one Herculean push might topple doorway, tower and dusty hymnbooks onto the sloping beach below. The building squatted just above the tide-line on an uneven bit of land. Sand blew across the gravestones and into the nave when Owen opened the blackened door. Inside it was quiet. The world standing still. Light flooded from clear glass windows and he could see, framed beyond them, a seagull hanging in the sky.

He flicked through the leaflets and books piled on the table next to a wooden honesty box. He read that the church was part of a pilgrimage route and that nearby was an island with so many buried saints, the place was once thought as sacred as Jerusalem. He climbed up onto the edge of a wooden pew and stared out of the window to the flat island. It looked too small for monks and pilgrims. And the sea seemed calm enough, though the leaflet said currents were dangerous: boats sank, people drowned: sometimes, the prayers muttered in this church were the pilgrims' last before final baptism. Perhaps the island he could see was not the pilgrims' one. He carefully folded the leaflet and pushed it into his pocket, then pulled out his mobile and tried London. Even if a connection had been possible, in this vault the signal would probably not have penetrated. The walls were as thick as a prison. Out of the corner of his eye, near the doorway that led to the tower, he saw a swish of black, like a priest's robes.

'Hello,' he called softly and moving across to the dark opening, peered up into the blackness. He could see nothing.

On the way home, they were all unhappy for different reasons.

'Wrong way, Dad. It's left here.'

'I'm cold!'

'Why can't I go to the disco? I'm sixteen. I can walk home...'

'I feel sick.'

'What's for dinner?'

'I hate you.'

'You were supposed to make it. Perhaps there's nothing.'

'He's looking at me again. Tell him mum.'

'I feel sick.'

They stopped the car briefly, changed places, wound down windows. In a field a tractor towed a sharp-toothed blade that turned and curled black earth. Seagulls, like some patchy feather cloak, spread in the vehicle's wake, and rose up into the air to wheel across the sky, then dip down to the ground, savaging insects, worms, each other. Owen, arm resting on the open car window, imagined soldiers rising from the ground, as though in the Greek myth. And then he thought of the children he produced who populated his world with the same ferocious rapidity.

'It's a small gully mounted plough,' said Flinn. And they all looked at him. 'Gully mounted,' he repeated. 'I'm going to watch a bit more.'

And they left him there, a lane or two from the cottage, waving goodbye, receding into distance. Just before they turned left down the last lane, Anna saw Flinn climb up onto the gate and the tractor halt. The picture stayed in her mind—Flinn on the gate, poised as if for a rodeo ride. Back at the cottage they spilled out, still arguing.

'I'm not God. I can't make the sun shine.'

'I've said I'll make the bloody dinner.'

'What can happen to me in a village disco?'

'I feel sick!'

Jan was struggling to make the car boot stay open while hair whipped across her face and into her open mouth.

'For God's sake, carry something up to the house!' Her voice was flung by the petulant wind, missing her family and depositing itself, instead, on two old people planted by the front door. They had appeared, as if from nowhere. She loaded herself up and hurried up to the porch. They introduced themselves as the owners.

'We thought you'd like some cake,' said the woman, offering a greaseproof wrapped bundle to Freya. The woman and man were old, perhaps in their seventies, perhaps eighties. But they were robust, too, standing there with the wind tugging at them, as if they relished its flap and the tang of salt air. The man was wiry, with a handsome aquiline nose; the woman plumper with a pretty face and wavy white hair. 'We always come to see how people are settling in, if there's anything they need.' She spoke as if she was translating the words—her accent odd and thick, unlike any Welsh they had heard so far. The man said nothing, looking across at his empty barns and pigsties.

'We know it's a bit basic, here,' the old woman said, 'but it's better than it was. We had no electricity till the sixties. No water, either.'

Jan put down bags, caught Anna's eye, warning. She fixed on Owen next—silently urging him to complain, hoping he would know that she wouldn't.

'My husband biked up to the village well to fetch water— for drinking and for boiling the nappies.'

'You had a child, here?' Jan asked, registering what a feat it must have been, to cope with washing all those nappies and sheets in such primitive conditions.

'Six,' the woman said with an edge of superiority. 'Five girls and one boy, all in this house. Our son runs the farm now.' And she nodded across the fields to a distant white house, a new bungalow, a cluster of outbuildings and barns. Jan could feel the old man's discomfort, his boredom with the Londoners. She wished her children made a better show—that Freya would stop idly kicking the wall, that Anna would stop glaring.

'Huw will be wanting to mend the oven for you, I expect.' She introduced her husband whose eyes were fixed on the bits of crumbling wall.

'Thank you,' said Jan. 'Come in.' And she felt all the oddity of inviting people into what was once their own home. Owen, fumbling for the key, looked at Jan. Neither knew how to thrust the alien language of consumer rights into arms that held out cake.

Mrs Evans paused on the doorstep before leaving. She had wound up the clock and shown how the hot water could be encouraged. Mr Evans had set the oven to rights.

'We didn't expect you until today, see. When I rang your husband he said you would be coming late Saturday, not Friday. We would have done a clean through.' She shook her head, perplexed.

Jan looked quizzically at Owen. He frowned, as if concentrating on something important. Mrs Evans looked from one to the other, perhaps understanding how it was possible to live together yet never communicate the vital.

Jan noticed how the woman somehow 'fitted' the cottage, whereas she, Owen and their children were filling it up, demanding too much space. Even her family's emotional complications and confusions were too unwieldy. Mrs Evans looked around (wistfully, Jan decided) and took in the piles of books, scattered magazines, hairbrushes and vacuum cleaner still not put away. Jan was not sure if she was critical or interested in their different and messy world. Anna plumped down on the sofa, fiddling with her straw-like hair, sulkily plaiting the ends. Mrs Evans directed her a look that contained, Jan felt sure, vestiges of impatience.

'If your girl has fixed on the disco, I'll make sure my Alun gets her home safe. There's not much else on for the young ones. My son always brings back Alun and the others who live up the lane.'

Anna stopped plaiting. She scrutinized the woman who stared back with an equally critical eye.

'You were in that craft shop, weren't you? You were the one who told me about the disco.' What Anna didn't add, was that all old ladies looked the same to her. She'd assumed—when she'd been in the shop earlier and people asked where she was staying—that knowing everyone's business was a feature of country life, along with cow-pats and unfashionable clothes. The old lady smiled dryly, as if she read the unspoken.

'I'll send Alun up with some eggs,' she said, briskly. 'He can introduce himself to you. And then there's Bethan, up the lane. I told her to come and say hello to your youngest.'

Freya looked alarmed.

Flinn came tramping back in an hour after the Evans had gone—just as Jan was getting worried. He was muddy and satisfied, talking farm technicalities, as if he had known these things for years. The family drank milky tea and silently cut slabs of Mrs Evans' wonderful chocolate cake. Crumbs spilled onto the table, their laps and the floor. In the oven, jacket potatoes hissed. The galley kitchen sent its hot, cosy beams of light into the dusk, like a temporary beacon.

This was their pattern. Freya spent mornings, afternoons and evenings with the girl in the cottage just beyond their paddock. Flinn cranked off each day, on a rusty bike (found in the corner of the barn) and helped Alun and his father on the farm.

'I'm thinking of agricultural college,' he confided to Jan one morning, before opening the door onto pale sunlight and a raw, guttering wind. Anna had become one of the crowd—helping in the beach shop, lounging on the sea wall, impressing local girls (and boys) with her nails, clothes and ignorance of rural life.

Jan and Owen, without the cement of children, were startled by each other's proximity. Sometimes they did not know what to talk about. They tried going for long cliff walks and often saw Anna, shrieking at the sea's edge, playing beach games or draped around Alun. This particular morning, they had attempted a difficult and steep climb across the peninsular edge; the wind blew strongly, the path often seemed unclear and, in one place, the route plummeted into sea. They were forced to climb up through the heather and brambles, then slide and scramble their way back down again. Jan said she was glad the children were not with them.

Coming around a bend, puffing and exclaiming at their unfitness, they saw, far below, a secret, tiny cove: yellow wet sand, a thin waterfall tumbling down, like crystal, only two people walking across an expanse of wet and lonely sand.

'Paradise.'

'Paradise would be warm.'

'We could have our picnic there, if we could get down.'

'It looks like you can only get to it at low tide. Look, they must have walked around that headland; they'll have to hurry up and go back—the sea's creeping up.'

The two of them watched the couple gazing into the caves and rock-pools. Jan peered. She pulled the binoculars roughly from around Owen's neck, put them to her eyes and trained them urgently on the tiny people acting out their little drama.

'It's Anna—with some boy I don't recognize. It's Anna.'

Jan broke away and stumbled on along the path, beginning to shout as she did so. Her voice was shredded by the wind, broken into useless fragments that scattered all around her. Owen began to shout too. Both of them, their backpacks, the binoculars, clumsily banging up and down as they ran, breathless, shouting. Jan's breath was coming out in short, sharp shrieks, the sound like a bizarre and alarmed tropical bird.

The sea, its white breakers beautiful and restful was unrolling up and up the beach—a carpet of fizzing white, dragging behind it the Atlantic ocean. Down there, the two had their backs to the narrowing space between headland and glassy sea. The girl had her hand on the boy's back as they both looked down into some shallow pool.

'Have you got your mobile, Owen?'

'No signal. I tried when you went for a leak.'

They stumbled on. Once, Jan caught her foot in a knot of bramble. As she shot forward, precariously close to the sheer cliff edge, his hand caught at her, dug fingers into her arm, vice-like, pulling her back. The hand shook. Despite the strong grip, Jan could feel, through Owen's skin, an animal-like palpitation. His breath and words came in short urgent gulps.

'Get closer. Throw stones.' They scrambled on, the bumps and jerks of baggage accommodated, moved with as if part of their anatomy. Jan, asthmatic, was now behind Owen, whose lean torso, bent forward, was scuttering over the paths as agile as the dirty sheep angled on ledges, staring at them with startled yellow eyes.

The path led back inland. Owen halted, assessed the lethal gradient straight ahead. Jan noticed his hesitation, then saw him bound out of sight back inland. Seconds later, she watched stones and boulders flying over bushes and over small trees out into the sky. When she found him, she realised that he was pulling at the rocks of a house, or maybe it was a hut, a shepherd's hut, ruined, with trees and bushes growing out of it. Sheep, startled by him, were trying to scramble out of the gaps at the back. As she too started to haul at smaller rocks, earth wedging down beneath her nails as she clawed at the stones, she noticed one sheep throwing itself again and again at a window that was too desperately small for its woolly body. Down in the cove, Anna and the boy were kneeling beside the rock-pool, tenderly poking its innards with a long stick. But if only they'd look up, they would now be able to see Jan and Owen, hurling the boulders, heavy, sharp, clacking on the cliff edge as rocks caught and spiralled onto soft sand down below. The deafening of sea and wind acted like a mute, but Owen kept up the bombardment, bound up in some atavistic action for survival.

When Owen exhausted the first supply, he returned for more. Now Jan saw, through the binoculars, the boy look up and casually touch Anna on the neck—a gentle and sexual gesture, revealing and intimate, that made Jan at once concerned (Anna was only sixteen) and embarrassed that she had observed something so private. The boy—whoever he was—helped Anna up and turning, gestured casually at the sea, the delicate sea fingering grey rocks at the foot of the headland, spreading out in a shining shallow lake. Jan waved, shouted nonsensical warning shrieks, pitching them out past seagulls hanging in the void, only metres away. She had given birth to this child making a sound like a trapped and lowing cow. Would she watch her die making the whooping sound of some other distressed bird or beast?

The pair below had set off at a lolloping run across the beach by the time Owen returned. They now paused on their way across the cove, backs towards Owen and Jan, to look out at the sea and take a careless kiss. Up above, Jan cursed their nonchalance; her mouth was dry, her chest constricted, her throat rasping sore. Would they make it? Did the boy know the coast well? Was there a next headland, more coves where they could be trapped? Owen had brought bricks this time—part of the chimney—and he persisted in chucking them down, still shouting, still trying to get his daughter's attention as she floated across the beach. It was barely five minutes since they had first caught sight of Anna, yet it felt like the world had turned upside down. Anna—whom Jan had snapped at only that morning, might die, while they watched, useless and impotent. Jan was biting at her finger until it hurt, her brain receiving, yet making no sense of, scrambled, oblique messages. A memory of her past had been triggered and messed into the nowness—some race lost at school, her throat burning, the physical and emotional pain of public and private humiliation. And curled within this memory was something else—the erotic and salty taste of youth and new love. Owen was swearing—fuck—shit—fucking shit, as he threw the bricks out into nothingness. They were both caught, separate, yet roped together in this never-ending fragment of time.

Just before Anna and the boy reached the shallow water at the headland, swirling around their legs as they paddled through, Anna looked back. She stared for a moment at the debris raining down from the cliff, the two dots on the cliff's edge, one waving. The boy had halted, was examining the entrance to a dark cave, as if he might be tempted inside. His back was to the rushing, frothing sea that lapped at Anna's calves. Anna looked at the people on the cliff, then down at the water getting deeper moment by moment. She grabbed for the boy's hand and pulled at him urgently, making him see what she had been shown. He looked out to sea, then down at the frothing water. He let Anna pull him away and the two danced along the ragged edge of sea, making for a cove beyond, two young and vital animals, foolishly believing they were too young to die.

'We should have done something sooner,' said Jan the next day. 'She might have drowned, got pregnant, disappeared.'

'In that order?' enquired Owen, sounding more flippant than he felt. He offered Jan his hand, helping her to jump down from the bank where she had been pegging up sheets (Freya had spread mud and horse muck from her shoes across the bed when she'd stretched out there to read). 'We can just thank God she didn't drown,' and as he saw Jan's face, accusing, he added, 'and girls get pregnant in the city just as much as in the country.' Owen looked out to sea, at the dinghies far out in the bay. 'There's not much we can do—people have to be careful. We'll just have to talk to her.'

And as he walked back to the cottage, past the duck pond, he crossed the fingers on both hands: one for Anna, one for himself. Behind him, the sheets set up a rhythmic thwack-thwacking in the wind.

Owen asserted that cliff walks were a bad idea. Jan could go shopping or something; he needed to work—to complete some research, finish the book he'd been writing ever since he'd got the lecturing job. People were beginning to talk— and not just about his lack of publication. He dutifully sat outside, sheltered from the tug of wind, huddled behind the bent and weathered hedge that defended this stretch of garden. Around him he stacked his art books, the Burlington magazine, a monograph on Ribira, his notepads and pens. But each time he opened the new monograph on Tintoretto, the one he feared would say everything he'd been planning to write himself, his mind began to empty. He was aware of insects, the stray bleat of sheep, a buzzard circling overhead. The sun (which on the beach gave no warmth) was unbearably hot in this arbour. When he squinted at the blank sheet of paper and attempted to write, the heat melted away meaning and understanding. His ideas, like spilt water, seeped into the dry, cracked earth. The sky spread above. He lay on his back, opening his eyes to immensity, to everything and nothing.

And he let himself remember. The blueness and islands of cloud became a room in Venice. A room with a simple bed, a desk and a cracked mirror in which he could barely see himself. Lying with the spiky grass beneath his shirt, he could smell polish, the garlic and tomato sauce cooking in a kitchen far below him. He half wanted to be back there, half wished that Venice would sink, taking its paintings, cafés and calles into oblivion. He got up and left his books to prowl about the cottage, listening for the clock, as if its random tick, its perpetual cheat of time were a signal of hope. From the cottage window, with its view of hills and sea, he saw paved streets, misty rain, that tiny room. Venice in June.

It was a strange family holiday, all of them split up, going about their own business, but it was probably their most harmonious. Sometimes, when Owen went on solitary walks to churches and holy wells, he thought he saw Jan in the distance—astride a fat little pony. She was a blob of black, winding up the hillside, like a monk on a pilgrimage. The image of her (or perhaps someone like her) would stay imprinted on his mind for years—and sometimes even haunted his dreams.

Half way through the second week—the middle of the holiday—they heard of a market on the far side of the peninsula. Freya and Anna wanted to go. When they got back to London, markets would be boring, but for now they were an adventure. Jan was washing her hair. Owen, outside, spread an OS map he'd found at the back of a drawer across the picnic table. Sheep were grazing in the field to the side of him and cows and a scruffy pony moved in the field beyond. He sucked in air, like he might inhale a Marlborough. The map showed three islands, two in the bay and one somewhere to the west, hidden away behind distant cliffs and out in open sea. He poked at crenellated brown lines, worn from decades of fingers sliding across the folds of paper.

'That's it. That must be the pilgrimage island.'

Suddenly, Jan appeared in the cottage doorway, soapy hair piled on top of her head, foam trailing down her face and back.

'Now the fucking water has stopped working. First it went all brown. Then it dried up altogether.'

He rose reluctantly; wishing that Flinn had not already left for the farm. 'What can I do?' he asked, thinking of the island.

'What can you ever do?' she shouted, squashing her eyes shut as the soap stung.

He followed her to the downstairs bathroom where she dripped over the carpet and pale yellow sink. He ineffectually twisted at both the taps.

'Useless!' she said 'Don't you think I've tried that?'

From behind a veil of black, wet hair she flung at him the London arguments they had both packed: she had no money, no status; she did all the domestic work; she was the one lumbered with the child care. He did not reply but trudged out to the car where he kept water for the radiator. In the kitchen he boiled saucepans because the kettle had stopped working that morning. He took the warm water in—sloshed it in the sink. She did not even thank him.

'I don't think you're very fair,' he said.

'Fair?' she cried out. 'Since when did fairness come into it? All you ever talk about is your career, your book, your trips to Venice. When do you ever ask about me?' She bent over the cracked sink, wet hair dripping down her night-shirt, inhaling the smell of lavender shampoo and her own sweat. More in self-pity than accusation, she went on, 'And if I stop cooking, cleaning and running around for everyone, this family falls apart.'

But that was only the London truth. She struggled to find anything to complain about here. She had stopped making packed lunches. No one made beds any more. They wore the same dirty clothes each day and the vacuum cleaner still lay behind the sofa. She turned toward him, about to say something, and caught her head on the edge of the tap. Tears mixed with the water, the soap.

'But you've got a job,' he said clumsily, attempting to help her, dabbing at her face, her head with the white towel. Eyes still closed, she flung back.

'Walking two miles to a kitchen shop? Being bossed by Saskia? What about my career, my painting? The only chance I get to put a couple of pieces in an exhibition you swan off to Venice and make it impossible.'

She had hit a nerve.

'Why are you always so fucking emotional?' He could hear the echo of his father's voice—but could not stop himself. 'And it was you wanted children, anyway,' He turned to shut the door so Freya would not hear his betrayal.

'I should have realised I had one already.'

'What?' he asked, suddenly roused. Her red eyes and wet hair pulled back from her face made her look old. He came closer to deliver his own taunt. 'If you were a real artist you might have produced something good by now.' For a moment he thought she was going to hit him, but then she turned away.

'Bastard,' she muttered softly to herself. 'You know how to really hurt.'

In the living room the grandfather clock was chiming. Mentally, they counted. Nine not ten, they both registered; the clock reminding Owen of his mother's house, Jan visiting in the university vacations, when they had first been lovers. He looked at his watch. He'd said he'd phone London before midday, had not even registered the grandfather clock was slow again. On its face were beautiful pictures of sailing ships, blue waves about to break, cherubs puffing and delicate gold italics stating North and South. Owen hurried past, noticing how the billowed clouds were growing darker day by day. Upstairs he thought he could hear a plaintive siren voice, singing faintly. Anna never sang. Freya was already outside. He called up the stairs more sharply than he meant.

'Hurry up, Anna. We're waiting for you to get a move on.'

The voice, if it was a voice, became the whistle of wind. A door crashed shut.

When he came back in with the last kettle of water, seeing Jan take a breath, he said, 'I think I'd better go.'

'Go where?'

'I'm making things worse. You're better off alone.'

'You're leaving?' She had wrapped a white towel around her head, but water was dripping down her neck and across her shoulder. He reached across and gave her a dry one from the pile. 'You're going back to London?'

'London? What do you mean?'

'Why does this make me feel adrift? So stupid?' She shook her head, as if surprised by what had come out earlier.

'What's London got to do with it?'

'You said you're going home early. Leaving.'

'Don't be stupid. We're on holiday! Or, do you want me to go?'

'I'm sorry,' she said. 'It's no good.' And he didn't know if she meant the plumbing, their arguments or the marriage.

'You're still handsome,' she said, at last; one of those illogical and irrelevant twists he found so difficult to follow. He helped her rinse off the last of the soap and remembered how, when they were first together, he had helped, in just this way, dye her hair blue for a student dance. She kissed him. Gently.

When they made love on Sunday mornings (the only time they had, these days) Jan sometimes pretended she was having an affair with Owen or that he was her doctor or her

34

priest; she had not been to church for years, but could remember the quiet administerings of Father Rowthorne, the sureness of his touch as he wiped the communion cup. As he flicked his eyes over her, she'd sensed something hidden. As though he was performing for his congregation, but keeping his real self in reserve, a self that was too intelligent, too critical. Sometimes she imagined that it was Owen having the affair; once, so she could feel tender, she'd given him a terminal illness. But now, with the door bolted against the world, he became the old Owen and a new Owen, too. Much later, this remembered moment—even as she tried to censure it—would visit her as she woke beside other men. They were pulling their clothes back together, the argument washed away, surprised by themselves, embarrassed in case anyone heard, when Anna hammered on the thin door.

'What are you doing in there? I need to do my face,' she shouted, rattling the knob.

Outside it had transformed into the first really hot day. The air was thin, the sky and sea bleached of colour. In the distance, like a great cloud, something white hung across the sea.

'Whatever it is, it's getting closer,' said Flinn.

Owen squinted out, beyond the scrubby field of sheep and the distant headland.

'This could be one of those apocalyptic moments. Perhaps we need to start running.'

'It's a sea ghost!' Jan said, imagining the cloud billowing over the rough ploughed fields until it enveloped and ate them. Anna said she'd pack her umbrella. In the car Jan and Owen held hands, as they had in the beginning. Freya and Anna scrambled in, then out, because they'd forgotten things: make-up, purse, fluffy toy, sun-cream. Still holding Jan's hand, Owen revved the car and pretended to drive off. Freya, in the doorway, holding a teddy that was really a rucksack looked worried. Anna, sauntering down the path, gave a V sign. Owen watched his two fair-haired daughters in the driving mirror.

35

'Anna will soon be as old as my students,' he said, to no one in particular.

Through the open window, the smell of thyme came thick from the banks.

'It smells of Venice. There was a woman, selling bunches of herbs. I bought some.'

'Why didn't you bring them home?' Jan was smiling at him.

'I gave them away. I'm sorry. I should have brought them for you.' Owen sighed and stared out at the sea. Some dinghies, like delicate moths, were passing the distant headland.

A goose honked them off as the car bumped down the drive with the family packed inside. The sun shone, the sea shimmered for them. Jan was fingering the dusty bit of lavender Owen had just picked her. She wondered if tranquillity could be transported, like holiday fudge, to sweeten their London life. They made it to the town without arguing or going wrong once. Freya sang songs, staring out of the window for glimpses of ponies, an island, choughs, the sea.

My beese Mary Ann wed-dee breevo,
An Dahv-ith uh gwas thim un yach.
My-ur bah-bahn un uh creed un cree-oh,

She sang as they flashed by holiday cottages with surfboards and wet suits piled up, signs offering bed and breakfast, fresh crab or new potatoes. Anna, after a pitying glance at her sister, plugged herself into a CD player. She stared out the window vacantly, occasionally mouthing lyrics, closing down the outer world of family to focus on the smell and feel of the new boy's skin, the touch of his hands.

In the market town it was still 1955—a setting for post-war family drama. Only the double-parked cars and clothes gave away the real decade. People talked in Welsh, queuing for carrots covered in earth and strawberries weighed straight into brown paper bags. Pots of homemade jam lined the rough wooden shelves of small shops. Anna bought lavender bags and a knitted tea cosy—things she might have binned in London. In the ice-cream shop, she exchanged a satisfying fragment of Welsh for a toffee crunch.

'Diolch,' someone called out, the voice threading after her. In the market square, Freya, as usual, asked for a doll in cellophane with a bottle and nappies. Owen had gone off to find a bookshop, disappearing up a steep street flanked by pubs and antique shops. Jan, watching him go, thought he looked pursued. She pulled out money for Freya and smelt the lavender stuffed in her pocket. She could still smell it as she bought Freya a paper parasol, exquisitely painted, probably by an underpaid child in the third world. The sun was burning the backs of their necks yet when they turned a corner they could see, out in the estuary, that mist had swallowed up the tilted boats and tractors, had even erased the distant islands.

Standing in the telephone box that smelled of urine, Owen paused with his hand over the receiver. He did not want to spoil things. He did not want to make this call. If only things been different and Owen's grandfather had never moved to England, he might have grown up here. He might not have gone to London or even to Venice. And in that case, he would not need to make this call or find out if a girl in London had told him the truth. But as he looked out on the emptiness of the sea-side town with its cheap bric-a-brac shops, he knew he'd probably have made the same mistakes wherever he'd lived.

Outside a child scraped the metal of her spade along the pavement. Owen frowned as it cut at his thoughts—I'm digging my own grave, he suddenly thought. He watched, as if it was a normal event, a man trying to pull a collared cat with a lead up the street. Then he dialled. The London number.

While he waited, he flipped over a calling card lying on the black shelf. Aphrodite, it read. Available Tuesday and Wednesday. Discreet massage only. Just near here, he thought, this woman would offer me sex. One day, perhaps, he might need an Aphrodite. More honest than living a lie. The phone was ringing—ringing too long . He hoped no one was at home. But suddenly it was picked up. Not her voice. Someone else—a girl. Breathless. She had been running.

'Sorry!' the young voice apologised. 'I was in bed.'

It was nearly midday.

'Is Beth there?' He attempted to deepen his voice, put her off the scent.

'Is that Owen?' the stranger asked, knowing, impertinent.

'Is Beth there?' he asked again, forgetting disguise. Worse than he had thought. Rumours spreading.

'I'll get her,' said the voice and there was a long gap when no one came. Then:

'Why haven't you phoned? You said you'd phone.'

At the sound of her voice, he felt, all over again, the cocktail of excitement and exasperation she always produced. He wanted to stay in the phone-box, hearing her voice, imagining her cluttered room with its art books piled up and postcards blu-tacked to the wall.

When he finally blundered out of the phone-box, he turned left into a narrow alley. He fixed on the uneven cobbles, the plastic sandwich wrapper tossed in the gutter. People were going to find out. Maybe not for a while, but soon. He needed to get back to London. Victorian houses were leaning over the cobbled lane. On one side of the street Alcoholics Anonymous stretched its upper floors across to caress a beer-making shop with hops and pint glasses in the window. Half way down the street, a pub nuzzled up to a Baptist church. He could see now, quite clearly, that he had stepped from one side of a line across to another.

Like an apparition, Anna was suddenly there. She rose up out of a shop doorway set below some steps. In the window were wooden toys: pull along cars, nameplates for doors, a Noah's ark with animals neatly paired, safe in their flooded world.

'Dad!' she said. 'I thought you were with Mum!' And then as she saw his face, 'Have you rowed again?'

'Certainly not!' he said with the only certainty he had left. 'I need something to drink!' Not bothering to see if she followed, he led the way to the worn steps of the pub.

The thick white mist enveloped them as they drove slowly home, compressing distance and perspective. They veered from left to right, hedges coming at them when they least expected it, appearing with a vividness and clarity that was startling.

'This is what driving in London fog must have felt like,' Owen murmured, but no one answered. If they undid the spell of concentration, anything might happen. At each cross roads someone wound down a window and listened, straining to see and hear other cars, while damp, soft air pressed their cheeks, like delicate kisses.

Yards from the cottage, coming around the last snake bend, as they had begun to relax, a red van appeared out of nowhere, materialising in the middle of the lane. Owen braked hard and they jerked forwards like puppets. They were aware of butterflies dancing along the hedge, the twigs and branches vivid, while in the car everything was frozen, even as papers moved. The map on the dashboard was sliding—but only in slow motion—down to the littered floor, while the car kept skidding inexorably on. Anna grabbed for the seat in front and slung her arm out to protect Freya, but walloped her sister in the stomach. Freya yelped at the same time as they hit the van, ramming the bumper and slewing both it and their own car at right angles in the bend. The van bounced forward, giving no resistance, easing the impact, as if the handbrake had not been on. But they felt the thud of impact as if they had all been shot. The noise sounded out in the stillness of mist and countryside.

'Dad!' They could hear, in Flinn's calm voice, accusation, suggesting he would have driven differently and saved them from this latest disaster. And although this incident, unlike the others, was not Owen's fault, they all somehow felt that he was the cause of their continued bad luck and, especially, that he should not have been drinking at lunch-time.

The postman found them examining the two broken headlights. He dumped the bag of letters on the road and went to look at his own van. He dismissed the marks and dents on the bumper, saying he wasn't sure which were old ones and which new.

'It's a bugger, these country roads, you'll be finding!' He did not acknowledge any blame, but gave Owen his details and took the ones he was offered. 'You should be staying off the roads when it's misty.' He was rummaging in his bag and pulled out a letter. 'Owen Griffiths?' He handed him the package and everyone looked amazed that they had been found so easily.

'Who did you leave your address with? Who's writing to you?'

Owen stuffed the letter in his jacket pocket.

'They said they'd forward details of a report I have to write.'

'But it's hand written!'

Flinn, Anna and Freya said they weren't interested in driving anywhere. The mist had settled, thickened each day with reinforcements from the sea, blanketing them in short-sighted silence, becalming them in the cottage and fields around. Owen was morose and withdrawn—they all thought it was the accident. Sometimes Jan walked down dripping lanes or crossed drenched fields to an abandoned church. The snort of a cow, close by but hidden, made her jump, as if something stalked her.

They had been in North Wales a life-time—two weeks. Their London world had begun to feel insubstantial or invented, a thread they could snap and not even miss. On Sunday Owen and Jan tramped across the steep fields that led towards the mountain. They were scrambling up the steep path so Jan could make a sketch of the abandoned church. Owen would not let her go alone.

'Too isolated, too hidden,' he had fretted. 'It might be dangerous. You never know what sort of person hangs out there.'

She had scoffed, packing her pencils and pad into the canvass bag. But the seed had been planted. She was afraid. Let him come, then, she thought. And they set off together, striding out because, at last, the mist was thinning. They could finally see where they were going. When they arrived, they lingered in the overgrown graveyard. Owen started to look for his great grandfather's grave. He tore aside weeds and grass and scraped at lumps of earth and stone. Jan barely listened as he read out the names: Evans, Williams, Jones, Davies, Himmel. She was watching birds that flitted in spots of sunlight between the trees. That's what I can't get, she thought, life and movement—perhaps I can't really draw or paint at all.

When they scraped open the worn door, it felt cold and dank inside. The vaulted roof and pale yellow slabs of stone seemed even more decayed than they had been two days before. Jan no longer wanted to draw. They moved around disconcerted by some smell or atmosphere the church seemed to hold. The past was hung there: birth, death, denunciation and decay, all rolled up. Owen stood at the altar, church guide in his hand. Jan guiltily stuffed a curled postcard in her pocket to remember the place when they were back in London; she had forgotten to bring money to pay for it again.

Tracing her finger around the stone rim of the font, Jan thought that for centuries, babies must have been baptized there, must have wailed at the first touch of cold water. Then this place, too far from real roads, had been bypassed, cast aside by travellers and congregation.

'Have you ever been baptized?' she asked Owen, suddenly remembering her own scrolled and coloured certificate carefully glued in the front of her dead mother's photo album, although she was not sure where that album was any more. She could not imagine Owen's agnostic father giving in to the ritual of white gowns, vicars and family assemblies, whatever Owen's mother might have wanted.

'Only by fire,' he replied, wanting to make her laugh. But she did not. She saw his awkward look, his inability to carry off the joke. He looked away.

'In what way?' she asked, fixing him, reading his unease. He looked at the naked altar, the Norman pillars, the rows of plain wooden pews, then back at her.

'I've had an affair.' The words had been sucked out of him, as if the church had need of confession or the heat of guilt. He started to mumble something—about not wanting to spoil everything. 'I was going to tell you when we got back. I was going to tell you.'

She let the words settle, stared at the cracked windows, the uneven rows of black wooden pews, then stared back at him. Like a boy he was; a foolish, stupid boy. She noticed his lip twitch and saw that he seemed appalled. At one window there was a flutter of wings and a bird dipped across the nave between them and up into the vaulted ceiling. A nest was up there somewhere, beside apostles and gargoyles. She did not know what he said next, did not know if she replied. There was a plaque with something like the name he searched for near the font. She could not speak.

'It was nothing—a stupid one-off thing. She was a student. I don't know how it happened.'

She stared at him hard, working out how much of this was true.

'That's why you've been trying your phone all the time! When Anna was down in the bay drowning, you were up on that hill phoning someone.'

'That was before we saw Anna, Jan. I wouldn't have…'

'But you were trying to phone her?'

'Only to tell her it was over.'

Jan scrutinized him.

'Liar.'

She tore ahead of him down the rough track—loose stones tumbling and shooting sideways. Once she almost fell. He caught up, reached out to help her and she slapped at him, as if he were an insect buzzing. Across the fields, drawing closer and closer to the distant cottage, he had to jog to keep up with her. All the while he kept up a flow, like a sermon, of apology and confession. He thought if he could slow things down, talk to her before she reached the house, he might have a chance she would listen.

'Which one?' she asked once, briefly stopping, rounding on him with the loaded question. The name seemed to confirm something, satisfy her in some way. And she set off again, with him in pursuit.

Inside the cottage Jan locked herself in the bathroom. She sat on the wobbly chair and fixed her gaze on fake plastic tiles covering one side of the bath. Owen knocked on the door.

'Jan, Janet—please open the door. Please.'

She half wanted to snort a laugh; she had not been a Janet for years. Owen posted a note under the door. Jan snatched it up and pushed it crumpled into her coat pocket, crushing the postcard that was already wedged there. When she stood up, her legs shook so badly she had to hold the edge of the cracked sink. She fished for a tissue in her pocket, her fingers brushing the dusty lavender. She stared at the dirty frosted windows, the dripping tap and could not work out why the sink was grubby or what the horrible smell might be.

And he had not told her the worst.

He spent the night in a Bed and Breakfast in the village. When he went to buy a paper—and all they had was the *Daily Mail*—the women in the village shop whispered in soft, evasive Welsh. The older woman was stringing white paper bags onto a hook by the till while the younger packed cigarettes in neat piles. Owen abandoned his paper, leaving it on top the freezer. He could not face those women. At the country garage, the man greeted him in Welsh, but cheerfully. If news had spread this far, he bore Owen no grudge. The parts of a bicycle were spread across the floor—a puzzle of disconnection, of bolts and levers and screws resting on newspaper, ready for cleaning or reassembling. To one mind the diverse bits, the spaces on the floor were all part of a glimpsed pattern, already coherent and connected. To Owen's mind the jigsaw of random metal could never reveal its meaning or interconnections. Owen had a sudden desire to stay and learn how the different shiny bits, smelling of cleaning fluid and WD40, arranged themselves back into working order. The garage man was wiping his oily hands with a rag.

'So you're having a good holiday? It's good weather, eh?'

He spoke slowly, chose his words with care. There was no answer to this. Owen mumbled something that could have been in either language but he felt oddly grateful, like an outcast dog, for any scrap of companionship.

Driving a different way home, a route he only vaguely recognized with signs offering holiday homes, riding lessons and boat trips, he passed a solitary phone-box. He stopped the car because he needed train times, some idea of a route back to London. But as he stood inside the old-fashioned box, trying to make connection times and train details substantial in his mind—asking the woman on the other end of the line to repeat it again and again because he had no pen, no paper—a collection of people began to queue under the shade of a nearby tree. There were no houses nearby and Owen had no clear idea why they were there. Waiting for the phone? Waiting for a bus? Waiting for enlightenment? An old man, a teenager in a long skirt and a woman with a red scarf tied under the chin all formed a Corot scene. They queued silent and patient, splashes of colour in the washed out morning light, watching him, the unshaven, gesturing man, perhaps fixing him in their minds forever.

Back at the family cottage, ejected, he sat on the bench outside. Jan was inside with Flinn and Anna, sometimes sending out messages or questions about practicalities: how he was going, when he was going. Flinn appeared briefly, slopping a cup of instant coffee. He dumped it onto the table-top, as if disgusted that he had brought himself to show even this much pity.

'Mum says leave a contact number.' And he turned away again, refusing to look Owen in the eye.

Freya had been dispatched to play with girl down the lane. On the line her sheets flapped again. This time she had wet the bed—something she hadn't done since she was four or five, when Owen and Jan had last argued like this. Anna appeared. She tipped Owen's packet of cigarettes and slid one out, gesturing that he should light it for her. He could not protest, somehow.

'I didn't know you smoked.'

It was like they were business associates, making casual conversation.

'I don't.' She half grinned, drawing in the smoke. 'Honestly, Dad. What a mess. And to play that video to us all, with her in it. How tacky.'

For a moment, he didn't understand. There was no television here—certainly no video. And then he remembered. Someone had taken a video of the Christmas social, staff and postgrads together. He had brought it home because he'd sung in the Karaoke, dreadfully, and had been the star turn. But just before, he remembered he'd been caught on camera dancing with the girl, as he'd danced with others. Danced with her out of kindness because someone had said she was upset, had been dumped by the latest man. He barely knew her then, though he remembered, for days after, the feel of her dress, the smell of her perfume when she'd pressed up close.

'It's not like you think,' he began, but saw how 'tacky' any explication would be. 'Do you think she'll forgive me?' he asked, noticing that he had smoked half a packet already.

Jan was to stay at the cottage for the rest of the week with the children. Owen would leave the car with Jan and go back to London, then pack and move out of the house in Kilburn.

'Why don't you go and see Nanna?' asked Anna, not quite as nonchalant as she appeared. She was folding the OS map, bending it, not according to its original creases, but into a new and lumpy shape.

'Stop it, Anna. You're making a mess. It doesn't even belong to us.'

'You could talk to Nanna. Nanna could talk to Mum, perhaps?' Anna's voice tailed off.'

Owen took the map out of her hands, then ripped off the corner and rolled it into a narrow tube. But his hands were shaking so much that Anna took the roach from him. He watched his daughter expertly stick three papers together, break up a cigarette, sprinkle in the tobacco and then hold out her hand for the little bag of grass.

'For fuck's sake. You don't smoke these too?'

'Not much. Although you're not setting me a very good example.'

'In anything.'

'In anything.'

He got up and walked across to the pigsty. Anna followed.

'Down in the village some people were dressed as clowns—selling trout they'd just caught in the bay. Proceeds to charity. I almost bought some. Then I remembered I had nowhere to cook the fish. I'm not on holiday anymore.'

'Neither are we.'

'No.' Owen thought about Jan locked in the cottage and Beth waiting in London. He thought about the abortion he needed to sort out.

But it was not so easy to get back to London. Engineering work on the line had been specially planned to make his life difficult. He would have to wait a day. He would take the chance to be with Freya before he transported himself (temporarily or permanently?) out of her life. Jan's idea, really, that he should be with Freya. Even betrayed and sleepless, she was managing, as usual, to organise them all. Lying awake in the stuffy Bed and Breakfast, he'd told himself it was better everything was split apart. Now he and Beth could be together. But he was no longer sure this was what he wanted.

The day was breezy and cool. Gales had been predicted elsewhere, but here the sea was calm, as if the storm had come and gone. It was early morning. Freya and Owen tramped down the uneven track, walking boots crunching along, stones skidding out from under, birds singing high up on vertiginous banks. Freya did not ask, as she might have done the week before, what the yellow crested bird was called. Questions were unwise. Language seemed dangerous; it could call up the same giddiness she'd feel perched up on that hillside where straggly trees clung, hanging out into space.

When they arrived in the sheltered cove, they found him already there. The fisherman was putting something into the bottom of a beached boat near the sea's edge and looked up and gave a curt nod. He trudged back up the beach towards them and disappeared into a thick stone building just out of the tide's reach. Owen wondered if this was where fishermen smoked their fish. Possibly it was a primitive shelter where medieval pilgrims had once huddled, breaking bread and taking wine before pushing out into the void.

The sand squeaked as they walked down to the water's edge where waves sploshed or hissed over stones and into deep rock pools. It was not a beach you would swim from— too many black edged rocks and cold looking patches of water. But the cove was nicely sheltered, tucked in between grass-green cliffs rising on either side. And it was a quiet place, somewhere to picnic.

Freya picked up a flat stone and tried to skim it across the sea, squinting out at the pale horizon. She was small for her age. Today she had dark shadows under her eyes and Owen noticed how her socks didn't match. He found her a flatter

47

stone and showed her how she should crouch low and give that little flick as she let the stone go. She concentrated, whipped back her arm and flicked the stone out evenly across the dark water. The missile hit, bounced up, dipped, bounced up again and then plunged down and sank. The child half grimaced, half grinned, staring out at satisfying, fading concentric circles.

The man came out of his hut and padlocked it shut. He pushed in front of him a platform set on wheels and scrunched it down across the sand and stones. With a shove, he pushed it out through the waves and up against a largish boat that moved in about four foot of water. But the fisherman had not timed the tide quite right and to reach the edge of the platform, Freya and Owen still had to take off shoes and socks and splash into the ice-cold sea. They gasped at this cold baptism and tiptoed, wincing, across sharp stones. Owen held Freya's hand, smiling at her an assurance he did not feel. They clambered up onto the platform, feet numb, and then down into the rocking boat. Here they sat and hauled back on socks and shoes over their cold, wet feet. Owen wished he had thought of thicker socks.

Meanwhile the fisherman waded back to the shore, pushing away the trolley, leaving them to the shifting boat. They could feel beneath their bodies the slop and slosh of sea. The man strode about the cove as if it belonged to him—kicking aside lobster pots, moving chains and rope, peering into beached sailing boats. He was in his late forties, perhaps. He carried back to his boat a pair of battered red life jackets, wading into the water and tossing them in.

'You'll be needing these,' And then his well practiced joke 'Or should I say, I hope you won't be needing these!'

The wind had picked up. They could hear the plosh of water sucked into black cragged rocks as sea fretted in the bay, just beyond the calmer waters of the cove. Beside the launch, a moored dinghy kept up a metallic ting, ting as wires tapped urgent messages against its mast.

The fisherman didn't address them directly. Each comment was more like an aside. He seemed to be in conversation with his boat or perhaps invisible companions. When Freya froze, her lips curled back over her teeth, the fisherman winked across. Perhaps it was only a twitch, but she unclenched, gave a smile back. Owen squinted out across the bay, scanning the misty and distant cliffs, attempting for Freya's sake to look as if he were completely relaxed. The man still splashed around in the clear water, checking the sides of his boat. With a heave he pulled the boat and passengers toward him. For a second it felt as if he might give them an almighty shove out into the sea's emptiness, but he hoisted himself up onto the boat's edge and slung his legs into the hull. It lurched wildly. Freya grabbed at the handrail. Owen grabbed for Freya. The vessel was swinging and jerking from side to side while the agitated sea sloshed up and down as if it would rush over the sides and cascade in.

When the rocking subsided, Owen hurried Freya into the too-big life jacket. He wondered if the man were insured and if he held a license for what had been advertised in a local window as 'safe, family sea-trips'. The fisherman untied wet ropes and hauled them, dripping, into the boat, then started up the husky engine. They could smell fish and salt and seaweed. As if his boat were full of tourists, the man advised that passengers should remain seated at all times. But Owen had no intention of jumping up and down; he was glued to the wet bench. The man's battered woollen hat was pulled down over his ears and the collar of a thick and muddy jacket was pressed around his neck.

Beyond the shelter of the cove, Owen and Freya felt the first bite of sea breeze and the green sea began a chop, chopping at the side of the boat. The fisherman revved the throaty engine, increasing speed once he had cleared the rocks. The chopping sound increased, as if something kept up with them, knocking the barnacled hull. Perhaps it was the buried priest from the cottage desperate for rebirth, desperate for a second chance. Across to the left, Owen and Freya saw, a long mile away, the wide sandy beach and bent church that marked their nearest village. Dots that must have been people speckled the beach. Directly behind the boat, as they headed out into the middle of the bay, was their own little cove and then somewhere up behind that, the cottage where Jan and Anna huddled. And somewhere beyond that was Flinn working the fields. The boat slowed. Reading the buoys, the currents, the invisible signs that only sailors know, the fisherman chose the moment to swing the boat out and around to face the open sea. At once, with a lurch, the boat rose up and down, climbing the steep waves and slapping down the other side. Owen pressed Freya's hand—too tight, a grip that communicated the opposite to what he wanted to say. So he pointed, as if to make a joke.

'That grey seagull's following you.'

'It's the one from the cottage,' said Freya, 'Looking after us.'

'Perhaps he's got two homes,' said Owen, 'One on his holiday island, one on our roof.' Then he wished he had not spoken. Two homes. A split life.

Owen had thought the water rough enough in the broad bay. When they finally met the open sea, it was as if they had only been playing before. Now the boat really rocked and dipped and creaked. The sight of an island—his island—black and low, out in the open sea failed to excite him. He felt sick. Freya, meanwhile, seemed to have got the hang of the launch's swash and buck. As the boat ploughed on, sometimes juddering as a hard wave hit and seemed to halt them, she became excited. The binoculars were slung around her neck and she cried out when she caught sight of seals swimming, sleek heads just out of the water.

'You'll see more on the island,' shouted the fisherman over the throb of the engine. This time he talked directly to Freya. He gave a curt nod at Owen. 'You'll need that life-jacket on.'

And Owen felt foolish: he'd been attempting to be cavalier, a city dweller thinking he knew best. He shuffled the garment on, glad of the extra warmth it gave him.

'Chough!' said Freya pointing out at a large black, red beaked bird that made its way inland. 'Lesser black backed gull.' She offered Owen the binoculars so he could see what she saw. But when he put them up to his eyes, all he could make out was disconnected sea or sky. He gave back the binoculars, feeling sicker.

They slowly drew nearer to the island, its massive bulk looming inhospitable and savage. The boat flung itself first with and then against the waves. And just as Owen thought he had the measure of its plunge and rise, it would suddenly jerk strangely or dip and roll as if it had given up and the waves had beaten them. Owen's breath was held tight, as if death rode with them, yet he also felt intense physical pleasure—a sense of his body and mind brought utterly alive. The fisherman was concentrating on holding the wheel. He looked out to left and to the right, involved in some tricky procedure with rocks and waves. If that man has a heart attack, if he makes one little mistake, Owen thought, we're all dead. He wished he knew something about how engines worked. He wished Flinn were with them.

'Look Dad,' shouted Freya. She jumped up and leant against the side rail of the boat where spray was flung up and across her. A second behind, he was protectively there.

'Look, a whole family of seals.' And sure enough—spread over the rocks were whiskered seals, small and large. At first they looked completely lifeless, great rolls of blubber abandoned, just left out to dry. But then Owen saw an open baleful eye.

The fisherman, whose lobster pots and nets were temporarily slung into one corner, slowed the boat down, as he probably always did to circle the rocky island. But today the wind was strong and it was hard to hold a straight course at so slow a speed. Once, the engine faltered and seemed as if it might cut out. They were perilously close to jagged rocks, to the white edged waves breaking close to indifferent seals. Owen was watching the side of the fisherman's face. He could not read if the situation was serious or not. He imagined having to swim for the shore and that somehow he would save Freya's life. Then it would be alright with Jan again. When he had asked her earlier if she thought she might forgive him at some point, she had laughed back.

'Forgive you? Don't be so stupid. It was bad before. Now it's impossible.' She would not stop pulling first one sleeve and then the other down over her hands, so that her T-shirt was pulled out of shape. And then she had said 'I used to hope this would happen and now that it has, it's horrid and I wish it hadn't. And I hate you more than ever.'

'We're not going to land,' shouted the fisherman back to them, as they floated close to an inlet that had a harbour wall and stone path up into the interior of the island.

'Too dangerous?' shouted back Owen, casually.

'I can get you in there,' bellowed the man. 'But we wouldn't get out. There's a storm coming.' And he looked out to sea, as if pinpointing the exact spot where that storm might be. He revved the engine, pulling against the current that sucked them towards the harbour wall.

What had seemed a sandy beach that first day Owen had glimpsed his island was in fact bleached rock. When the tide went down, a circle of exposed stone tricked people into thinking the place hospitable. But it had no beaches at all, just razor sharp edges that boats veered too close to, a windswept interior with scrubby grass and sheep, gulls screaming and birds perched high on the guano cliffs, some with wings spread like capes. Owen and Freya were both lashed to the back of a wild sea, with a stranger to guide them in an endless rodeo ride. Perhaps in centuries gone by people had known there was no point in having an easy pilgrimage.

Peering up, Owen saw the remains of the monastery: the arched and roofless walls of a chapel and outbuildings that had long since crumbled and fallen. He thought he saw, close to a belfry, a man on a pony staring out at them. The horse was in shadow and the man seemed to be wearing black. But as the boat dipped down the man was gone.

'Does anyone live there?' he shouted at the fisherman over the rush and roar of the sea dashing against the island.

'Only ghosts,' shouted the man back, grinning at him, hauling the boat around so they were on the other side of the island and they faced the distant mainland once more.

When he delivered Freya back to the cottage, Jan left Owen for the afternoon so he could pack. The car, filled with his family, scrunched down the driveway, dipping up and down as it lurched over potholes. Owen waited until they had gone and then started to make flapjacks, stirring together what he could find in the cupboard: some ancient looking flour, Jan's muesli, spice, cupfuls of sugar. Upstairs he shoved belongings into bags debating what was his, what Jan's. It was impossible to peel apart the layers of their entwined life. He could still feel the dipping and swaying of sea beneath his feet. When he lay down and closed his eyes, the bedroom spun around, as if he were drunk. He pressed his face into the pillow breathing in Jan, a worn and sweet smell, musty and familiar. He could smell, too, his improvised cake baking in the oven. There was something reassuring in the warm and spicy smell that filled up the house, yet something not quite right either, a metallic edge. He presumed that was the dope. Tomorrow, he would eat his way to London, blanking out what he would have to face when he arrived, blanking out what he had left behind.

Waiting for the taxi, he looked around at the familiar outhouses and tubs of geraniums, then tossed his cigarette stub aside, kicking it under a hedge. It had started to rain. He drew in the cold, clear air. He could hear the geese and ducks in the next field and the thwacking of sheets in the wind. He would miss this: the sound of the sea, the sight of twisted and tenacious trees, growing despite a battering. He would miss the calm. He felt he was setting sail, not for home (he was no longer sure where that was) but for some misty future. All afternoon he had tried, and failed, to piece things together. He could not imagine what the days ahead held.

When the taxi finally bounced up the track, Owen left a hasty note on the kitchen table, like any casual visitor. 'I'm sorry,' read the note, 'sorry for ruining the holiday. I'm sorry for ruining everything. I love you all.'

He could not think what else to write. It was cold and raining more heavily. He hauled his heavy luggage out to the taxi and the driver helped him stow bag after bag into the wide boot. He was not leaving the art books to bother Jan. Anyway, if she binned them, they'd be impossible to replace.

'Travelling light are you?' The taxi driver puffed with the effort. 'They'll have to put on an extra London train for you!'

The man, like everyone in the village, seemed to know where he was going, seemed to know his story better than Owen. It was probably already being circulated as a cautionary (perhaps humorous) tale for the next batch of tourists. And should he ever return, he too would be told the saga, but an embellished and painted version, more real and finite than anything he felt now.

Before the taxi had even turned the first sharp bend, Owen was unwrapping the crumbly mixture balanced on his lap. With the windscreen wipers softly swishing and the thrumming of rain, he settled himself for the fifteen-mile journey to the market town. As he chewed on dry flapjack, crumbs scattering over the back of the car, he saw through the window a tractor ploughing. He watched it as it churned the clods of dark and fertile soil, trailing in its wake a cloak of fighting gulls.

Aftermath

If this were not the story of her life, Anna thought, things would have gone according to plan. She'd missed her train, missed her coach and couldn't get through to tell Nanna or Gramps to pick her up from Taunton. She was using her initiative—making her own way to them. She remembered doing this walk once before, with her parents, but it hadn't seemed so far that time. She'd not been carrying a heavy rucksack and it wasn't as hot.

On her left was a large field, the gate propped open with a rusty canister; she went in and flopped down, pulling the water bottle from her bag. The liquid was tepid and tasted of plastic, but she was too thirsty to care. She poured some onto her hands and wiped it across her hot face. Over the other side of the field, a boy was mending a fence. She hoped he wasn't going to come and tell her to go away—or worse, come over and chat her up.

The summer that Anna's mum and dad split up Anna had taken Freya down to Nanna and Gramps to be out of the of the way in the week before school started. The girls had both been miserable, but Nanna had taken them on trips each day, probably so they were too busy to spend time thinking. Each night they'd toppled into deep sleep, having walked miles, hunted in junk shops for treasures, caught trout on a fish farm or been swimming (once in the sea). Nanna found cafés at the right moment or produced picnics with cakes they never got at home. When she waved them goodbye after that first summer, she'd said the visit had made her young again, that they should come for a week or two every year. So that's what they did. For the next three summers—sometimes with Flinn, sometimes without. But this year, it wasn't just Flinn who didn't come: Freya wouldn't either. She'd joined the Brownies and was on a camping trip in the grounds of some monastery or castle.

Anna could see the boy making his way over, so she heaved up her bag and set off again down the narrow road. There were high hedge-banks on either side, with birds bursting out and fluttering along, as if showing the way. Bits of her route felt lonely, even though it was the middle of the day: parts where trees shadowed the road and she imagined a hunter hiding in the dense undergrowth. She hurried, knowing that should she need to run, her chest would tighten and the air in her throat thicken and block each new breath. That had happened once before, when she'd taken a short cut at dusk through a London park. She'd seen someone in the bushes watching, then following. By the time she reached the park entrance, she was hyperventilating, gasping at thick, resistant air. She materialised into a world that continued as if nothing had happened, as if she hadn't almost been grabbed and wasn't standing there retching, unable to shout for help. There was a busy take-way over the road where someone joked through an open window. She'd hurried across and stood by the taxi rank, looking back into the shadows where the man had transformed into a smudgy shape under a tree. Safe in the glow of neon, she cursed herself for her stupidity.

The village was still a mile down the road, but this part of the route had houses dotted along, so she could speed up in the quiet bits and walk more slowly passing the cottages and neat bungalows. When she reached a small pub, she went in. She didn't have enough for a drink, so bought crisps. Six or seven men were standing at the bar or drinking at small tables; they stared as she walked up to the counter. The men did not exactly intimidate her, but she was too hot to pull herself up into a more feisty self, or to explain who she was and where she was going. She bought the crisps, asked for a drink of water and left.

The walk had already taken over an hour and she was surprised at how slow the journey was proving to be. She stopped briefly by the ruined abbey to rest. Watching a child hopscotch across the huge flagstones, she thought about her brother Flinn, who'd messed up his life big-time. But she wasn't sure if she doing any better. She'd been at university a year and hadn't done much work. She didn't like studying Geography or living at home. Given everything that had happened to Flinn recently, being at home wasn't an option anymore. She'd applied to transfer, but hadn't told her mum.

When she'd tried to phone her grandparents from Taunton, their line had been permanently engaged: someone had forgotten to put the receiver back, or else Gramps was trying to block the sales calls telling him he'd won a holiday or needed to change his gas supplier. Anna had been about to trudge into Taunton town centre to get lunch and wait for the evening coach when she'd seen a man with a placard:

Tourist steam train to Minehead. See the scenic route and travel in style. Connecting mini-bus leaves every hour.

This might be a method of getting closer: the train passed a few miles from her grandparents' village and she didn't want to spend a day in Taunton waiting. Scenic turned out to be expensive. The man sold some tickets and then turned back to her, lowering his voice; she could pay a child's fare and he'd square it with the conductor. He smiled at her as she'd climbed aboard the bus with the other passengers, but she sat at the back and fixed on her book, ignoring his toothy grin, glad when he didn't follow them onto the platform.

On the steam train, Anna sat on a rough seat that scratched her bare legs, and stared out of the window at the patterns of fields and pretty villages. She liked the rattling carriages, the puffs of steam, the funny card tickets that a serious young boy was taking and studiously clipping. He wouldn't quite look Anna in the eye, as if he didn't want to be reminded of the world he'd temporarily absented himself from. He might have read, in her expression, a questioning as to why a conductor was even needed, since no one could have got on the train without paying. But Anna could understand why he might do an unpaid job for the love of it. The train tooted its way into a green and sky-blue past, beyond that of her parents' lives and deep into the post-war hollows of her grandparents. Out to her right were the sea and a wide bay curving to hold one or two sailing boats making for land.

Anna's first mistake had been getting off at the wrong station, her second hitching a lift with someone who didn't seem to understand her accent and dropped her off in a strange place. She must have added at least another mile to the journey. She couldn't believe she was still walking and no one had noticed she wasn't where she was supposed to be. She kept expecting a call, but half of the time her mobile had no reception. Whenever a car passed Anna had to squash into the hedgerow. Her bag, which had got heavier bit by bit, dug painfully into her shoulder. To her left and right were tilted fields and hills: yellow crops growing in the distance, a horse looking over a fence, flies dancing viridian. She had stepped through a door leading to the 1950s, but she knew that the yellow fields were some new brushstroke, a contemporary colouring of rapeseed. An ancient sport car passed with the sunroof down. The woman passenger, with her scarf tied jauntily under her chin, raised a hand in greeting. I'd rather have had a lift, thought Anna, as the car sped away in the direction of her grandparents' village. She imagined the vibrating telegraph of village gossip: a pink-haired girl is on her way; a punkish hoody is infiltrating our rural lives.

Anna rested again when she reached the first straggle of houses announcing the long winding village. She sat in the shadow of an oak tree, sipping water and watching a girl on a horse who could not make the animal go over a packhorse bridge. The girl's legs came out wide from the horse's side and kicked at the beast's flanks in a desperate way. But the horse kept slowly backing until it stood, trembling in the middle of the village road. A car eased by the obstruction while the girl held up her hand in thanks, as if she were in control. The horse eyed the car and tossed its head making the metal bits of the bridle jingle. It set off backwards again, as if wound up and fixed in reverse, its hooves scraping at the ground, inching back toward the grassy bank.

Anna bounced up, swinging up her rucksack, and the horse, startled by the sudden movement, shot forward across the pot-holed road and up onto the bridge. In a second, it had skidded over the rise and was trotting calmly away as if it hadn't seen, seconds before, demons in the nettles and Himalayan Balsam.

'Well done, missis,' came a voice from a garden. She looked up to see a man resting on his spade. 'I was about to come out and give im a wallop meself.'

Near the middle of the village, a woman Anna vaguely recognised intercepted her as she took a short cut over the green. The person could have congratulated Anna on her marathon, but she enquired, instead, after Anna's family, asking if she was down for the summer again. Her grey hair was strained back into a pony-tail and she was walking so briskly Anna found it hard to keep up. The woman's dog, with one of those leads that expands or is reeled back in by the click of a button, kept twisting its legs up in the slack cord. When the woman stopped to untangle the animal, Anna bent too and vaguely petted the thing, while it jumped and licked her hand. Anna thought it would be nice to tumble onto the soft ground and never get up, rolling in a bed of green grass and dandelion.

She heaved herself upright while the woman went on fiddling with the lead and talking. They were standing by the pond, where Anna could see pond skaters and water boatmen. This was where she and her dad had searched for damselflies, tadpoles and whirligig beetles. The dog was snuffling at the edge, as if it could sense the teeming mass of secret life: newts and fish tucked beneath the sluggish surface.

'It's a shame your mother and father don't come with you anymore.' I suppose it's too much work for your grandmother to have all of you there.'

'I don't suppose mum and dad would want to come together, now he's married to someone else.' Anna didn't mean it to sound like a wise-crack.

'I had no idea,' June said, pulling herself up. 'Your grandfather never mentioned it. I was asking after everyone only the other day.'

'I didn't mean to be rude. I just thought people knew. He's been married to Lois for a couple of years. He lives in Cardiff now.' The woman tried again: 'I didn't know. And your brother? How's he? Such a handsome boy. Your sister too, with that golden hair—beautiful—like an angel.'

Anna did not say how the angelic Freya had quite a temper, was dreading High School and spent her time playing with dolls. Neither did she mention her brother's girlfriend and baby, how Flinn had not finished his A levels and had a mindless job.

'Flinn's fine, just fine. And Freya, too—she's fine.' The woman nodded, as if that was what she wanted to hear.

Ten minutes later, when Anna arrived at the cottage, her grandparents said they didn't know anyone called June, and were surprised she'd not called for a lift; they'd been sitting by the telephone, waiting.

The days sped by. With Anna to herself, Nanna spoiled her more than usual, buying her clothes and books on their shopping trips to Taunton. They traipsed around to visit the old ladies from the church and WI, and Anna put up with the same medley of questions each time. Gramps was pleased to see her too. She was, he told her, his favourite grandchild. Then he tapped his nose to indicate that this was their little secret. Anna suspected he said much the same to her siblings. She and Gramps went for the usual long walks in the woods and along the beach (though now he needed a stick for support) and he took her to an open garden day where he bought her a plant—Blue Ensign that he said she should plant in shade; it would brighten her gloom.

'But I'm not gloomy,' she said.

'I can tell,' he replied. 'Not gloomy exactly, but like a packhorse with a load. Sometimes I feel the same.'

But after the first week, when she'd often sensed he was trying to confide something, he began to avoid both her and Nanna. At the dinner table and in the evenings when they sat together, he shut himself up in his book, something to do with astronomy and black holes. And the more time Anna spent with her Grandmother, the less Gramps sought her out. Sometimes it felt like the pair of them were competing— or using her as a distraction from some problem that worried them both. At the end of the week, Gramps told Anna he wouldn't be going on any more walks, he needed to catch up on gardening. Then he pressed a fifty-pound note into her hand.

'That's for passing the exams, but you'll have to pull up your socks next year.' Her dad had disclosed, then, the dreadful grades she'd been trying to keep secret. 'I thought going to university and doing a subject you liked was going to make all the difference?' She wasn't sure if he was joking or not; he was staring over his glasses, like a doctor examining a patient. She wanted to say that just because you like something doesn't mean you're good at it and that sometimes when you like a subject you end up being worse at it.

'I like geography—it's just that I was running a student newspaper, too.'

'Were they paying you?'

'Not exactly; it will be good for the CV, though. I'll probably go straight into a job.'

'Glad to know you're thinking of working some time. When you do, you can start giving me pocket money.' The crushed up money was tight in the palm of her hand and she wasn't sure if she should offer it back. He winked at her and went back to his paper. Anna wondered what he thought about his grandchildren as they all got older and their untidy lives sprawled up against his own.

'Thanks,' she mumbled and pocketed the money.

When she'd been young she'd got on better with Gramps than with Nanna. Nanna always seemed to be fussing around her father as if he were still a child, or else tidying and cooking. Anna was left to trail around the garden after 'Bamps', picking strawberries or helping to weed. Gramps would invent reasons to fetch kindling from the woods or stones from the stream and reasons to go searching for the huge grass snake. They were pioneers, escaping laying the table, escaping into the wilderness.

Now it was her grandmother she spent time with. Since that first summer she and Freya had come down together after the split, the balance had shifted. But this year, things were changing in a new way: she was beginning to feel she was not very close to either.

One morning Nanna appeared at breakfast wearing a blue linen dress and pretty earrings. She didn't bother to sit down with Anna, who was still in her nightdress, but just stood, nibbling a chocolate digestive and quickly drinking some tea. She didn't even bother to clear up the table, which she usually did promptly. Anna assumed her grandmother had planned another trip to Taunton and waited for Nanna to say what time they should leave. But Nanna barely spoke and seemed preoccupied; she fidgeted with some spiky blue flowers in a vase that Anna had thought were weeds. Then the doorbell rang and Nanna jumped, as if she'd not expected it. She hurried across to the door and turned at the last minute.

'I should have asked you to come, Anna! I feel mean, now. But Grace won't want to wait. I forgot to tell her you were down. We're going up to Porlock.' Anna was about to say she could be ready, when she sensed she wasn't wanted. Nanna was ignoring her, gathering her things up in a determined and systematic way. Anna shrugged.

'I'm fine, Nanna. You go and have a nice time. Perhaps you need a break from looking after us?' But she felt a bit hurt when Nanna did not even reply. Gramps got up from the table, leaving his plate with the toast half eaten.

'Will you be back for dinner? Or do you and Grace plan to eat out again?' He made it sound like the worst crime in the world.

'Of course I'll be back. Anna's here! I've left a list on the table—if you could nip to the village shop?'

'But you don't always remember to come back. You say one thing and do another.'

'Do I?' Nanna looked genuinely surprised. 'When?'

'Last week. And the week before.'

When her grandmother had gone, Anna thought she would make things nice for her return. She cleaned up the dishes, swept the kitchen floor, vacuumed and then went to do the shopping. She wondered if Gramps got jealous because Nanna had a life of her own, or whether Nanna had been mean to Gramps again. Sometimes Anna had a sense of distance between them, like they were satellites on different orbits, scared of accidentally colliding. True there weren't many flashes of irritation, but there wasn't much affection, either.

When Anna came back from the shops, she flounced into the cool of the house, sweaty from carrying the heavy bag. She'd had to wait ages to be served, and then the shop woman had made a fuss when Anna changed her mind about which biscuits she wanted. The woman had muttered something about needing to make the sale void and that it was difficult when it was paid for with a credit card. The shopkeeper had appealed to other people in the shop who'd all stared at Anna's pink hair and orange top.

Anna dumped the bags on the kitchen floor, wishing she'd been invited to Porlock. She couldn't be bothered to unpack and only rummaged for the crisps and the magazine

63

she'd bought for herself. After she'd wandered around the empty house for a bit, she carried out tumblers of Lemon Barley Water into the back garden, feeling pleased as ice clinked against the tall glasses and sunlight shafted through the trees. She put the tray on the round metal table and called across to her grandfather. Gramps, working on his vegetable patch, did not even look up. His shiny spade spliced crumbly earth while he dug some sort of trough (or shallow grave). She spread the magazine across the table, looking at the autumn styles, imagining herself in heavy long skirts, 60's brash shirts or baggy, tweed trousers. The idea of fashion seemed odd in this backwater, where even she did not bother about appearance.

A robin—this was one of the first birds Gramps had helped her identify—perched above her on a branch. When it sang, the rich notes entered her like strong liquor. Gramps plodded over in his Wellingtons and vest, and the bird, with its little dipping flight, flew to his newly turned earth. They watched as it wrestled with a worm, half in, half out of the earth. He drained his glass, then threw the ice out onto the lawn.

'Has Nanna said anything to you?' he asked. 'About things?' Anna looked at him, unsure. His voice had a new sort of seriousness.

'About the things we should cook tonight?' She knew this was not what he'd meant. Much later, she wished she'd asked something probing, something that might have unlocked the secrets shut away. Gramps frowned and stared up the hill towards the farm perched on its crest. Without much enthusiasm, he pointed out a buzzard that circled in the distance over the woods and fields. When he looked back at her, Anna felt he was still up there in the sky, escaping into the bird's endless circles.

'I want to talk to you about your grandmother. I also want to ask you something.' It sounded too formal. And after a pause, 'Perhaps I need to tell you something, too.' Her

64

grandfather watched the robin, sitting on his spade handle, as if it might give him a clue about how he should proceed.

Gramps absently brushed at the crumbs on the table and a livid spot of red dripped onto Anna's magazine. They both stared. Another drop fell onto the grey table. Her grandfather turned his hand up and examined a small cut at the base of his finger.

'I'd better get a plaster and sort this out. We'll talk later.' He seemed relieved to be able to leave. Usually he just flicked his hand up and down when he had a cut, or sucked it if his skin was clean. Gramps went inside and Anna stared at the pages of her magazine and at her drink with the melting ice-cubes. When her grandfather eventually returned he had three bourbon biscuits in his hand. He handed two to her, like he used to in the old days.

'You need to put that milk away you've left in the shopping bag,' he said, placing binoculars on the table for her, so that she too could escape and be with the buzzard.

'You wanted to talk to me about Nanna?' He considered for a moment.

'It can wait, love. It won't be going away.' He slowly pulled his shirt back on and trudged away. Anna pulled a face as he waded across the earth to work. She wondered why nothing was ever straightforward. She had come down here to get away from hidden psychological stuff, from people getting het-up.

Anna pulled her chair up close to the table, flipping over the pages of the magazine one by one. But she could not pay them proper attention, could not insinuate herself into the easy prattle. The glossy pages had already dispatched the present and were full of next season's scarves and coats and heavy leather bags; even looking at them made Anna feel hotter. And when she thought about what autumn held for her family—the upheaval, the recrimination about her leaving—she became more uncomfortable. Anna stared up into the leaves of the tree, squinting into the blue of sky, trying to decide if she needed to be worried about her grandparents, too.

Eventually, she went to find Gramps; he had moved down to the bottom of the garden and was busy tying something onto a row of canes; it could have been raspberries, perhaps blackberries. In the greenhouse she could see trusses of red and green tomatoes—Nanna always made chutney out of the last of the tomatoes, the ones that would never go red because the season had turned and the sun had lost its heat. When Gramps bent down and attempted to untangle a strawberry net spread over his ripe fruit, Anna bent too, thinking about how, in university, she had not found it easy to work hard. Gramps was right when he said something would need to change. Perhaps it was because she was always having problems with boyfriends. The latest wanted to spend all his time in bed with her and she usually agreed, despite needing to do other stuff. Men are such jerks, she thought. But she wondered, all the same, why he still hadn't phoned. She flipped out the mobile and checked on the battery, then checked messages. She helped with the net in such a desultory fashion that her grandfather became irritated.

'Not that way. You could once do this with your eyes shut. Does everyone forget everything?'

She was dragging at the net so it snagged the fruit, making the berries scatter. She gave a heave and the net caught on a twig and ripped.

'Anna, what's wrong with you?' She stepped onto the soft ground to pick up the berries, so ripe, so inviting, but sank into the pale earth, leaving the imprint of her trainers, just as once, at nursery, she had pressed painted palms to paper. 'Anna, get off. Move!'

Her grandfather went to get his rake to erase the imprint. Anna sat on the tangle of grass beside the plot, letting the hot sun tan her legs and arms. For some reason, as he worked, Gramps began to talk about the refugees in the village. He might have been hoping to appease, to smooth over the irritation between them by mentioning something he hoped would interest her. They were learning English well; they'd lived in London when they first arrived and Nanna saw them in church every Sunday. They were fitting in well, Gramps told her. The woman had joined the bowls club, though she wasn't much good. She talked constantly, like she wanted everyone to be her friend.

And then, by some shift in the conversation, they were on to, of all things, marriage and abortion. If Nanna had been outside, she would have instinctively diverted them.

'It's just too bloody easy now,' Gramps said, and then perhaps wanting to hurt her, he continued, 'Look at your father. He walks away from one marriage and it's you children who suffer. Look at Flinn. And now there's Freya too...' And although he did not say it, she knew he included in the catalogue of family disasters her own failure to do well in her exams and the fact that she'd told him she was shifting to a less prestigious university.

'What's mum been saying about Freya?' she asked. He did not reply but went on raking, bending to tug out a weed. Anna ripped at tufts of grass and dug the nail of her finger into the dry soil.

'It's not Freya I'm worried about; it's that student's child. Nanna said the girl wanted to keep it; your father said he didn't want any more children.'

For a moment Anna held her breath. She had not known this, but that was years ago, before their lives had skittered off in different directions.

'If he was going to leave your mother, he could have at least stood by the student.'

'Perhaps the student didn't really want a baby.' She did not know why she was having this argument so long after the event. But she had a vivid picture of her father, dancing up close to that girl, his body moving against hers. To brush the picture aside, she added rather ineffectually, 'I suppose a woman has the right to choose, though.' She was not thinking of the argument so much as trying to shake from her mind the image of her father and the girl on that video he had once brought home. Yet even as she attempted to expel it something in her was peering closer, trying to make out the girl's features. Would Anna recognise her sallow skin if they walked past each other? Would the student recognise her— see her father's image in Anna's surprised face? She felt a complex and painful stir of emotions, outside any notions of right and wrong and blame. She imagined the vacuum cleaner device sucking out an embryo life, that complication of half brother or sister that none of them wanted. Her grandfather snorted, but instead of chasing the argument and kicking aside her objections, he shook his head at her.

'You're such a sweet, ignorant child,' he said at last, his watery blue eyes narrowing as he squinted into the sun. He said it gently, not meanly. He was looking beyond her, back up the wooded hillside to some distant place. She felt, not so much patronised, as cast aside by a bigger issue, beyond her reach. But Anna would not let go.

'So how do any of us know what the girl really said? And if dad didn't want the baby, then it was important to tell the girl.' There was a flutter of fear behind her words.

'Somebody decent might make a difference,' Gramps said, slowly, fixing her with a look she could not fathom. 'Wouldn't you hope for someone decent to help you out?'

He stared at her a long time before she looked down, wondering what point he was making. Eventually he slung his rake down onto the ground, squashing the leaves of a vegetable Anna could not recognise.

'So who are you to say my dad's not decent?' She did not know why she could not let things go. Especially since she often thought that her dad had not behaved well—by any of them.

'Decent? None of you have the slightest idea about decency. It's hard work, Anna, such bloody hard work.' He turned away, his face red from sun or exertion and he wrenched at the net, scattering strawberries across his newly raked earth.

Anna got up and strode off, not understanding why she had been drawn into somebody else's argument. She thought about packing her bags to go, but mostly, she wanted to make up, wanted to find out what was wrong. In the cool of the kitchen, feeling dizzy from the heat, she stood for a while letting Gramps' words settle. She did not know why he was so cross about her father, nor what he wanted to ask her about Nanna. Looking out of the window she saw her grandfather stamping across the earth and plants, like Rumpelstiltskin, squashing fruit and leaves beneath his green boots. He grabbed his jacket from where he'd left it in the fork of a tree and strode away, banging the garden gate and walking off up the track that led to the woods.

Anna never told her grandmother about the argument, although perhaps Nanna guessed. For the rest of the week, Anna and her grandfather were studiously polite to one another. But they didn't have a chance to be alone and mend things. One day he stayed in bed saying he felt unwell, the next she went to Taunton to visit a university friend. Then, when she said she needed to go back to London earlier than planned, Gramps looked relieved and pressed a cheque into her hand and told her it was to help with her studies.

'You never know what's around the corner. Take your chances now. Rosebuds and all that. Hard work, but a bit of fun too, eh?' He did not look directly into her eyes but patted her on the back, like she was some un-trainable animal that could not help its waywardness. She wondered at the time if he was buying her silence, hoping she would not mention his outburst. But later, she decided that he'd felt sorry for her, coming down into the winter storms of his marriage. She banked the money in her savings account, feeling uncomfortable about it. When she was short of cash for her holiday in Greece, she took the first bit of money out and bought clothes, suntan creams and contraceptives.

Flinn was glad when Anna moved to Bath. He thought his mother probably was, too. In Anna's first year at university, she'd come home late all the time waking everybody up as she banged the bathroom door or set off the smoke alarm burning toast. She'd been gone now over a month and everyone seemed to be getting on better. He was glad he wouldn't have to listen to her telling him that working in a garage was for dimbos, that he was stupid to leave school. Take your AS levels again, she'd said. Don't be such an asshole. He didn't know if she felt sorry for him or if she just wanted to rub it in. And it wasn't like she was any great success either. But he knew too, one of the reasons he got so irritated when his sister kicked off, was he suspected she was right, he was doing fuck-all with his life.

During his lunch-hour, Flinn often lingered in the garage, talking to the owner or fiddling out the back, telling Mikkis he'd get life sorted soon and perhaps open a garage of his own—though this was not something he wanted or even believed. Sometimes Mikkis listened or replied, sometimes he just pushed another little job at Flinn: You get nothing without learn to work—learn to work, and Flinn would take the piece of metal and start to clean it, wondering why he hadn't gone out for his break. He'd been in the job six months and his hours were getting longer and his pay was shrinking.

This particular day, he escaped into sunshine once it got to twelve o'clock, calling back to Mik that he was going out to buy cigarettes and a sandwich. It was autumn, a clear, sharp day. The trees were almost bare and the air smelt sooty. On the pavement, piles of curled leaves scrunched under his feet. He'd always liked that when he was a kid, scuffing them up and crunching the crisp ones. He was not sure at what age he'd stopped being a child. Sometimes he thought it was when his parents broke up, but if he was honest, it was probably when he stopped playing with toys and started with machines—about ten, he'd say.

Flinn passed the local shops—hairdresser's, newsagents, sandwich bar and Spar—then turned into the High Street and kept going. He walked for almost a mile, tracing a route that took him back to his old life. After his dad left, his mum sold the old house and bought a cheaper one, further out of London, so he didn't spend much time in Kilburn anymore. They'd all had to move schools too. None of them had liked that, especially Freya. He was thinking about his sister as he walked, and about what she'd told him the night before. He'd been babysitting again, and had taken her up hot chocolate and biscuits so she wouldn't keep coming down and interrupting the film he watched that would probably have given her nightmares. But after he'd slopped down the drink for her and turned to go, she'd started to cry.

'I can't sleep,' she said. 'I don't like this house; it's haunted. It's giving me horrible dreams.'

'It's bigger. I like it better here. And the garden's bigger, too.' Flinn wasn't really listening. The DVD player was broken and would not pause, and if Flinn didn't get back soon, he'd miss the killings.

'It's like this,' Freya had said, fixing him. 'We're driving on a white road—so smooth it's perfect, even though it makes me car-sick. Then, everything goes bumpy and jagged and dark and I can't breathe, and then I realise …I can't breathe because someone has put their mouth over mine. Something is pressing hard against my body and my nose, so I can't breathe or even speak. It happens all the time. Lots.' She had slumped back on her pillows and stared at him triumphantly.

'Tell Mum. You must tell Mum.'

'No. She wouldn't understand.' And she had scrutinized her brother to make sure he was paying proper attention.

Flinn walked on, as if directionless, hands stuffed in his leather jacket and chin pushed down into his red scarf (a

71

present from his new girlfriend). If Freya was cracking up, he decided, it was not his affair. And maybe she just wanted attention. When his mum and dad were together, she'd always been the spoilt one. Now nobody seemed to notice her. Flinn was passing a park where in the distance, under a row of beeches, an orange dust of leaves lay like a sheet pulled up over the muddy grass. He looked across to see if anyone walked in the softness under the beech trees.

Along the residential streets, there were more trees; some so big that they had pulled up the pavement, their roots swelling the tarmac so it looked like they had great webbed feet. In a few of these streets the houses were big and set back, many of them converted into flats. Occasionally there was a house lived in by just one family. These houses had chandeliers in each room and curtains drawn back to show off the paintings on the wall and the grand fire-places. Later Flinn passed clusters of smaller streets and blocks of flats. Here, there was a more run-down feel, but that didn't bother him. He knew why he was walking this way, why he was spending his whole lunch hour going back to the streets he'd once played in. When he got to the busier roads, he glanced inside all the shops he thought Kylie, his old girlfriend, might drift into, then he wandered across to the small park with its slide, swings and toddler section. He was searching for someone with big hoop earrings, someone plodding along and pushing a fat-wheeled buggy.

Other mums with pushchairs were manoeuvring in and out of shops, laden plastic bags hooked over the handles of their pushchairs. A dad was carrying his baby, pointing out the pigeons that were scavenging around people's feet. Office workers queued at sandwich bars and school kids hunched under a tree, passing a cigarette around, talking loudly so they got noticed.

Flinn reached the entrance of Mr Khan's store, near his old school, and then stood back while some boys pushed their way out. Heads down, hands in pockets, the herd forced themselves through the narrow entrance. As they spilled into the street and made to walk away, Flinn called out after one of them.

'Hey, Akkie. Akkie!' The shortest boy looked up and recognised Flinn.

'Hey, Flinn. What's up, man!' The other boys were striding off, talking at one another and laughing. 'How's the job?' asked Akkie, not looking Flinn in the eye. 'I saw your mum up the Family Centre. She said you were doing fine with everything.' They let the word 'everything' settle a moment between them.

'I haven't seen you in ages,' said Flinn. 'I thought you'd come round.'

'It's a long way, man—and I wasn't sure…'

'Kylie says you've been to visit her.'

'I've been down once or twice.' And then seeing Flinn's face, 'But I don't take her nothing. No drugs, man. It ain't me no more.'

'I didn't say you did.'

'But that's what you think.'

The door of Khan's opened and an Asian woman came out, covering her head when she saw the two boys who were nearly men, the boy with the ginger goatee, the good looking Asian boy with his soft brown eyes.

'You want to go for a beer?' asked Akkie. 'I've only got Key Skills last thing. Shite, that is.'

'Okay,' said Flinn, 'I need some fags, though. You coming in?' He guessed what his boss would say when he didn't make it back this time.

'I'll wait outside,' said Akkie.

In the shop the owner seemed pleased to see Flinn. He said he remembered him from before, when he came in on his way home from school. 'Must be years ago,' the man said, piling tins on a shelf. Flinn smiled back, noticing that the big boxes full of crisps, with the cut-out holes where you put your hand in, like a lucky dip, were still piled near the door. If he put his arm far enough through that hole he might be able to reach back into a simpler past.

'Prawn cocktail,' said the man. 'Two packets a day—see, I don't forget. My wife would say—here comes prawn cocktail boy—here comes the addict!' Flinn remembered. He didn't tell the man that he'd gone off those crisps, or that his family's life was just like everyone else's now. Messed up. Flinn shoved the cigarettes into his pocket and was buying some chocolate when Mrs Khan emerged from the rear of the shop where the DVDs were. She seemed angry or upset. Mr Khan turned to Flinn and explained in English.

'The girl has left her baby again. She comes out shopping with it and forgets to take it home. She put it here twice last week.' From the far end of the shop came a thin wail, as if the thing were confirming the injustice of the situation. Flinn knew straight away it was Macie. Kylie would have left her.

The woman hurried back into the depths of the shop and Flinn saw Mrs Khan, on the black and white monitor by the counter, pick up the monochrome baby and soothe it. He recognised the pushchair, the snowsuit, the child. It was not just any baby: it was his baby

'And she's only a schoolgirl. Not married!' said Mr Khan, disgusted. Flinn stared, transfixed at the screen, that crystal ball, cupping his future. Kylie was no longer just leaving Macie in the clinic or the doctor's; she had started leaving her in shops and in the park too.

Flinn believed Kylie had been a good mother in the beginning. When Macie was born, she'd managed all the feeding stuff, had even breast fed a bit before she put Macie onto formula; she'd gone to the clinic regularly, with Flinn in tow, and had been quite cheerful, even though she'd had to leave school and not sit her exams. What does it matter, she'd said at the time, I'll get to run my own business later. But that was before she got so low. Now Flinn couldn't sleep sometimes, worrying if Macie was alright, if Kylie had done her some harm, dropped her on the floor or let her choke on a bottle. He knew he probably wasn't a good father either: if he were, he might have her all the time. But he did his best— tried not to do so many drugs; didn't go out late the nights before he had Macie next day.

On the screen, Flinn watched Mrs Khan kiss the baby on its forehead and felt a tug of jealousy. He was about to announce he was the father and then, catching sight of himself in the mirrored counter, decided there was no point. He guessed what they'd think of him. He was wearing scruffy clothes. He had a nose stud and lip ring, dyed blond hair and a tattoo on his arm. He didn't think they would put a baby in his arms; they'd never let him take her away.

Holding the chocolate he had not yet paid for, Flinn went over to the door and called across the road to Akkie, sitting on a low wall.

'You'd better go.' Flinn sounded calmer than he felt. 'I gotta stick around.' His hands felt strange as he held the open door. A man in a suit pushed out past him, irritated that Flinn blocked the way.

'You gonna be here all day?' The man's West Indian accent was smooth, but irritation flickered at the edges. Flinn stood back.

From the other side of the road Akkie signed he'd stay put, then settled back down on the wall and turned his collar up. Flinn let the door swish shut and turned to Mrs Khan who had appeared with Macie. Macie laughed when she saw her dad, then pulled Mrs Khan's hair. Flinn felt a huge tenderness, and surprise too, that she could do this to him each time. Macie, at six months old, was getting sturdy and strong. She was a replica of Kylie, with her curly hair and green eyes, but she had Flinn's colouring and would be tall like Flinn. She was bundled into a padded blue snowsuit and her pink face was shiny from heat and tears. She stretched out her arms to Flinn, but then looked up into Mrs Khan's face, her attention caught by dangly earrings and the woman's green nose stud. Perhaps she remembered her from before.

'I'll get the police,' said Mr Khan. 'They can take it home. It's not my job.' He waved a hand impatiently at Mrs Khan who tended to the child. She had pulled off the thick hood to reveal curly ginger hair, wet with sweat. 'It's not your business either,' he said to his wife. 'Police will take her home.'

'I can do that,' said Flinn. 'I'm… I was at school with her mum.' They both stared at him, as if he might want to abduct the child. Other people had come into the shop and were buying papers, cans of coke, sandwiches. Someone was asking if they could fax a letter. Mr Khan needed his wife's help. For a moment he seemed tempted by Flinn's suggestion. But then his wife spoke in Bengali, her bangles clattering as she gestured with one arm, while with the other she held the baby tight. Mr Khan translated for Flinn.

'She says we must get the police. The baby must be with its mother.' Flinn thought he had not translated all that his wife had said. The man hurriedly gave out change. Phone cupped to his ear, he dialled a number then tapped amounts into his till and served more customers.

Flinn moved aside as someone pushed a CD and tins of cat food across the counter. He wanted to hold Macie, let the wisps of fuzzy hair touch his cheek. He tried smiling at Mrs Khan. The door swished open letting in a burst of cooler air. Akkie slid into the shop, standing back for people coming out. His hands were in his pockets, his hood was up, half covering his face.

'Gotta go,' he mumbled, and then, noticing Macie held by Mrs Khan, 'You gotta stay?' But it was not really a question.

Eventually Mrs Nixon, Macie's grandmother, arrived. She was quite young and wearing a fashionable black coat; she could almost have been the baby's mother. The shop had emptied out after the lunch-time rush and there were no customers left. Mr and Mrs Khan were totalling up receipts and talking quietly to one another, every now and again glancing across at Flinn. When he had told them that he was the baby's father, they had looked him up and down with disgust, just as he expected. But they had let him hold her, had watched the way she gave excited yelps when he took her in his arms and they had smiled when she laughed as he played round and round the garden. Flinn liked the feel of Macie nestled close against him, the milky smell of her breath.

When Mrs Nixon saw Flinn holding the sleeping baby, she strode straight up to him.

'What are you doing here? I told you to keep away on the wrong days.' She hardly gave Mr and Mrs Khan a second glance. 'You've done enough damage,' She attempted to wrestle Macie from Flinn's arms. Underneath the unzipped snowsuit was a pink babygrow, grubby at the collar from dribble and food. 'Don't you think it's hard enough for me and Kylie,' she said, standing back, 'without you meddling.' She was not as tall as Flinn, but she had squared up to him. Under her make-up, Flinn could see Mary Nixon's skin beginning to flush and it looked like she might suddenly cry. Her green eyes were fixed on him and he could smell the perfume, bought mail order that Kylie also wore.

The baby began to wake. Mrs Nixon, with surprising strength, pushed up hard against Flinn and slipped her hand around the snowsuit so she could get a better grip. Flinn could feel her sharp knuckles against his chest. She pulled. Flinn pulled the other way.

'Careful of the baby,' said Mrs Khan, coming around the counter. 'Be careful of the baby.' When the baby's head jerked suddenly sideways, Flinn let go. In his mind, he imagined his daughter snapped in two. If Mr Khan knew the story of Solomon, he should announce at this point that Flinn, who had given up the child so she would not get hurt, was the true parent. But Mr Khan kept his head down when Flinn looked at him in appeal.

Mrs Nixon took possession, with a flutter of triumph, and the boy noticed she looked older than when they'd last met.

Flinn's emptied arms were tired and limp after holding Macie for so long. He kept silent, as the woman crooned at the child. He sometimes hated Kylie's mum. But he also knew it must be hard for her—with Kylie messed up and Macie who didn't sleep. He wished he and Mrs Nixon could go and have tea somewhere and talk, like they often used to. The woman looked up at him, as if she sensed his thoughts.

'She'll be alright now.' And he noticed how Macie cuddled into the familiarity of her grandmother and quietly fell back asleep. Mr and Mrs Khan talked in low voices, furtively watching the spectacle.

'But you know your days for seeing Macie,' said Mrs Nixon in a whisper, shuffling the child around so she could hold her securely. 'What on earth have you got her for?' She looked Flinn up and down in exasperation, but he sensed, too that she wanted to say something, to ask him something important. The last time he had collected Macie, he had felt the same.

'I was buying some chocolate,' Flinn said, not mentioning the cigarettes. He knew she blamed him for the cigarettes, the drugs and the baby. He had never somehow been able to tell her that Akkie was the first person Kylie had sex with and the first person to give her drugs. 'Then I found out that Kylie had left Macie again.' He said this as if he'd known for some while that Kylie had been leaving the child. In fact, he'd only learned about it from a friend the night before.

'Rubbish!' said Mrs Nixon, looking frightened. The baby shifted and started to cry again. Over the top of the noise, Mrs Nixon asserted to the Khans and to Flinn, too. 'She's just nipped into another shop, I expect.' But she could not look anyone in the eye.

'We phoned the police,' said Flinn. 'They must have contacted you. I've been here an hour.' And then he regretted he sounded so superior, so accusatory.

He followed her at a distance, down the side streets, passing the burnt out house and the rec. ground where he'd played football as a child. He wanted to make peace. Kylie's mother did not look back. She pushed the buggy along, bumping up and down the pavements. Flinn could just make out Macie's padded arms sticking out either side stiffly, like a doll's. He hung back, wondering what pills Kylie had been taking. He couldn't understand why she had become a victim, why all the rest of them had managed the business of drink and drugs. It had been fun looking over the edge of things, knowing just when to pull back. He didn't know why Kylie had toppled over.

When Flinn passed the road where his old house was, he gave a wistful look up the tree-lined street. It often seemed his life up there had substance, whereas now he existed in the cracks of life, the bits he really ought to jump over. Five minutes later and they had reached the estate and the seedy row of shops. In a doorway, a man covered by a blanket asked Mrs Nixon and then Flinn for change. A black and white dog curled up beside him wagged its tail optimistically, though no one stopped. It was getting cold. Flinn could see the man's breath coming out in white puffs, like he was pretending to smoke, like Flinn and Akkie and Kylie had once pretended to smoke in primary school. He had almost caught her up and it was then that Mrs Nixon spotted him. She stopped and shouted.

'Flinn, I'll get the police again if you come round our house when you shouldn't be there.' And people turned to stare at them both. A man going into a betting shop paused in case the woman needed help. Flinn let Mrs Nixon go, watching as she reached and crossed the busy junction near her house. When she disappeared down her road, Flinn started to follow again. He turned into the familiar back lanes littered with bin bags and broken furniture. A burnt-out car had made an appearance since he'd last been there. Near the block of flats, he propped himself against the flaking plane tree. Somewhere on its trunk he and Kylie had once carved their names, using his new Swiss army knife. He could see a light on in the back kitchen and someone moving around behind the nets. He could hear voices and just make out Mrs Nixon taking off her coat.

That evening in his attic room, Flinn lay on the floor beside Macie. The baby was on her side staring into Flinn's face, making noises that sounded, to him, approving. He ran a finger down her downy cheek and felt, yet again, all the trouble of tenderness.

'What's going to happen, then Macie, Gracie?' he asked, blowing onto the white skin of her neck so that she squirmed and chuckled. The wet nappy Flinn had taken off was on the floor next to a plate of toast, a cold cup of coffee and a dummy with fluff stuck to the teat. He could smell the ammonia that clung to Macie's skin. He was waiting for his mum to finish work. She would probably make them all supper and liquidise some baby food, like she usually did.

Macie rolled onto her back, liking the feel of the new, dry nappy. Flinn pushed the old one aside and placed his blond head down next to hers. He lay there in his baggy jeans and ripped T-shirt, looking up at the ceiling, thinking it might, after all, be nicer to be a baby.

'It'll be all right, Maze,' said Flinn, hopefully. 'Just you and me now.' He wondered what he would say to his mum. He found words slippery, especially those to do with emotions. He preferred labels, like the ones he put on the back of files and computer equipment; they were simple and transparent. If life were slotted together like lego, or could be programmed like computers, he thought that complication might be ironed out, that people would be happier. Macie had labels: baby, small, vulnerable. These labels were in lower case. In capitals, she had bigger labels: DAUGHTER, and, more shockingly, MINE.

By the time Kylie had announced she was pregnant, she and Flinn were not going out anymore. They'd had a big row a month or so before, and she was back with Akkie, going clubbing all the time, making sure she was rude if she ever bumped into Flinn. He, and everyone else, had expected the child to be dark skinned and dark eyed. Instead she was obviously Flinn's, with his grandmother's rich strawberry hair—his hair. Flinn had always thought he'd be a father some day. Only not a teenage father. Once or twice he'd imagined how he'd visit his Nanna in Somerset, piling the family and dog into the fancy car with its nice baby seat and good DVD player. In that daydream he was already rich. In that version his wife wore baggy student clothes and made him laugh. Other times he erased this wife and took one who was beautiful and sexy—only that left the niggling problem about why she had chosen him. He could get girls—but not any girl.

Macie was moving something to her mouth. Flinn opened the tiny fist and extracted a cigarette butt, and then flicked it across to the far side of the room, where his dirty washing was piled. Perhaps imagining wives was like having a test drive, preparing you how to steer things in life. Macie rolled back onto her front—her party trick—and dribbled onto his blue rug. He remembered how he used to lie on the carpet in his Nanna's house tracing patterns, the circles within circles. He wondered if Macie would layer herself into this house. He could not imagine what her reflections on childhood would be, or how he would feature in it.

In the silence between his CD tracks he heard the doorbell, then his mother's muffled voice. He caught something about not seeing someone for ages and wondered vaguely if his dad had at last come to visit. He could hear, wrapped in his mother's words, an edge of annoyance and dislike over and beyond the usual impatience at being interrupted—perhaps it was his dad. He heard footsteps on the stairs.

'Mind if we come in?' Akkie poked his head around the door. Behind him, other lads filled the hall and doorway.

'Is that it?' said one, staring at the baby's fat legs, waving in the air.

'What do you think it is?' said Akkie, 'A dog?' Flinn scrambled to his feet.

'I was changing her nappy,' he said, because he couldn't think what else to say. He felt caught out, exposed. These were the last people he expected to visit. Over the top of Flinn's music, Akkie apologised.

'Sorry about going off earlier. I didn't think I'd wait for the police.' He grinned sheepishly and Abdi, from behind, nudged him in the ribs, muttered in his ear and then laughed.

They had filtered into the room, circling around the edges, taking up their positions. Jason Floyd, the boy with the eyebrow rings, stood running his hands across Flinn's CDs, taking in the names, assessing Flinn's taste in music. Another boy stood looking out of the window. Wasim squatted down and put his finger into one of the baby's hands. Immediately the pink fingers closed around the brown skin, attempting to draw it to her mouth. Wasim laughed at her and tickled her under the chin. Akkie was looking as if it had not been a good idea to come mob-handed. He didn't seem to know what to say to Flinn.

'I'm in a band—with Jason. You should hear us, man. Come to one of the gigs. We could have that drink.'

'Sure,' said Flinn, but he did not know if there was a place any longer for either of them to meet. In his head was a cliché about water under a bridge or a bridge that had got burnt, and even if he could remember the sayings, they weren't quite right, weren't quite complex enough for all that had happened between him and Akkie and Kylie.

'Want to buy some DVDs?' interrupted Jason, noticing that Flinn didn't have many on his shelves. 'Brand new. Half price,' he added, slinging his bag down and opening the top.

'No thanks,' said Flinn. He looked up at his own DVDs, checking they were all still there. Someone was lighting up, taking deep draughts of smoke, someone else was about to roll a joint.

'Hey man, not with the baby,' said Jason, and the boy with the cigarette put it out in a saucer.

They all looked at the baby, the complication that did not fit into any of their lives. Flinn felt years older.

'We was going past—down to the pub with bands. Jason's got some stuff to do, stuff to sell. Thought you might like to come.' Flinn was grateful that the child, smiling up at the legs and faces, gave him an excuse.

'Cheers—but I'm a bit busy.' And he nodded down, as if it was an engine he was in middle of fixing.

The lad by the window suddenly leaned forward, watching something in the street below.

'The police,' he said, turning accusingly to Flinn, as if Flinn had set them up. 'They're coming in here.' Jason rushed to the window. He looked down at the policeman and woman standing before the door. Through a moment's rest in the music they all heard the bell ring. Jason grabbed at his bag, bulging with DVDs, swinging it close to Macie's head and then over his shoulder.

'Out the back,' he said, as if he were in a movie. Flinn carefully picked Macie up before anyone stepped on her.

'You can go through the kitchen,' said Flinn to Jason. 'There's a gate out to the back lane. You'll have to climb over. We keep it locked.' The boys thundered down the stairs as a voice shouted up.

'Get the door Flinn. I've got a client.' The bell rang again and Flinn watched as Akkie and the others grabbed at shoes left neatly at the bottom at the stairs. Jason flung open a door but it was the downstairs toilet.

'Here,' shouted Akkie, pulling open the kitchen door and rushing out, shoes in his hand.

Collecting up Macie's changing bag, clothes and little teddy, Flinn carried the baby down the stairs. Flinn's mother was standing in the hall staring towards the back of the house. Through the open door she could see bodies scrambling over the back wall.

'What on earth...' she was saying when she registered Macie. She stopped. 'Why have you got Macie?' she asked. 'It's not Saturday.' The door to the counselling room was ajar. A short man perching on the edge of an uncomfortable looking chair stared out at them. Flinn stared back and wished his house were not always filled with such hopeless people. The men who came for counselling, spilling their self-pity and guilt over the living room, disgusted him. He was not sure they were any different to the men his mother complained about, going to brothels and paying for their sex. From the front door there was an aggressive knock, then a voice.

'Would you mind opening the door, please. It's the police.'

Flinn had not expected that his mother would come too. In the back of the police car he sat jammed between her and the policewoman, who held Macie. Macie was rigid and about to cry because the woman was not holding her right. Flinn knew she wanted to be upright, looking at things going by, digging hard heels into his lap or pulling his hair. He didn't feel he could say this to the policewoman who looked straight ahead, stony-faced. His mother seemed worried and flustered because the policewoman would not let her hold Macie either. And she had been forced to send her client home, offering him a free consultation another time. Flinn had watched the man leave and wondered if it might be reassuring to him, to glimpse the chaos of other people's lives.

It was warm in the car. Sunlight filtered through the windows. Flinn's mother was still talking at him, the policeman was smoothly changing gears, accelerating, talking into a radio the language of alpha, bravo, fox-trot, translating the name of Flinn's street into police-speak for those who sat scribbling or typing elsewhere. Macie had gone red in the face and was now crying. The policewoman looked too young to know what to do with babies. She was gradually going red in the face herself as she wrestled with the struggling thing on her lap.

'Why on earth didn't you talk to *me*?' his mother was saying. 'I could have contacted Kylie's social worker. We could have gone through the courts. Why did you have to steal her?'

Flinn didn't really know why. Except that Kylie had been asleep on the settee, with the television on when he let himself in through the back door. Mrs Nixon was no longer there and Kylie hadn't woken when he'd got Macie out of the playpen and fed her with the jar of baby food he found in the fridge. He'd gone across to check Kylie, but she was just asleep, making little mutterings and snorting noises. She had on a low top and he could see her flesh rising and falling, creamy and soft. Kylie still had not stirred when he went upstairs to change Macie's nappy and found the sheets of the cot wet and smelly. Even when he eventually let himself out through the kitchen door, letting the door bang soft-shut, he assumed Kylie had not heard, for she did not call out. No one followed. He left the buggy and carried Macie in his arms but didn't think to write a note. He could not say any of this to the policewoman, since, if he mentioned the drugs or Kylie not looking after Macie, it might mean that they put his child in care. And anyway, no matter how loud he had shouted, Kylie would not have heard. They would never hear one another again. That time was past.

'Shall I hold her?' he said to the policewoman, because he could not bear the shrill cries. And the woman, giving a look that suggested he was capable of leaping from the moving car with the baby in his arms, shifted the child away to the other side, nearer the window. He wished someone would notice that he was good with his child.

'I took her because her bed was wet,' he said, more to himself than his mother, watching Macie stop crying now she could stand and look out the window. He caught his mother's exasperated sigh and heard her demand again.

'Why didn't you talk to me when you came in?'

'Because,' Flinn said as they drove into the police station car park, 'you were talking to someone else.'

Owen put the hotel phone down. He had been speaking to his mother, apologising for forgetting her birthday again. He'd put a red ring around December 5ᵗʰ in his diary, but it hadn't helped. His wife, Lois, had gone on ahead to order breakfast, taking their son, Ben, with her. The child had been so tired he'd made raspberry noises at his grandmother and wouldn't join Owen singing *Happy Birthday*. The three of them were staying in one of those anonymous hotels in London: all rooms the same; en suite bathrooms with complimentary shampoo; tea and coffee making facilities; a TV (with adult channel). Lois felt comfortable somewhere like this: it was clean, neutral, it reached a certain standard. Owen found it suffocating; he would rather have been staying in the Quaker Bed and Breakfast with its walled garden and eighteenth century lounge; there you took simple breakfasts in a room with French doors and dusty chandeliers, sliding the toast in yourself and waiting for it to pop up while you talked to other guests. The Bed and Breakfast had no TV, no en suite and you made tea downstairs (dropping your money in the honesty box). Lois had shuddered when he'd suggested staying there. Walking across to the window, Owen tried to make out the narrow street that led to the place, but an office block that looked like a beached ship blocked his view. He supposed the stranded building was some sort of architectural trope, a reference to the river that ran just behind. When he came back up to the bedroom with Lois, he must remember to ask her what she thought of the corny design—if he could hold onto the thought long enough.

Owen's memory had great holes in it: he was bad at giving back student assignments; never remembered the milk when he was asked to buy it on the way home and all his holidays had merged into an indistinct summer where he was young and old, happy and miserable. One holiday, though, stood out from the rest; the one he tried most to erase.

What Owen did let himself remember, was the journey back from North Wales. As soon as he was on that packed, tiny train, he'd had to dash for the smelly loo, with its slop and crumple of paper towels. Before this, he'd been nicely stoned in the taxi to Pwllheli, but later he was so ill he thought he'd have to get off the train and find a hospital. In the grey mirror, when he hung on the edge of the swaying sink, he saw a drained face that stared back at him miserably. That was the summer Owen gave up buying dope. Now, if he was ever passed a joint at parties, as he drew in nicotine and greenness he was back on that train, hurtling through tunnels, plunging down ravines, flying out into open sea.

It had been stupid, Owen thought, to have given up his lecturing job in London so promptly. Back then, he had thought he was about to be fired. Beth had complained about him and had passed on things he'd said to her in confidence, things he perhaps should not have said about his colleagues. She'd also told them that he'd bought dope from her. So he'd assumed it was the end of his career. But these days, he often thought back to the last conversation he'd had with his Head of School. Perhaps he'd misinterpreted the gaps between the man's words, the serious looks and the silence as the man shuffled paper on his desk, then sighed across. Perhaps the deal hadn't been, you go and we'll give you a good reference; perhaps everyone at work had been as surprised as Jan when he never went back and moved away.

Owen's old friend ran the University Adult Education department in Cardiff, so he'd called in a favour and got some part-time work. Paul also had a spare room and contacts in the Art College. It hadn't seemed like running away. He fully expected he'd be back in London before the end of the year. But things hadn't worked out that way.

When Owen had been in the Welsh capital a month or two, he met Lois at a party. She had a design business and was funny and energetic. Perhaps because Lois was American and saw things differently, it made Owen look at the world in a fresh way. He hadn't meant to move in with her so soon, but everything sped up. And then she got pregnant and they had Ben. And now Ben was two and a half and his eldest son, Flinn had a child too. Owen sometimes wondered why he had swapped one set of family tensions for another.

Owen had come up to a conference on teaching and learning that the English Subject Centre was running—he was giving a talk on the use of Art in Creative Writing—and he'd booked extra days at his hotel so he could stay for the weekend. Since it was December, he'd told his London children that he'd take them out to buy Christmas presents. Then, at the last minute, because he'd been given a double room, Lois said she'd come too with Ben, and see the sights.

Later that morning Owen collected Freya and took her back to the hotel. She said she didn't want to go on the London eye after all, nor to the tower of London. She waited until Lois set off with Ben and announced that she and her dad should go and see the Lewis Chessmen at the British Museum.

Freya barely spoke as they tramped around room after room, not stopping until she found the chess pieces. These, she gazed at intently. She examined the intricate stone people riding their stone bridled horses, the long haired men wearing pointed helmets with ear flaps and carrying shields patterned with circles and other heraldic designs.

'Norwegian, Mid–twelfth century,' read out Owen, encouragingly. He remembered how, when he'd brought Flinn here as a child, the boy had only been interested in weapons. Owen had been worried that Flinn might turn out to be violent. But Flinn, in fact, was the only one of them who never lost his temper.

'They're small,' Freya said. 'Not like in Harry Potter. Let's go.' And they traipsed back through the rooms, Owen trying to read snatches of information as they passed the labeled vases and pillars and artifacts.

Outside it was too cold to walk in the any of the parks, so Owen suggested West Kensington where there was a good bookshop. Inside, the staff trailed around after them, making unhelpful suggestions. Freya chose a book telling the nativity story with gothic illustrations.

'Topical, I suppose. Would you like this one, too, about a girl detective in Victorian London?' Freya picked the book up and examined the front cover, then turned to the first page. She began reading the opening words, then the next paragraph. 'Lois gave this to her niece in America. She's eleven like you.' Freya closed the book and put it back. They went into a toyshop and then a place that sold stereo equipment. Freya seemed to be looking for something, but wouldn't say what. Owen was hungry and pointed out the cafés and bars they were passing. Freya dragged him into four more shops. 'You could just have money for Christmas. Make up your own mind later.'

'If I tell you, don't laugh. I want a karaoke machine. I want to practice the songs I have to sing at home.'

'What songs are those, honey?' Freya examined her father.

'Honey? Why are you calling me honey?'

'Because I'm fond of you, I suppose.'

'Fond?'

'Because I love you.'

'Everyone keeps saying how much they love each other. Actually, it's really hard to love.'

They had lunch in an Italian restaurant that he had once taken Beth to. It wasn't until he was inside that he remembered. Freya approved of the pizza with its crisp base and the melting mozzarella that pulled into strings as she tried to eat it.

'You should come down and stay more often, Freya. You're always doing something else.'

'You could come up and see me.'

'Well, that's what I'm trying to do.'

'But I want to see you alone, not you with Ben.'

The waiter had brought ice-cream for Freya, coffee for Owen. He was craving a cigarette. 'How's things with everyone else, then. How's Flinn? How's Macie?' Freya put her spoon down and then slid her finger into the last scrap of ice-cream. She messed at the pink stuff a bit and then pulled her finger out and licked it. Owen frowned at her. Freya looked at him from under her fringe, as if she were assessing something.

'Flinn's fine. Macie's fine.' She went back to ice-cream.

'Is that all?'

'Macie cries at night when she stays. Mum has to get up and take her into bed. I feed her, help give her a bath.'

Freya said all this mechanically, as if delivering what Owen might want to hear. She picked up the spoon again and concentrated on getting up the last bits from the silver bowl, making a scraping noise that put Owen on edge. He was watching out of the window for Lois while he drank his espresso; he'd phoned her, but her battery had gone dead before he could give exact directions. It was early in the month—a cold but bright day that seemed to have encouraged the hibernating world to erupt into the streets to buy. People were rushing past, laden with bags. He felt he had not been paying proper attention to Freya. He tried again.

'Anything else happened? Anyone been abducted or shot?' Freya considered him a minute. She was about to say something, but then changed her mind.

'No. No one's been shot.'

'What's been happening, then, since I last saw you?'

'I don't like the girls in my new school. And... if you want to know, Lois has just walked past on the other side of the road. She's gone down that alley.'

By the time that Owen came back, carrying Ben, Freya

had started reading her book. She didn't look up when they all bundled into the restaurant, talking and laughing.

'Are you going to eat something Lois?'

'Thanks, Honey, but we've eaten already, haven't we Bensy? We got noodles a while ago.' Lois pulled out a chair next to Freya and plumped down.' Hiya there, sweetie. How's life?' She gave Freya a hug and Owen saw his daughter stiffen. 'That looks good ice-cream. You want another?' Without waiting for a reply, Lois ordered coffee and pudding for them all, then spread a pile of leaflets and postcards across the table. 'We had such good fun. We could see nearly all of London. And an old woman was in our pod and wouldn't stop talking; she kept showing me all the places she knew, telling me as if I was a foreigner. The river looked brilliant.'

Owen liked the way Lois made places come alive. Other people were smiling across and the waiters had immediately sprung to attention. He didn't know how he could have missed her. She was wearing a pink and black coat, with a bright green scarf slung over her shoulder and was tall: stately with her high cheek-bones and dark hair coiled up. Freya had distracted him while he'd been keeping watch. Something she'd said had been important: something to do with school. Ben had clambered on to Owen's lap and was grabbing at the sugar that Freya inched out of his way, bit by bit, so he could almost get them, but not quite. Lois turned back to Freya. 'Was the museum good, too, sweetie?'

'Brilliant,' said Freya, taking several sugar lumps. 'We spent ages there—went around everything, and I've got a book about Jesus.' She turned back several pages to show angels appearing across the night sky. A red flush spread across her face, as if she expected to be mocked.

'That's nice, hon. It's the Christmas story, isn't it?' Ben leaned over to look at the shadowy pictures that danced in the biblical text.

'Jesus brings me presents.'

'Bensy! That's Santa, not Jesus.' Owen was putting Ben down on his chair and gesturing that he was going outside to smoke. He pulled out his cigarettes and asked,

'What shall we do tomorrow, Freya? Lois suggested a film.'

'I go to church on Sunday, dad. I sing in the choir now. I'm busy Sundays.'

Later that month, Lois went off to Belfast, taking Ben with her. She had discovered some distant relatives that she'd started writing to; they all had the same great grandfather. She said that going before Christmas was a good idea, she wasn't busy at work. Owen had marking to do and because Anna was staying, it would give the two some quality time together. She had not added, although Owen knew it was part of her reasoning, that Anna irritated Lois, with her views on American politics and the way she made Lois feel personally responsible for everything any president did.

When the phone call came, he was deeply asleep, in bed unusually early; retreating from the problems and pressures of his marking—cocooning, Lois called it. He'd been in the pit of dream where he was swimming but being pulled back by a strong current. Lois screamed at him to save Benjamin who was drowning, but he could see Ben sitting beside her on the boat wearing a crown and eating ice-cream. And he's not called Benjamin, he had wanted to say. I would never have called my child Benjamin.

When he woke, he knew the call must be from Lois. The phone downstairs was insistent. As he ran, fumbling for lights, pulling at his dressing gown cord, he worried that someone had been in an accident, someone must have drowned. People often thought him reckless because he drove too fast, but in truth, life's precariousness terrified him.

'Not Benny. Not Lois,' he said to himself, reaching for the shrill phone. It was an Irish voice, mumbling and incoherent. In the background there were shouts and cheers, glasses clinking. He heard himself saying,

'Where's Lois? Is she all right?' There was a pause the other end.

'Mr Griffiths?' It was a voice with a strong Southern Irish accent. 'Is that Mr Griffiths?'

'Yes. I'm Owen Griffiths,' he said, impatient. It had to be about Lois. His mouth felt dry. He had told her not to go to Belfast. Not to take the child there. But Lois had assured him that the threat of terrorism lay elsewhere: they were more likely to be blown up in London, in Cardiff even. He was already mentally packing his case, wondering how long it would take to get to the airport.

'This is the Celtic Club, Mr Griffiths,' said the voice at the other end of the line. 'I'm ringing about your daughter.'

'Benny!' cut in Owen. 'He's a boy. My wife won't cut his hair. Where is he? Is he all right?' In his mind he saw blood clotted on the boy's curls.

'I can't hear you very well.' There was a surge of noise, the word fuck screamed somewhere near the mouthpiece. 'It's somebody's birthday!' the man said. Then a glass smashed. 'Your daughter!' the Irish man repeated. 'She asked me to phone you.'

And it was then, standing on the black tiles, lifting first one foot then the other off the sea-cold floor, that he realised it was not Lois. Not Benny. It was Anna. She had gone out earlier, promised not to drink too much, to let herself in quietly and to be back by one.

'She's outside on the pavement,' said the Irish voice. 'I don't think she's very well. When she came around I asked her if she wanted me to phone an ambulance but she said to phone you.'

'Came round?' said Owen. 'What's happened to her?'

At the other end of the line, an eruption of singing drowned out the voice of the barman. A roar of voices bellowed, *For he's a jolly good fellow* then, without pause, broke into *Auld Lang Syne*—the party spirit rolling up the dead year,

93

although it was only December 21st. Even as he was revising the airport plan, inserting instead a hospital dash, something about the singing snagged at his conscience. Then he remembered. He hadn't booked tickets to the New Year Eve's dance, though Lois had already bought a dress and planned the baby-sitter. He had not even bought Christmas presents, apart from those he'd got in London. In the distance he could hear a tired voice pleading, a voice that epitomised his own weariness.

'Drink up now please. Let me have your glasses. It's two am, we're closing.'

'Is she hurt?' Owen asked more urgently.

And the barman's patient voice repeated, 'We're very busy. She asked me to phone you, okay? One of the bar staff is with her. She's just sick. You'd better come as quick as you can. I have to be going.' And the line went dead.

On the table, beside the wilting flowers, was the empty bottle of whisky Owen had finished earlier that night. He was expecting more—probably duty-free Irish—for Christmas. He could smell Glenfiddich rising from the empty glass. He felt sick, had the beginnings of a headache.

'How did Anna get so old?' he asked himself, staring at dead flowers in a vase. He remembered her as a baby, waking him at night with her crying. Then an ocean of time had swept along: lectures to write, papers to prepare, exhibitions to visit, students to supervise; he had wanted, he supposed, more than family life, for his name to be known academically. Now it was known at his old university—for making his student pregnant, smoking her dope and paying for her abortion.

'Oh God!' he said. 'I hope the fucking mechanic has brought the car back.' He shuffled into his slippers and went out of the back door to peer into the gloom of the side alley, looking for the white Volvo. Innocently, as if it hadn't been cutting out daily, it waited for him, parked in a yellow pool of street lamp. In the back, where he had carefully put down the seats, he could just make out the shadow of the sofa that he really should have taken to the dump. The mechanic must have returned the car, bill tucked in the glove compartment and keys posted into the outhouse. A sudden gust of wind iced through Owen's pyjamas. Trees swayed and eerie shadows danced. Drips of wet fell from above. The back door slammed.

'Shit!' he said, knowing at once he was locked out. But he still tried the door, hammered at the glass, as if his wife or the cleaner might be hiding inside. The outhouse, which he'd promised to lock each night, was miraculously open. He stooped to pick up the bunch of silvery keys, and then, with a practicality that surprised him, grabbed the old enamel bowl, used for piling weeds in when he and Benny gardened.

Though Lois had designed their house (design was, after all her job) and managed trips to specialist plant centres, it was Owen who did the digging, planting, weeding—and cooking. When they'd first been together, Lois had swept Owen into her whirl of parties and meals out. But then, after having her first child at thirty-nine, she'd come to a standstill. She said she was in shock. When they both came in from work, she'd flop and tell him to take over.

'Honey,' she occasionally said, 'surely you must be used to this family stuff by now.'

Clods of earth and shrivelled weeds clung to the bowl's surface. He swilled it out under the outdoor tap. The weeds and dirty water splashed to the ground dousing his cold legs. Dark patches spotted the navy and white cloth, as if he were incontinent. All the way into town he kept the heater roaring.

He thought about Freya as he drove fast, feet sliding off the pedals when he changed gears or accelerated. He could not work out why she had taken up religion, why she talked about forgiveness and redemption. When he had tried to discuss the subject with her, she remained silent, staring mutely out, as if she suspected words would trick or manipulate her. He asked himself why he was only ever given fragments of information about his children. He phoned London every week, but the kids were always dashing off somewhere or watching telly or in the middle of something, so the scraps they threw his way were inconsequential and wouldn't coalesce.

Owen was driving the same way he drove to work, racing there, after dropping Ben at the crèche. He should have been able to negotiate the route with his eyes shut, but he was beginning to feel that he had lost his way. The familiar was thickened by darkness. Trees, which by day he never registered, filled black space above and all around. The sleeping houses, those great blocks of stately brick and slate, appeared grander and further set back than they did by day. It was as if, in the brief space of night before the world once more turned, he was being shown the secrets of the city's Victorian past, just as once, in a museum in York, he had been trundled down a passage through time to glimpse the Viking world.

He turned right; his daily short-cut. At least that was familiar and automatic; the plunge into the shadow of a railway bridge, the gaining of a few precious seconds. And then, as the car was swallowed into the dip, from overhead, came the ghostly clank, clunk of trucks, trucks that in Victorian times would have been laden with coal.

His foot slid again and the car, like some stupid fairground ride, juddered and bucked. Life a rodeo, he said to himself, life a journey. Life a cliché. What was he doing at Christmas, driving in slippers in the middle of the night, philosophising while drunk? He jerked a gear change. Up at the junction, Owen braked, slid his slippered feet back into place and curled his toes so they firmly gripped the metal plates. He wondered if he might be better driving in bare feet or not driving at all. Then the car stalled.

On the other side of the road was a pub, closed up, curtains pulled tight. But, though it was nearly dawn, Owen could hear singing. A door opened briefly to spill first light and then a man into the street. Seeing the halted car, the man gazed wonderingly across—as if Christ or one of the three Kings had miraculously appeared. Behind him, as he swayed, the man trailed what looked like a woman's scarf.

'Taxi?' he mouthed. Owen saw that one of his bosses— usually austere, reproving, esoteric—was flagging him down for a lift, and that behind him in the doorway a woman, who was not his wife, clung to the frame and giggled. Owen could smell whisky on his own breath as he ducked his head and restarted the car.

Beyond the university area the streetlights were brighter and the roads busier. He kept an eye out for police, aware he could not afford to be breathalysed. Just before he joined the wide road that swept into town, he swung around a tight corner. He slowed first, checked his mirror and changed gear carefully. But at that same moment a boy lurched into the road. There was a girl with him, his arm heavy across her shoulders. Owen braked and swerved. The car shuddered, then slewed sideways. He was aware of trimmed hedges coming towards him, of the car bumping up a low pavement and of a clock somewhere striking. His eyes mechanically shot to the rear view mirror, anticipating the car that might hit from behind. But it was Jan's sofa in the back of the estate—huge, velvet, unwanted and obscuring his view—that hit him first. It must have broken the cotton ties before it slammed into the back of the front seat—hard. Owen's hands began to shake. He could smell whiskey, sweat, the disgusting fake floral air-freshener Lois liked.

Outside, the couple stared mildly at the car, skewed at an angle, with its crazy settee in the back. The boy was grinning, pulling from his pocket cigarette papers. The scruffy child, with his crooked and appealing smile, his shoulder-length hair and clothes cloned from the sixties (or was it the seventies?) had a careless nonchalance, like some echo of Owen's earlier self. The boy put his arm back across the girl's shoulders and they set off, past the car, drifting along the street, their wide trousers dusting the ground like road sweepers.

I must tell Anna how much I love her, Owen thought, taking deep breaths and trying to remember how to reverse, how to manoeuvre a car when his hands were damp on the steering wheel. It surprised him that the car actually bumped back down the pavement and he was suddenly off again, steering and changing gears smoothly. Yet whenever he changed lanes, it kept feeling like he was driving a heavy, lumbering hearse. Only what filled up the back of the car was not a coffin; just the ugly settee he'd been storing in Lois's garage. He was nearing the castle now, on the outside of three lanes and needing to get across so he could draw in by the club. But the other traffic propelled him onward. Unable to see out of the mirror blocked by the settee, all he could do was keep driving in a straight line. Above him a lace-work of Christmas lights, with a few dark patches where bulbs had blown, danced across his vision. To the side, the blare and dazzle of headlights made him afraid of blundering into another driver's path.

Ahead he could just see the hotel and club, a clutch of people standing outside on the pavement, a body sitting against a wall.

'Oh my God,' he said, 'she's dead!' He swung the car left and almost hit someone overtaking on the inside. He veered back again, struggling as his feet slid on the pedals. His palms were still damp on the steering wheel and he did not know where all the cars had suddenly come from. He was being carried past the hotel, past the person helpless on the steps.

He drove, pursued by a car behind and one to the side. Half a mile further on he managed to get off the main road and turn back again. An ambulance, siren wailing, lights flashing, overtook him. Almost in the slipstream of the flashing vehicle, he sped back up the carriageway but realised there was no right turn. He saw the hotel ahead again and the same crowd of people. He wondered if Anna glimpsed the white Volvo as it flew this way and that. The ambulance turned right past the club. Owen followed, although the turn was illegal. He was immediately in a traffic jam. But at the sound of the ambulance, the cars were parting like slow water and Owen made out, up ahead, a man on the road, a motorbike splayed.

Driving away from the accident, the wrong way down a one-way street, Owen emerged near the hotel. Slowing, he put on the hazards. Even as the car bumped up onto the pavement he was out with the engine still running. The barman, in his thin black and white uniform, looked frozen. Anna, by contrast, seemed indifferent to the cold, despite her sleeveless and low cut black top. Her hair, brown these days, corkscrewed into dreadlocks, seemed messier than usual. She was no taller than her mother and clothes were generally too long for her, but her short skirt exposed her thighs. The glittery, black top had risen up and showed the silver stud just below her tummy button, the one she had kept hidden from her father for almost a year. She grinned crookedly at him as he approached.

'What you doing here, Dad?' she asked. The waiter and the group, who Anna might or might not have been drinking with, stared at the man in pyjamas.

'Are you okay?' he asked, blanking out their looks. 'What happened?'

'Forgot that bastard lived in Cardiff,' she answered, as if he would know which boy she spoke about, of the hundreds she saw, or chose not to see, in London and Bath. The people around her began to disperse, perhaps disappointed no fight broke out, no ambulance arrived, and that just a man in pyjamas had been sent as entertainment. From the floor, Anna gave a regal wave at the people melting into the night. The barman tossed away the cigarette he had been smoking and looked Owen up and down.

'She passed out for a bit,' he said. 'We gave her some water, thought she'd just been drinking. But some lad said she'd taken some E. You'd better watch her.'

Inside the car Anna lolled first one way then the other. Owen made sure she was belted in, that the door was securely shut and that the bowl was on her lap—just like when she'd been a child. He drove carefully, not noticing that the hazards still flashed. Anna rambled: something a person had said or done, how she hadn't met someone or had met someone, how 'that bastard' had once really messed her about.

Suddenly, with a great belching noise, she was sick into the bowl. For the first time that evening, Owen felt some relief—the poison was out of Anna's body, and it wasn't even sloshing across Lois's car.

'Disgusting,' said Anna, when she had finished, as if it belonged to someone else. They stopped at red lights. With a speed which shocked him (he thought for a minute she might be about to run off) Anna flipped up the catch, opened the door and poured the steaming contents onto the ground, while the exhaust of cars behind and in front billowed up, like fog.

'Thank God I didn't do that in front of Evan,' she slurred, shutting the door. 'Can't you stop or something. Wash this out?' She waved the foul smelling bowl toward her father. He drove on and started looking for somewhere to stop. They were passing the river. It flowed oily and slow and there were quiet roads he could disappear down, park where no one would see them.

When they got out, he took her arm and walked her up and down, making her drink from the emergency water bottle he kept in the boot. They paced this way and that. Through the railings to the left of them they could just see the smelly river with its scum of plastic bottles and paper, the half drowned supermarket trolley that poked out at an angle

'Look at the silver river, Dad. There's a moon in it. The moon's fallen in the river.' Then she pointed out a house across the road with mattresses stacked in the front garden.

'Pretty house,' she said, smiling into his face flirtatiously. 'Shall we go and sit down?'

'No,' snapped Owen, appalled at her lipstick mouth and the words spilling out. He was holding her up, touching her flesh, the flesh that other men touched. It was something he tried not to think about. Anna was drenched in perfume and the smell mingled with that of sick. His daughter had large brown eyes just like her mother, and she fluttered them at him, in some pastiche of courtship. He propped her against the car and washed out the bowl, making sure that the sick splashed over the scrubby grass and not him. He had found an old jacket in the back of the car and put it on himself when Anna refused. She had looked at the thing with contempt, as if even dead, she would not lower herself to look so ugly. Owen remembered when he'd been young himself, taking so many pills—speed or acid in his day—that he thought he'd never unslow his heart or make his edgy body sleep. He remembered adolescent sex—in bedrooms, in cars, under hedges, down coal cellars, anywhere and everywhere. He felt embarrassed by his own sexuality and by Anna's, too. He wondered what Anna had been doing and taking; she said nothing—much.

'I'm glad it's you, not Mum,' said Anna, leaning up against him. 'She'd assume I'm a drug addict and want to counsel me.' She started to giggle at some picture that came to her, and Owen refrained from the concerned, paternal, 'Are you?'

'And that boyfriend of hers! He'd just tell me off. He's yuck.' It was the first Owen had heard of a man; he felt a moment's jealousy.

'Boyfriend?' he queried, casually.

'Whoops! Wasn't meant to tell you. Not your business, Mum said.' The words tailed off. Anna turned and vomited across the car tyre. Owen rummaged in his dressing gown and then jacket pocket for a tissue.

Anna dabbed at her mouth, pulling a face at the bitter taste of beer and bile and staring in surprise at the smear of red on the tissue. 'Old prude,' she mumbled through the tissue. 'Like a Victorian. Thinks he can sort us out! Full of shit.' Owen was going to ask if he was a counsellor, like her mother.

'Your mum and I got things wrong,' he said, and knew he stated the obvious. 'But I got it the most wrong.' He paused to see if she was still listening; her eyes were partly closed. 'I'm still here if you need me,' he continued. 'I want you to come and stay more often.' He hoped Anna did not think it sounded as cheesy as it came out. He thought he would explain to her, as they drove home together, how he had been stupid, drunk with the idea of youth and freedom. And that now he was beginning to grow up.

In the car, Owen tried to keep Anna talking; he thought she would be all right so long as she stayed awake.

'How's Flinn? How's he coping now he's a teenage dad?' His voice was jolly, but he felt irritated that his son had made him into a granddad. They were driving via back roads, winding through dark streets where he had to guess his way, moment by moment, but also he had to keep talking, hoping the shape beside him would occasionally talk back.

'Flinn's fine. He's a good dad to that baby. The police let him go: they knew he was a good dad and wouldn't really steal a baby.'

'Flinn stole a baby? Do you mean that Flinn stole his own baby, stole Macie?'

'It's not really stealing is it, if it's yours already.'

'When did this happen? Why did no one tell me?' That's so like Flinn, thinking he could be a baby's mother.' Anna was instantly awake, alert.

'It's not just the girlfriend's baby. It's Flinn's baby too. He's good with it. Anyway he's sorted. More than the rest of us.'

'But he's got no qualifications.' In the darkness, he felt her incredulous look.

'Is that what you think being sorted is?' The full weight of

102

her scorn. 'At least he takes his responsibilities seriously.' She was almost slurring her words, concentrating on each syllable so she would not.

'I'm trying to get it right this time,' he said lamely.

'Leaving Mum with no child care when she was trying to re-train as a counsellor?'

'It was hard having Benny little; now I'm trying to make up for things.'

'He's spoilt. We all think he's spoilt, even Nanna.' And Owen had been stupid enough to think Benny might heal things! 'Freya can't stand Ben,' Anna added, 'That's why she never wants to come and stay anymore—well, mostly that, anyway.'

Owen pulled the car to a halt near the park where he often took Benny on a Saturday or Sunday when Lois caught up on sleep or work. The abandoned swings and slides hung, waiting for morning, the overhanging trees drenching them in darkness. Owen stared down at his hands holding the steering wheel. He had meant to say so much to Anna, but it was Anna who was serving up revelation to him. Once, when she was a child, Owen had read her a story about a boy who steps into the past. In the same house and garden he inhabits and wanders through by day, he discovers, at night, a past world that helps him understand himself. It seemed to Owen that in this no-man's time between day and night, he was glimpsing truths that were invisible to him by day.

'Anyway I'm sick of kids,' Anna added. 'Freya's so like a baby. When I go home there's doll stuff or baby stuff all over the house. Mum's all over Macie. When I come and see you, it's Benny, Benny, Benny.' She turned and pronounced, as if it were the greatest of her revelations. 'I'm never going to have children, or a family. You know what? I'm going to have servants.'

When they were almost home, Owen suddenly remembered he was locked out. Before he asked Anna if she still had her key, he found what he had wanted to say all night.

'I'm only just beginning to know how much I miss you all.' And silently in his head, he added—and that other life too. To him this seemed different to any of his other confessions; this time it felt like the truth. He wanted the night to continue, so they could talk more, so he could listen to his daughter, so he could re-discover his lost world. At the prospect of understanding himself, of life being simpler, he felt excited—the same sort of stir that the first gin gave him—or spliffs used to.

'Could I come and see you properly in London?' he ventured, 'Perhaps rent somewhere in the same area?' When Anna did not reply, he wondered what else she was preparing to tell him. But then she made a grunt as a snore bubbled out of her. She shifted in her seat, muttering something.

He turned into Meadow Way, already planning how he would make Anna sit up all night and drink sweet tea. He would sacrifice the next day's Christmas shopping; keep awake all night to watch over this precious child. All around them the stylish modern houses were respectably quiet. His was the only car in the close. And then he noticed something in the wing mirror—a blue light quietly flashing. He wondered how long he had been followed. As he pulled up sedately outside his own house, his slippered foot shot off the clutch and the car jerked forward and stalled. He noticed for the first time that the hazards were still flashing. When the police car stopped behind him, a policeman got out. Coming across to Owen's car he put a hand on the top of the car and leant down to Owen's opened window.

'Would you mind stepping out of the car,' he asked in a bored voice, taking in the pyjamas, the slumped girl, the white bowl with its traces of sick. Anna opened her eyes and hugged the white bowl to her chest, as if she loved it.

'Sorry about the drugs, Dad,' she moaned, once more starting to be sick. Owen got out of the car, wondering where he should begin.

Christmas was not a great success. When Anna went back to university, she did not see her father again until spring, and even that was not a planned meeting. Her grandfather died suddenly of a heart attack and she travelled down from Bath to be with Owen and Jan at the funeral. It was Anna's first funeral. A boy had died at school, after an overdose, but she hadn't wanted to be at that graveside. It wasn't really a sense of decency that restrained her, an awareness that teenage sobbing might make it harder for the family, it was the fear that once she'd begun to cry, she might never stop. So now, standing in the spring sunshine, waiting for the black hearse, she fixed on the comings and goings in a neighbour's garden, the shout of a child chasing a ball, the bike squeaking up a dirt track opposite. And just behind the distraction was her mantra—*I will not cry, I will not cry*. She could feel the sun on her back and the black dress beginning to stick to her skin.

Outside her grandparents' house, waiting for the black cars and twisting a beaded ring around her finger, Anna was haunted by that last summer she'd spent in Somerset. She had written since the argument with her grandfather, and she'd spoken to him a couple of times, but he'd seemed deafer recently and the phone conversations hadn't amounted to much. She tried to think of happy memories, but her black shoes were tight and pinching, forcing her back into the cramped present. Opposite, beside the lane where a tangle of ivy grew over an empty cottage, wound a rivulet. She dreamed about escaping to sit in the shadow of trees, letting her feet dangle in the ice of stream. In the damp grass, she could find a stick and poke about for grass snakes and toads.

It was these same tight shoes Anna had worn the year before when she'd gone for an interview at the university she'd later transferred to. She could still see the small office at Bath Spa with its wave of trees and span of fields out of the window, could see the lecturer's photos of family, his books on the shelves, his papers spread about. There had been a faint smell of male sweat—she supposed her dad's university office must once have been pretty similar.

Outside the office a bird was piping, as if it had been wound up and set going for background effect. And the long drive she'd tramped up with feet hurting, seemed only there to make students aware of how far from the city they'd come, how deep into the country they'd fallen. She remembered thinking (although it was a thought that never came to her again once she was there, writing essays, missing deadlines, drinking late into the night and rushing to tutorials and lectures) that it was all pleasingly quaint on this country campus. She had wanted a fresh start, a spell to erase the past. She had stared out of the window, noticing dots of sheep and it came to her that there weren't really academic reasons for wanting to leave London, and the truth was hardly appropriate—boyfriend trouble, lousy exam marks and not wanting to live at home. And if she had nothing academic to say about the old course, how was she meant to respond to any of the lecturer's questions? She certainly didn't understand what he'd just said about meta-narratives.

Anna stared into the man's blue eyes, noticing he had a scar on his ear lobe, as if he had once worn an earring. She smiled at him shyly, making up an interest in fiction.

'I liked this course especially,' she lied, 'because there are so many texts I haven't yet read or thought about.'

And she gave him an eager look that suggested a hunger to learn. And when he smiled back, as if that was exactly what she should have said, she asked him what courses he taught and what he would recommend for someone transferring from a Human Geography degree. What she remembered most was the sense of power yet hopelessness when he flirted back and then gave her the place for the following year.

Anna's shoes (her only black pair, her only pair with high heels) were hurting badly. If there were to be more interviews, more funerals, she'd have to buy new. The summer before, when Anna had come down to Somerset—and she had felt her grandfather drift away—she'd begun to think that her grandparents were as cross with her as they seemed to be with each another. This was something new. Her mother had said it was nonsense, all in her imagination: all marriages had their bad patches; Nanna and Gramps were like everyone else.

Anna had not expected to be back so soon; no one thought Gramps might die—he was too fit. Anna registered that her grandmother looked dreadful, like she was scared or guilty. She was pacing up and down, looking at her watch and flustering between Anna's mother and father, both of whom were trying to take her back inside. Anna glanced across at the other old people, waiting outside for the cars because Nanna had insisted they must. Anna thought about their patchwork lives, inventing a soft trail of sepia images. She threw in some black and white pictures and a few garishly coloured photos for the sixties. Their lives, she supposed, were straightforward affairs: happy and dull, filled with routine. She thought about her mother speed-dating to meet men, her father making a student pregnant. It was different nowadays.

Though it was already March, the wind that whipped down from the moors still carried the threads of winter. Anna had been hot, now she was cold. She shifted from one foot to another to keep her legs warm, aware of the scrape of neat-heeled shoes on the road. In the black crepe dress and her mother's borrowed jacket she felt like someone else—a delegate perhaps or an interviewee. Each gust of wind sent a scattering of raindrops from the tall tree down onto her and the rest of the assembled crowd. They shook themselves each time it happened, like animals used to the itch of nature. She could smell wild garlic in the hedgerow and up in the woods ragged anemones, celandines and primroses would be bursting into life.

Owen was holding Nanna's arm as if she, like her husband, might be felled any moment. But it was Owen who looked frail—his face pale, his eyes cast down so he would not catch anyone else's. All around Nanna the immediate family—Anna's mother Jan, Auntie Bea, Uncle Harry, Pru and Geoff, old Aunt Mary, clustered in their black suits and outfits. Up in the wood they could hear crows circling and cawing while somewhere over in a garden, a bird sang.

Nanna had said they should come outside to get a breath of air, to enjoy the watery sunlight that had at last broken through the storms, and because the cars coming for them might have trouble parking in the narrow village lane. So they all had to stand there, making polite conversation, aware that Bea, Gramps' sister, and Nanna had not spoken for years; that Pru, who had cancer, must feel like this was a preview of her own funeral and that Owen and Jan, Anna's parents, were no longer married and probably not comfortable in each other's company.

'It's a nice day for it,' said Pru, shivering. She was so thin her clothes hung on her. Anna could make out shoulder blades through the black jacket.

'It's best to die back where you belong,' said Harry, tactlessly. Nanna threw her brother-in-law a look, then tried to change the subject.

'I'm not sure any of us belong here anymore. There's so many incomers, so many strangers now, new houses built on the farm land, no working farms.'

'You never belonged here,' Harry chipped back. 'You were always wanting something better! I was certainly never good enough for you,' and he attempted to make a joke of some old grievance that only the oldest of them seemed to understand. 'It must be half a century since you made that clear to me.'

'Not quite, Harry. And I'm not as old as the rest of you,

remember?'

'Of course, the teenage bride.' And Nanna did look young, compared to the rest of her husband's family. She was still in her sixties, whereas many of the rest were ten or twenty years older. There were none of Nanna's own family there—just Owen, Jan and Anna. She'd been an only child and her parents were old when they'd had her. Harry tapped his sister-in-law on the shoulder.

'When you take my brother's ashes up to the mill, back to our old home, I'd like to come too.'

Nanna snorted, like her husband might have, and turned her back, muttering something, shuffling her son around so that the two were turned away from everyone else. There was an awkward moment's silence, then one of the elderly women began to talk to Anna. Jan walked across and said something to Owen and three large black cars drew up in convoy.

Throughout most of the service in the anonymous crematorium, the square and cream coloured building with its neat gardens set high up on a hill above the sea, Anna remained impassive. They had driven slowly through the gates and up the long road and then parked, like royalty, outside the entrance. The small chapel was full of people Anna didn't know, and she thought for a minute that they might have been directed into the wrong building. But Nanna, held up by her son, nodded at one or two of them as she walked to some kind of altar, then took up her place in the front row before an empty table, covered with a drape. Strawberry coloured light spilled through an arched window. When six men carried the heavy coffin in and rested it on the table, Anna averted her eyes, as if the sight of death were indecent. And when, in between the hymns, the vicar informed her:

'We are granted but a brief while on this earth to do good and then are returned, in happiness to the bosom of Christ, just as John, our dear brother is now reunited and at peace with his maker,' Anna felt furious. She did not want to hear this litany of Christ and faith and God and absolution. Gramps, like her, had said that he did not believe in God. 'Put your faith in science, in progress,' he would say. 'Sometimes it lets you down, but at least it doesn't always let you down.' And he'd look significantly across at Nanna who was rubbing in pastry or beating cake mixture for the next church gala or W.I. meeting. It was probably what Gramps and Anna had most in common—the sense that this life was all you got and that you should use it up before it used you up.

Anna sat, stood to sing, then sat again, mouthing hymns, mouthing Amens, watching, out of the corner of her eye, the mass of people around. There were more friends than she would ever have suspected: friends from bowls, from his walking group, colleagues from his work on the parish council. Then the minister said something about Gramps' love of gardening, the solace and peace it brought him to nurture life and make things grow, to create his own private paradise. A picture of Grampy trampling his plants flashed into Anna's mind and then, uncontrollably, she was crying, trying to make no noise, trying to keep her shoulders from shaking. It was too big for her: life and death and the mess of people's lives. Anna rummaged for a tissue as her nose ran and her mascara, she knew, smudged itself down her cheeks. Jan, sitting beside her, touched her gently on the arm and passed over her own crumpled and twisted tissues. The vicar had been watching Anna as he talked, perhaps because she was in the front row, perhaps because she had purple dreadlocks. She had glared up at him as he droned softly on and he stared back with an expression like satisfaction as she started to cry.

Later, back at Nanna's with all Gramps' Somerset family as well as people from the village, Anna became confused about who was related to whom; they had never gone in for regular family gatherings where she might have got to know

110

her relations. Auntie Bea, her grandfather's sister whom she had never met before, beckoned her across to the chair where the woman sat in state.

'Where's the rest of the family?' she asked sharply. 'The other girl and that boy with the funny name?'

'My sister and brother stayed at home,' said Anna, 'if that's who you mean.' And then Anna looked pointedly away.

'I see they don't teach young people manners anymore,' she said. 'I can't get up for food. I'd like a sandwich—not ham.' And she turned to speak to someone else, dismissing Anna as if she were nothing to do with her. In the old woman's profile, Anna saw the lines of her dead grandfather, the same strong jaw, the long straight nose. She was sitting in his chair, near the little table with magazines and magnifying glass, but presumably didn't know it was his, never having visited before this day. There had been some argument with her, a family rift. But it was as if the dead man had sent his delegate to carry on the business of family intolerance.

'It's all right,' said Uncle Harry, 'I'll see to my sister.' And he winked at Anna but seemed about to cry.

Anna drifted around being courted by people she vaguely recognised who asked about her degree course and her plans for the future. They all seemed delighted by the coincidence of her doing a degree just outside Bath—the town that Nanna and Gramps had lived in most of their life, before retiring 'home' to Somerset.

'But it's not really Bath,' she kept protesting. 'I'm on the campus, right outside the town, and I don't really remember visiting much when I was a child. I just remember the play-park. She noticed out the corner of her eye that however much her mother and father attempted to distance themselves from one another, they kept being jostled back together. And whoever was in the same circle looked embarrassed but kept up a neutral stream of comments that would allow one or other of her parents the chance to escape.

Nanna gradually stopped looking upset; she smiled at everyone and bustled around, helped by her friends. Just like at the W.I. events, the women delivered teas and sandwiches, crusts neatly cut off, offering them to couples, groups and even stray children who had appeared through the side gate. Nanna knew the names of most of the village children and gave them treats, like she did stray cats, welcoming them while Gramps had shooed them away from his pond or plants.

Jan had once said to Anna that Nanna's nurturing was to compensate for only having one child. And Jan's sister, Rose, who was there at the time, said Jan sounded just like a crap psychotherapist. Once Jan had even suggested that Nanna needed to dispense affection in order to get crumbs back, since her son and husband certainly weren't capable of showing her much. But Anna, drawing a line, as she sometimes did, about what could and could not be said about the break-up, snapped that it was just that Nanna was kind and outgoing, like her own dad was.

The house still smelt of Gramps—his tobacco and astringent soap. On the back of the kitchen door his waxy coat hung on a hook. It seemed to Anna that in a moment he would emerge out of the throng, sling on his coat and tell them all he was off, going down to the green house because he couldn't bear the wittering of condolence; he might even look at her to say, 'Mind you spend that money wisely. Never a borrower nor a lender be.' And he would be gone to shoo off the mewing cats and gaggle of children.

Anna felt exhausted. She did not know how the grown-ups could manage this business of inconsequential talk. Nanna was moving around thanking people, handing out cake and telling children how much they had grown, how much like their parents they looked. Then Anna noticed Nanna kept getting names muddled. She told people the same thing over and over again; she smiled vacantly, even patted the vicar's hand.

'Thank you for coming to the wedding,' she was saying to him. Noisy children were running out one door and then in by another, slamming doors as they went. A boy wearing Wellington boots barged past Nanna as he chased a ginger cat. Anna moved over to her grandmother and took her by the arm.

'Have a rest, Nan,' she said, desperately wanting that for herself.

'After I've said goodbye to your father,' said Nanna, pulling Anna towards the hall and front door. Owen been acting as a chauffeur, taking elderly relatives to nearby villages. He would soon be driving back to Cardiff. They found him bending over, offering a hand to help Aunt Bea up from her chair in the hallway. Nanna avoided acknowledging Bea and instead brushed a scrap of dust from her son's shoulder.

'Your brother might not have liked his service but he would have thought the birthday party went well,' she said. Owen stood back up and turned.

'Are you all right, Mum?' he whispered. 'Shall I stay, as well as Anna?'

She was shaking her head as Bea hauled herself up, unaided.

'What are you whispering about?' Bea let her hand rest on the coat stand. 'You ought to tell him outright if you've something to say. It's about time you told everyone how you upset our family.' They turned to stare at Aunt Bea, whose sharp eyes were flickering over them all. 'Where's that oak table Pops gave you? Pops always gave you more than you deserved.' Anna noticed her mother hovering near the front door, wanting to say goodbye, but not wanting to be sucked back into her old family.

'Let me introduce you to Bea, your sister-in-law,' said Nanna, also noticing Jan. Nanna turned from Jan to Auntie Bea, half smiling at them both. Bea scowled and looked at Nanna as if she were making a joke in bad taste.

113

'No, Nanna,' said Jan, softly. 'She's your sister-in-law.'

'I knew it was a bad idea to come,' said Bea, jerking her arm away from Owen, who had grasped it, perhaps in an effort to get her out the door quickly. Bea moved as if to go past Nanna and then shoved her in the stomach, quite deliberately. Nanna crumpled, giving a little gasp as if the air and life within her were expelled. Behind doors, the other side of the walls, things went on as before. Someone was laughing with a silvery, tinkling laugh.

'Nanna!' cried Anna. Her grandmother was propped against the wall, holding her stomach, groaning slightly, grey in the face.

'Mum, are you okay?' Owen had let Bea go, had rushed to his mother.

'Like your father,' Nanna pulled herself up to say. 'You're just like *him*.' And she suddenly looked tough enough to hit Bea back. Owen quickly stepped between them.

'You silly woman,' Bea sneered, though she was looking less confident now, as if aware she had opened a Pandora's box. 'Why my brothers ever wasted their lives trying to marry you!' And she barged past Owen and out of the front door, perfectly able to walk unaided. Only the people in the hallway heard anything. They knew that something odd had happened, but knew, too, that it was easier, and more tactful, to pretend it had not. Owen sat his mother down on the hall chair, as if she were frail, but Anna thought that Nanna looked surprisingly unscathed, even pleased with herself.

'Bea probably feels guilty. Not making up with her brother before he died,' said Jan. People looked at her as if she had the authority to pronounce on such things. 'She doesn't deserve it, but I'll wait outside with her.'

Owen smiled back his thanks. Anna watched her father walk across and touch Jan on the arm. He was speaking softly, but loud enough for Anna to hear:

'You'll wait an age for a bus. I'll give you a lift to the station, after I've dropped Bea, then I'll have to shoot off myself.'

A door was banging somewhere upstairs. A woman came out into the hallway with a small child whose arms she was trying to push into a thick jacket. The people in the hall were dispelling the argument, flustering around the child, helping find his toy, the piece of cake he was taking home. Nanna sat on the chair by the coat stand and someone brought her a cup of sweet tea. In the living room, through the open door, Anna saw matronly women clearing up the debris of cups and saucers, bustling around, fluttering and chatting as if they had successfully completed their Friday WI sale.

'Yes,' Anna heard her mother say to her father. 'That would save me bumping around interminable villages.'

And they gave a nervous smile at one another before Owen came back to his mother. Anna sensed some new conspiracy, inexplicably evolving out of the other strange scene she had just witnessed. And none of it made any sense to her. She wanted to lie down on the crisp white sheets upstairs and sleep—drift away from all the problems and evasions.

She loved this cottage—the bedrooms, the food, the views from the windows, even its insistence on three meals a day, on routines and tidiness. And all the things Anna loved it for: the table laid with bone china, the slow ticking of the clock, the daily papers, the predictability—her parents seemed to hate. The fuss somehow tied them up or tied them down, while it set her free. It had always reminded her of her of a dolls' house, a miniature world she could play with or discard. So it was Anna who would stay for a week with her grandmother, while her parents, after they said their goodbyes, would hurry off. She saw them from the upstairs window shuffling Aunt Bea into the back of the car, while they sat side by side in the front and drove off down the lane, not even bothering to look back and wave to her.

On the way to the station, Owen and Jan barely spoke. Neither could have realised how awkward they might feel pressed so close. Owen must have been aware of Jan's hands in her lap, of her new chunky silver jewellery and the bracelet she kept twisting round her wrist. He would have noticed her wedding ring moved to her right hand, mixed up with pretty glass bands. Jan was conscious of Owen changing gears, his sleeve close to her arm, sometimes touching it.

'Shall I put the radio on?' She nodded. He put on a pop channel she didn't remember him ever liking and Jan felt it as a strange betrayal that his tastes and habits had changed. The country world flashed by: cows, sheep, pubs, a collection of hippy caravans parked on a wide verge. Jan imagined lives packed into a tiny space and then miraculously expanded each time anyone opened the door onto moorland, streams, lanes stretching into the distance, the sea.

The pair travelled for such a long way in silence that Jan began to feel rude.

'Has Flinn spoken to you about coming to see Macie? He says a visit once a year is too little. She's changing all the time'

'I was going to talk to him at the funeral, but he didn't come. I don't really think of Macie as a priority; it's hard enough to get time with Freya, Ben, Anna or Flinn.'

'I think he feels you're not taking him seriously enough — as a father, I mean.' Owen flashed a look sideways. Jan could read what was left unsaid: *of course I take it bloody seriously—being a grandfather, having a son with no qualifications, a son who steals babies for a living.* She stared away out of the window when she continued; it was not her job any more to read the unspoken, to fend off Owen's exasperation. 'I don't know why he didn't come in the end. He said he couldn't face it, but I don't know if he meant all of us together, or the actual funeral.'

'More likely he couldn't face having to wear smart clothes.' Her face must have tightened. 'It's a joke, Jan, a

116

joke.' But she was tired of him refusing her logic or thinking she had no sense of humour.

'I get jokes, Owen—when they're funny. You should ask him and Macie to stay with you in Cardiff.'

'I'll talk to Lois.'

The funeral had been hard enough for them both; Jan did not want to part on bad terms.

'Anna said she'd had a nice time at Christmas. Lois gave her a really pretty top.'

'She baby-sat for us a few times. It was good to get out. You know how it can be. You don't get out much when you have a young child.'

'I'd noticed.' They went back to being silent. Soon they arrived in the station forecourt. 'Thanks,' Jan mumbled, as the car drew to a halt.

'I'll park the car and come in.'

'No trouble. There's plenty of trains to London.' She did not want him to know her real plans, her altered plans. She hoped she sounded decisive enough. If he was parking the car, he took a long time about it. By the time she had bought the single ticket to Manchester and hurried up onto the busy platform, he still had not appeared. But she didn't trust him, not when he was upset and needed someone to talk to, not when he needed to smooth things over between them. If they argued when he came to visit the children, it was hard to get rid of him. He'd stay until he felt he was no longer at fault; that he couldn't be blamed for anything more.

She hid in the ladies toilets, looking at her watch—a man's watch with its no-nonsense face, ticking off life's seconds with efficient indifference. She had felt, when she'd bought it, that it would somehow make her more assertive. But all it did was slip around, so she could never easily check what time it was. The toilets smelt, but she decided to wait a full five minutes. She twisted the clock face toward her, reflecting on time's duplicity, its pernicious darting when you wanted it slow, its interminable drag when you needed some pace.

Scratched on the metal dryer of the toilets were the words *Mags and Tim*, placed inside an equally scratchy and wobbly heart. On the wooden doors cryptic or abbreviated messages spoke of trysts, of love or urged her to fuck off. She stared at the bobbled glass of the dirty window and tried to make sense of the argument back at the funeral; she wondered if that was what Owen would want to talk about and whether he'd be surprised to find she'd disappeared. When a woman with two small children bustled in, Jan took out a brush and pulled at her hair for a few minutes, staring hard at her clouded and obscured reflection.

Back on the platform, she hid behind a pillar and peeped out. The station was busy, but there was no sign of Owen. He must have decided not to pursue her and to drive back to Cardiff. The first train was for London. She almost took it, imagining her arrival back, Flinn putting on tea, asking how it went. People scrambled and ran for open doors and Jan stood back as holiday travellers, commuters, mothers and children piled off the train while other people pushed their way on. She stood there, watching the guard make easy jokes with a man in a wheelchair, wheeling him down the ramp, while the doors slammed and the whistle blew.

Flinn wasn't surprised when Jan phoned to say she wouldn't be back until the next day. He didn't mind looking after Freya, he said, because his new job didn't start for a week. But it seemed an odd and expensive thing to dash to Manchester—couldn't they all go for a weekend some time later? Jan wondered if he'd warn her sister, Rose, that she was on the way or if he'd ring his new girlfriend, ask her if she wanted to come over and cook them all a meal.

Jan clicked off the mobile. She needed the journey to think, to be silent and to nurse a headache. But the train north turned out to be far from silent. A tumble of lads pressed into the seats on the other side of the aisle, immediately pulling out cans of beer and a battered pack of cards. Behind her, an old man talked loudly. No one seemed to reply, so she couldn't help answering him in her own head: *Yes. No, I never read that paper; it isn't nice weather really.* She stared out the window. The journey became a fuzz of hedges, bushes, back yards and muttered replies in her mind: *You don't say—Well I never—Isn't life strange?* She could not turn the demons off. She stared out at playing fields with their smudged muddy patches and overworked goal areas. A wash of spring floodwater had left land bare and pitted; in some fields there were still deep pools. For a while, the train chased the river and Jan watched the cream swirl of water by a weir and, further downstream, the fizz of a waterfall. She would have liked to be the person walking in the dusk, along the still evening path.

Behind her, the bodiless voice sounded like her dead father-in-law. The man puffed out clichés and complaints, as if he could hold at bay mobile phones, drunken teenagers and the noisy children chasing up and down the carriage, shrieking when the sway of train toppled them to left and right. What was this man afraid of, she wondered.

'So they say,' she heard him grudgingly admit to a faint voice beside him. Her father-in-law, sitting behind. Travelling with her. Strange to go to the funeral, be a part of the family she was separated from and then carry away the dead man with her.

The train coasted towards a bedraggled station and she wondered what her real motive was for fleeing to her sister. Perhaps she needed mothering and counselling herself, just as Owen did. The train juddered to a halt and there was silence in the carriage, everyone staring onto the emptiness of buddleia and sycamore, the emptiness of a broken bench and a shelter with its glass smashed. Jan remembered lonely underground stations, patrolled by armed East Berlin guards that she had once swished through one summer. The brightly lit trains sailed from one West Berlin station to another, criss-crossing those areas walled off above ground. It felt to her that the subterranean world she traversed then was like her own subconscious; she lived day by day in the brightly lit West, but each time she plunged into darkness, shadows came trailing after her.

Jan had been lonely after Owen went, though she would never let him know that. She had needed to meet other men. Wanted sex. But the first man she had gone out with was her counselling mentor who had told her his marriage was finished, that he only stayed with his wife because she was ill. As soon as she was better, he'd said, he would leave. They spent Monday and Tuesday together and slept together one evening a week. After six months, Jan realised he didn't want to leave his wife. Being a counsellor, she grasped (perhaps that was what she had to learn) didn't mean you told the truth, or even that you sensed what truth was. She requested a new mentor—a female. A few months later, Jan tried speed-dating, then moved on to a computer version. It was exciting at first, like having lots of mail in the post every day. But the men seemed to ignore her own carefully thought out criteria—cultured man, over forty who likes children, walking in the country and enjoys art and cinema. The replies came flooding in from boys, lesbians and a man who wanted S&M. It was a full-time administrative job just to delete the daily flood.

She gave none of the men her address, but met a few in Bloomsbury or the West End—in public, anonymous places. She told Pete she was a primary school teacher and Roger that her name was Rose. She trailed around museums (wanting to jettison the men so she could look in peace) ate Indian and Italian and watched film noir. Most were boring but nice. Then Marcus, the counsellor, had phoned her ten days ago: he told her he had finally left his wife.

Rose would know what to do. Rose would no doubt tell Jan to forget Marcus or ditch Roger (who may also have been using a pseudonym) and then, as always, these injunctions would make Jan immediately see she had to do the opposite. Jan phoned her sister as the train drew out from the tunnels of Birmingham. Rose didn't seem particularly surprised that Jan was on her way.

'I was expecting you. Funerals always make you wobbly. What time do you get here?'

'You always do this to me! Make me so damn predictable. I thought, for once, I was being impulsive.'

'It reminds you of Mum. Me too.'

Jan's mother had died when Jan was seven, Rose nine. She could certainly not recall the funeral—despite Rose's insistence that she must. All Jan could remember (and she sometimes wondered if she'd deliberately blanked out the rest) was being sent to stay with a neighbour and playing, for a week, with a wonderful doll's house and rocking horse that Mrs Haskins had bought, years before, for her own daughter.

Rose and Jan's father was a kind man, though not communicative. When he started dating women again, he gave the girls a dog. The animal's mad pulling or refusal to move had been part of childhood, like unmade beds, indifferent food, telly and playing Pontoon with their dad on Sunday nights. On walks in the local park, in the mud and drip of autumn, the dog planted itself in the rain, skidding along on his bottom while they heaved at the lead, attempting to drag him back to the messy kitchen, to their dinner. And when they opened the door onto a steamy kitchen, the hot smell of watery potatoes, burning meat and soggy vegetables blasted out, like an unstoppered potion of their father's love. After their mum died, their dad made sure he cooked all the time they lived at home. When they left, he ate at the pub or bought in takeaway.

Jan could not tell her sister the truth about why she was coming to Manchester—man trouble. She knew that the boys opposite, dressed as Superman, Marge Simpson, a priest and something she didn't recognise, would have looked across pityingly at the woman who needed computers to get her men.

'I'll arrive in a couple of hours.'

'I've got a job on, Jan. Be at the pub by nine or you'll mess up my visit. I'll buy you a meal.'

'I thought other people did the mystery shopping. You're just the boss.'

'Sickness. And I think someone's been fixing this one—giving it too good a score because their friend works there.'

Rose had a business assessing restaurants and hotels. She visited, made notes and then reported back to the owners. In a way, this was the same service Rose offered Jan. She delivered her opinion, giving low marks for complication or dreaminess and scoring high for clear-headedness. It was getting dark, the train was racing through commuter towns with little box houses brightly lit and cheery, holding hands across floodplains and green belt. On the other side of the carriage, the boy dressed like Marge Simpson winked at Jan, smiling at her reflection in the darkening glass.

In Manchester it was raining. Splashes of cold cut into Jan's thin dress. In the North, spring had yet to arrive. She pulled out her black cardigan. Young people—girls in low cut tops and men in white shirts as thin as her dress—pressed past. Soon, most would be Friday-drunk, and in the thin light of bars and clubs, they would pair off, some just for the night, some for longer. Sometimes Jan told herself the business of falling in love was a necessary self-deception to get babies and safely bring them up—before men and women inevitably separated. Sometimes she half suspected she thought this when she'd been living with Owen, especially as she gradually grew out of love with him. But she'd not expected it to be quite so hard, or dull, once he'd gone.

A man in a suit, newspaper held over his head, running to get out of the rain, crashed into Jan, then steadied both her and himself. He gripped her arm and muttered an apology, smiled briefly. In that second she felt his assurance. And she wanted it, wanted him. She stood under a tree, watching him rush away, while girls without umbrellas squealed as the downpour drenched. People called out to one another, half bantering, half threatening.

'Come under my umbrella love; there's room for two—if you squash up close!'

'In your dreams!'

She missed this, in London, the way that life embraced you in the North, pressed up close. She stepped from under the dripping tree to run into an arcade, but a tram—she always forgot the trams when she'd been away too long—came thundering down. She waited while it passed, then slipped down an alley full of expensive shops, thinking about Tolstoy's novel, about how she had named her daughter after the heroine—Anna. She'd been given the book when pregnant, had breathed that Russian world the autumn and winter the foetus grew. But she was a slow reader, and, if anyone had told her about the ending, she'd long forgotten it. When she reached the section where Anna Karenin kills herself by jumping under a train, she was appalled. Jan wanted to drag the text elsewhere; re-write the heroine's destruction and her baby's chances in life.

Jan found the pub, known to her in her youth as the place where tramps drank, but now done up and re-named. Rose was sitting at the bar, looking cross. Jan stood for a minute in the entrance shaking off the wet, like she was a dog who'd just plunged out of a fast stream.

'I've been here half an hour; each time they've asked if I want a table, I've had to say I'm waiting. It will mess up the forms.'

'Don't bother with—hello, how are you?'

'Anyway, I've ordered you chicken.'

'You know I'm vegetarian again.'

'Well just eat the sauce.' It was like old times.

At the table Rose directed Jan to use the second hand on her watch to time how long the garlic bread, then the chicken chasseur took.

'Don't hold it ostentatiously like that. Put it down on your lap. Why ever have you got such a huge watch?' Rose started to scribble on a paper napkin, her eyes flicking over the other tables, over the buffet and the waiters hurrying back and forth.

'Are you cold?' she asked, and Jan thought Rose might have noticed she was wet and that they might be about to talk about real things.

'Actually, hot and cold. I've been rushing. But I'm okay, really.' And to demonstrate, she pulled off her wet cardigan.

'And is the music too loud?'

'Everything's fine.

'Be more specific; "okay" and "fine" is not the sort of vocabulary I encourage in assessors.' Jan realised, with a rush of irritation, that her sister was only interested in the questionnaire. Rose was scribbling something on the napkin and folded the words carefully up. She pulled up her leather handbag from the floor and stuffed the paper inside, then looked up and smiled, touched her sister briefly on the arm.

'You know, it's good you're here, even if you did make me wait forever; there's something I need to talk to you about.' She scrutinised Jan. 'It's a long time since we've had a good chinwag.'

'Ages. I've been so busy helping Flinn with Macie.'

'Sometimes I think I should have adopted that child.'

'Really?'

'Not really. It's Anna I always wanted.'

'You can have her!'

'I'd like her to come and work with me. She's got an aptitude for this business.'

'Tell her. After her degree finishes, that would be a good idea. Perhaps an even better idea if she never finishes her degree.'

'It's fate that you're here. I've been thinking about you. I even had a dream that you won tickets for the Orient Express and asked me to come.'

'I would. Only it's not likely to happen.'

'Well, you never have any money, but I do. Although I thought a cruise might be better, given my circumstances. Will you come?'

'What circumstances?'

'I'll tell you later.'

'I'd love to come on a cruise with you. But you don't seem very pleased to see me.'

'It's just that I had some bad news earlier, and I could have done without this job tonight. I'm too tired for it.' Rose was never tired. 'And it is too hot in here, you know; it's stuffy and overheated.'

'What bad news?' There were too many strands for Jan to follow at once.

A waitress in a little white apron came smiling up to them.

'Is everything alright?' she asked. 'Can I get you another drink?' The girl's eyes wandered off, checking the people on the next table, then checking her watch.

'Two halves of lager, please.' Rose frowned at the girl as she walked away.

'I prefer wine,' said Jan.

'She really should have taken my empty glass.' Rose was squinting across the room. 'Did you get the name? Check the name-tag when she comes back. I've taken my lenses out, my eyes hurt—and I've forgotten my glasses. I'd curse the team if they forgot their glasses or didn't get a name. I must be cracking up, Jan.'

Anyone sitting at another table would have probably found it difficult to guess who was the elder. Jan, with her dark hair and olive skin might have been thirty or forty. Rose was plumper, with wild curly hair, high cheekbones and the sort of looks that had been 'too much' when she was young. For boys they had been, somehow, as unmanageable as her bossiness, her refusal to defer to male egos. Now, she had a string of men: business associates, lovers, ex-lovers, gay friends. Sometimes Jan felt irritated that such an unpromising beginning: thick glasses, failure at school, no boyfriends and a BTEC in business studies, should have resulted in the sort of freedom and success that she, the pretty one, the one who was clever enough to go to university, had never known. Perhaps her flurry of courtship was just sibling rivalry, the desire to compete. Perhaps she was only here to show off.

'How's the mystery shopping business?'

Rose shushed her.

The aproned girl approached and slid plates of food in front of them, curls of parsley decorating the cream coloured sauce.

'Did she hear?' asked Jan, as the waitress moved away to get the salads and dressing.

'Course not! And I got the name—Chloe, like Uncle Ben's dog.'

'Do you still see them?'

'I see none of our family, if I can help it.' Rose forked at the thick sauce and smelled the steam that billowed out. 'Except you lot, of course.' She got out the napkin to write: No garlic bread.

With Rose, Jan slid into little sister. In Rose's world, Jan's minor successes were insignificant. She was still poor and unknown, the one who needed looking after. Her own counsellor had warned her about that sibling role—the dependent one. But then, what did his analysis count for, when he had his own dependencies, his own distortions? When she'd been going out with Marcus the counsellor, she'd often imagined little versions of both Marcus and her sister inside her head, fighting over her. It was like that comic she'd read as a child, where colonies of people live inside your head and guts. Don't listen to her, little Marcus would whisper, she's always bullied you. Don't listen to him, Rose would hiss, he only wants to sleep with you and control you subtly. Sometimes Jan was so exhausted by the voices, she was rude to the real Marcus, the real Rose, and they were shocked by her uncharacteristic aggression.

'Any sauces, condiments? Everything satisfactory?' The girl was stifling back a yawn, taking a look at the huge wooden clock that ticked its slow way to the end of the shift. Rose had told Jan that if the meal took longer to arrive than ten minutes, customers got a free drink.

'Have you ever had a free drink?' Jan asked when the girl had gone, and Rose was looking into her bag, and writing on a post-it-note stuck to the lining.

'It's not really free. Nothing's free in this trade. This company takes it out of the waiter's wages.'

'How mean!' said Jan.

'They give it back to them in bonuses if they get people to eat the expensive meals.'

'Are we eating the expensive meals?'

'Of course not. I know better than to believe the recommendations.' The bar and restaurant were filling up. Couples were claiming tables either side of them.

'Listen to me Rose. Look at me. I need your help.' But Rose was watching Jan mop at the congealed sauce on her sleeve with a red napkin. She frowned. Jan looked down and saw that the serviette was full of Rose's hieroglyphics—timings, codes, oblique references to things the waitress had and hadn't done.

'It's like taking a child out.' Rose snatched the crumpled red paper and placed it into a plastic bag she conveniently had in her handbag. 'Shall we ask for the balloons as we leave? Do you want face-paints? You could be a pirate.'

'Rose, I need to talk. It's important. Where's my sister—the funny, strong and kind one?'

'I'm sorry, Jan. I'm just exhausted. I've got to concentrate on this stuff first. And there's other things I need to tell you. I'll take you back home after and we can talk over coffee and cake.'

Jan liked the sound of that, being taken to a place that was a home; her own place always felt provisional. If she took her eye off the chairs and garden and paintings, the flowers on the table, they were likely to metamorphose or evaporate.

'If you're not well, Rose, you should see a doctor.'

'One of your better ideas.'

'Have you already?'

'Dr Crow told me I should ease up on the work. But she's not self-employed.'

The third beer began to relax Rose. Garlic bread late and with scowl, she wrote, under cover of her address book, then offered a fake smile to the waitress as she delivered plates of food to the next table.

'The food's not very nice,' said Jan, pushing the remnants of it to the edge of her plate. She watched the couple flirting on the next table and felt envious. A young boy came and cleared their table of plates and glasses. He was about to take the bread, until Rose stopped him.

'I haven't finished. In fact, I'd like more.' He slid the plate back on the table and shrugged, then wondered across to the bar and started chatting to the barman.

'Jan!' The tone was urgent. Jan hoped Rose was about to explain things. But instead Rose said, 'Have you seen what that woman's doing opposite?' Jan swivelled and pretended she was putting her cardigan back on.

'What's she doing? I thought she was just flirting?'

'She's nicking the cutlery. She's already got three spoons, two forks and six knives in her bag. Do you think she'll try for the glasses?'

'Are you going to tell?'

'Not my affair, to tell. Anyway, I don't want to draw attention to myself.' Not much, thought Jan.

'But I'll mention it in my report.' Rose buttered a crust of bread, watching the woman. 'Business is good, by the way. Too good! The competition has gone international—only big companies; I've got the crumbs—lots of them.' And she mopped up the crumbs on her own plate, as if to illustrate this. 'We're both doing well.'

'Both? I thought you had a team?'

'I've a new partner.'

'Who?'

'And what's up with Freya these days, Jan? Why doesn't she speak to me when I phone?' The waitress and an older boy had finally noticed that not just food was disappearing from plates on the table opposite.

'Has he got a name badge on?' hissed Rose. 'He's the manager.'

'She's that person on the telly.' Jan had, at last, recognised the couple. Rose put down her pencil and stared. 'The one that does the morning show.' Jan and Rose could see the woman clearly when she shifted in her seat, shrugging her shoulders at the waitress.

'I can pay,' she was saying. The man looked irritated—by the woman's words, the waiter hovering, the two women staring across. He spoke as if explaining to an idiot.

'It was just a game. To see if anyone would notice. Because the service was bad. We want the bill.'

The woman took off her glasses and stared at the waiter, half-smiling. She looked him up and down, registering the stubble, the dark eyes, the curl of his hair. He dropped his eyes, fixed them on the polished wood floor. The man was holding something out.

'My card.'

The manager, not more than twenty, looked up, then fixed on the credit card, as if it was an autograph he was being given.

'They live in Didsbury,' hissed Rose, as she made more notes. 'There's a section here for problem solving. I wonder what the boy will do?'

The boy took the card, along with the knives and forks and spoons and came back with a bill. When the man queried the price, the lad trudged back to his till, took money off for the half-drunk bottle of 'sour' wine and returned once more. The man, now standing, casually signed the chit. He helped his partner up, and she gently swayed as he rested a velvet jacket over her shoulders. She smiled out at the staring faces. When Rose and Jan left, unnoticed, a huddle of waiters and waitresses were talking and laughing near the bar. The waitress was at last enjoying herself and had given up yawning, had even given up serving at tables.

Back at Rose's, Jan went to the bathroom, tried on perfumes, opened bottles of lotion and dabbed different things on her face and hands. When she opened the white wooden cupboard she saw a man's shaving things neatly placed alongside dental floss and Rose's herbal medicines. She picked up a bottle of after-shave, examined the labels and the price. Usually Rose did not allow men to invade her space. When Jan went back into the lounge and called out to her sister (who was in the kitchen making lattes with a new machine), asking what the man's name was, there was no reply. Jan flopped onto the cream settee and started flicking through magazines. When Rose appeared with the tray, Jan asked again,

'So who's the new man?' Rose was wiping crumbs from her lips. She placed the cakes and coffee onto the glass table.

'There is no new man. Just a very old one.' She smiled at her own joke, picking up Jan's shoes and placing them tidily in a basket in the alcove. Jan could never make up her mind whether Rose's house was a hotel, a shop or a bordello: wicker baskets stored magazines; shelves displayed lamps and silver objects; throws and antique lace hung from doors and cupboards. In the bedrooms there were crisp sheets, soft towels and miniature soaps piled on the guest sink.

'I love it here,' said Jan. 'It's the home I wish I'd grown up in.' And they both remembered their tiny terraced house with the smell of dry rot and musty dog, the washing draped over banisters. Often they had to wear wet clothes to school because they'd left it too late to rinse their navy skirts and jumpers. All day Jan would be uncomfortably aware of damp clothes and the smell her socks gave off as they dried tight against her skin. Perhaps they were shedding those memories, those skins, when they renamed themselves. Jan and Rose. Not Janet and Rosemary anymore, those children forced to wear their difference like some badge of office, drawing down on themselves pity and aversion in equal measure.

'Have some cake,' said Rose. 'I won't, it's too rich. I'm on a diet.' Some things didn't change. Rose would have already have eaten hers, probably two or three slices, in the kitchen. Rose dropped some sweeteners into her coffee and stirred. She looked thoughtful. 'What did Freya spend her Christmas money on this year?' Her thoughts had probably been chasing along, pursuing problem families.

'Tell me what I should do about men, Rose. I'm worried about the effect on the children. I don't know who I like the best, or what I want.'

'You never did. You always waited for me to tell you what you wanted. That's why Owen was no good. He wasn't bossy enough. Go for the one who will tell you what to do.'

Rose had put some music on. She was singing along to Kate and Anna McGarrigle, gently swaying in front of the huge mirror that offered back her own reflection: greying wild hair, high cheekbones, black kaftan, hooped earrings.

'Freya bought some dolls,' said Jan. She half wished she had not come to stay in that too-perfect guest room. Rose's advice was predictable. Useless. She watched her sister move across to the computer and pull out the scraps of red napkin from her handbag to write up her report. On the desk were new artefacts—a silver fountain pen and a leather bound book—things Jan felt sure did not belong to Rose. Her sister noticed the fixed gaze, then sighed.

'He's sixty and rich. He's kind, retired and widowed. He's moving in. But don't ask me anything more. I'll tell you the rest tomorrow, when we've both had some sleep.'

Rose drew on her reading glasses, turned her back, resistant to questions and peered at the screen. The rigid shoulders, the stubborn back whispered familiar words to

Jan. *Leave me alone; you'll get nothing more from me, my emotional world is my own.* Rose could lock herself off now as easily as when she was a child. Jan picked up *Hello* magazine, began idly flicking through, wondering if it was too late to catch a train home or too late to phone Flinn and check everything was okay.

'Rose! It's that couple! Look! It's them!' Jan had fluttered the magazine up to show her sister. Rose got up and came around the back of the sofa. In the picture, the couple from the restaurant were sitting on a chaise longue, a vase of spectacular lilies on the table in front. The headline declared: Couple ready to play happy families. And a second picture showed a nursery full of dolls and toys and a cot, neatly and emptily waiting. Jan read out loud from the article:

'I'm fine now, says Mel. We want to get back together and start a family.'

'Perhaps that's why she needed more cutlery,' said Rose, and went back to her computer. Jan stared at the picture, the smoothed out shining life. There were huge trees growing in the garden, glimpsed through French window—an Eden of greenness. Rose's typing stopped. She swivelled around.

'Why's Freya buying dolls at her age? You're going to have problems with that child. Send her up to me; she needs to grow up.'

'I think I'll phone her,' said Jan, throwing the magazine down.

'Won't you wake her?'

'Perhaps we both need waking. She wanted to talk, then I had to dash off to the funeral. I should have gone back. I'm stupid, Rose. My youngest daughter's a mystery—I don't know who she is any more. That's the real problem, not the men.' Jan looked at her watch. 'I'll phone her, tell her I'll pick her up from school tomorrow, take her out to a café or something—so we can talk.' She turned to her sister. 'And you wanted to talk too. You wanted to tell me something. All I've done is go on about me.'

'It will wait. Actually, it probably won't wait. I've been meaning to come and see you all—I will, very soon.'

Rose almost came down to stay in the summer, but then changed her mind, said she had other stuff on. Jan had been looking forward to them doing things together. She and Freya had trawled though tourist leaflets and decided Windsor, Greenwich and lots of river trips; they'd even thought about hiring a boat. When Jan got cross with Rose for cancelling, saying she'd already booked tickets to an exhibition and asked her sister what else could be so important, Rose replied that some things were, like having your breast removed.

Jan had dashed back up to Manchester then. She'd stayed for three weeks, until Rose and Rose's friend, Max, persuaded her to go home. The operation had been successful, Rose needed rest and was craving quiet so she could re-cooperate for chemotherapy.

'Look on the bright side,' she'd said to Jan. 'It killed Mum, but these days the prognosis is good. You'll have to put up with me visiting for at least another fifty years.'

When Jan got home, she phoned every other day, and strangely, because there were serious things to talk about, they started turning each crisis into a story to make the other laugh. Sometimes when Jan picked up the phone, Rose would just say, Okay, what's funny? And that would start them, even before Rose got around to describing how the cold cap, which was meant to stop her hair falling out, ripped it out in handfuls, as the nurses struggled to pull the thing over, or off of, her thick curly hair.

Jan and Flinn were out shopping, Macie in the pushchair. Jan told Flinn how Rose had decided to go without the horrible cap and to let her hair fall out the quick and easy way.

'None of it sounds very easy to me, Mum.'

She knew that he could not make sense of what she and Rose were up to, the way they had made this momentous thing into an adventure between them, something exciting and funny. She barely knew herself what was going on.

'No. It's awful. I just hope she's telling me the truth about the prognosis.'

'What did she say it was?'

'Ninety per cent chance for full recovery. Unless, of course, she's making that one up. That would be her best joke yet.'

'Mum! Stop it! Did you check this with Max?'

'He'd echo what she wanted us to hear. Do as he was told.'

The summer sales were on and town was busy. The crush pressed in on them: women with grilled shoulders, young girls in tight, hot jeans, older women layered with shopping bags. Flinn stared at a girl wearing a tight bikini top. She kept heaving the material down, and her breasts jiggled around as she managed the manoeuvre. Flinn bent, smiling, and tilted Macie's sun-hat down so the brim covered her face.

'I liked Max when I met him. He seemed straight, sort of down-to-earth.'

'He's not my type. I'm not sure I'd call it down-to-earth. More like staid. Conservative. But I think he's strong enough. He can handle Rose, says he finds her rare.'

Every few yards Macie threw her teddy across the pavement and either Flinn or Jan bent to pick it up. They brushed off the dirt and handed the threadbare thing back. Neither was paying much attention to the child. Normally, they would have talked to her or told her to stop, but today both were preoccupied. Both were going out with new people.

Jan turned into the café where you could get good coffee and little pastries with dates or nuts in the middle.

'The rest of the stuff is bought in, but I think someone makes these; they're Middle Eastern. I wonder if they'd mind if I asked for the recipe.'

Macie stretched her legs wide as they tried to get the pushchair through the door; her sandals fixed firmly each side of the doorframe. The pushchair reared up for a second, and then Flinn had to wiggle it this way and that, and clatter through into the quiet café. People looked up.

'What's up with you, Macie? We're going to have a drink. Juice, Macie.'

They steered the pushchair across to a corner where last time, there had been a heap of toys in a box and a small blackboard. Those things had been removed and a wooden table had been rammed into the alcove. A woman sat there, making a list, writing with a fountain pen in loopy, embellished squiggles. She looked up and frowned as the pushchair came crashing around the pillar.

'Oh!' said Jan. Macie began shouting:

'Want fizzy, want fizzy.' She thrashed around in the buggy as Flinn tried to undo the straps and get her out.

'She always gets cross when she's hungry.'

'I think she's tired, Flinn.' Jan fished out her purse and hurried across to the counter, giving an apologetic smile to the woman as she squeezed back past. The table jolted slightly and coffee spilled into the woman's saucer.

'I'm so sorry.'

'No matter.' But the woman looked like it did matter. She scanned the other tables, as if looking for escape.

When Jan returned with a full tray, she slid coffees and cakes onto the table and then a plastic beaker of juice for Macie, who was drawing over the paper menu with Flinn's biro. Macie pulled a face when she saw her drink.

'They don't sell fizzy here, Macie, but I've got you a special straw.' Jan extracted from her bag a twirling, multi-coloured tube. Macie reached for the plastic straw, smiling. Flinn looked impressed.

'Genius, Mum.'

'Practice. I reckon we've got about ten minutes. Get drinking.' In fact, they had less than five. Macie bubbled more juice over the table than she drank. And she didn't like the crumbly pastries either, spitting out the bits of date tucked inside.

'Want icy cake, smartie cake.'

'No, Macie. They don't have them.' But Jan knew that Macie didn't believe her. Jan had been trying to make Macie eat healthily and the child no doubt sensed some sort of crusade. When Jan bent over to pick up the straw Macie had tossed onto the floor, the child stretched out and scratched Jan's face.

'Ow! You naughty little girl, Macie. What a horrid thing to do.' Jan's voice was higher and louder than she had intended. People turned to stare and the waiter, who may also have been the owner, came and mopped at the spilled pools of juice, muttering a little and curving his body, ballerina-like, to attend to the lady at the next table.

'Another coffee? Certainly, madam.' He turned back and tickled Macie under the chin. She laughed up at him, won over by someone so coolly charming and utterly indifferent. The man's eyes were flickering around the café, assessing the ebb and flow of trade, the tables that needed quickly clearing. A girl and man stood near the counter waiting for somewhere to become free. The waiter signalled to give him two minutes. He took away Macie's beaker and placed the straw down on a paper napkin.

'Bad, girl, eh, little cheeky one?' And he patted Macie on the head, ignoring Flinn and Jan.

Flinn was blowing on his coffee and drinking fast. Jan was collecting up her shopping so she'd be ready to leave.

'Just give her a clean-up, Flinn.' He reached over to wipe Macie's face and she threw herself sideways, crashing down onto the ground, while her chair skidded sideways. The woman at the next table, startled, stared down at the plump girl in her pink frilly top and tight shorts, screaming and kicking out at other people's shopping and at the table legs. Then the woman's eyes levelled at Flinn, whom Jan could tell, she thought might have pushed the child.

Jan and Flinn abandoned their cappuccinos and the haphazard puddle of juice dripping rhythmically to the floor. They collected up the rest of their bags as the waiter hurried over towards them. Flinn had Macie bundled up under one arm and was heading towards the door, the wheels of the buggy squeaking as he rammed it at the café exit. Jan tried to ignore the stares, but saw that people looked at Flinn, at his lip and eyebrow rings and dyed hair, and then took her in, too. She flung the door wide and they escaped into the flux of life.

'Why do these things always happen to us, Flinn? How can the rest of the world hold everything together?'

'They don't really, Mum. They're just better at pretending. I bet if we went back into that café now, the old ladies would have changed into belly dancers and the woman on the table next to us would be kissing the waiter. It's all crazy. It just depends whether you choose to see it. Isn't there a poem— something about, World is crazier…'

'Are you smoking dope again, Flinn?'

'Mum! I'm clearer headed than I've ever been.'

The crazy world rushed past: children, young couples, an old woman with a limp and a stick, a man with a metal detector. In the glare of light and the slight haze, the shopping precinct looked different. Jan hesitated a moment, as if unsure which way to turn. Flinn strode off down an alleyway between a bookshop and chemist. He turned to look back at his mother.

'What time is it happening?'

'Can't we just take this child home, Flinn? I'll come back later, alone.'

'We're there now. And I sort of want to see what all these cranky people are like. If she were my daughter, I'd ban Freya from that church.'

'Don't be stupid, Flinn. That would make matters worse. And she has the right to be a Christian, just as you have the right to reject it.'

'So how long is she being one today?'

'Heaven knows! All day, I suspect. Moira said she'd take Freya back for tea too—Freya leapt at that.'

Jan could hardly keep up with Flinn's leggy stride. She sometimes wondered how she had never noticed him growing so tall. He still looked, when he smiled, like the little boy she remembered squatting on the floor, busy with Lego. He stopped and turned to her, smiling now. She was absently pushing her hair, cut in a new short style, wondering if it looked foolish.

'What are you grinning at, Flinn?' She was defensive.

'You said, Heaven knows—you know, Heaven. Freya's singing hymns!' Flinn bent to tickle Macie, who squirmed and laughed, then threw her teddy at a passing man. She seemed happy now she was out of the café. 'Hey, Macie thinks my jokes are funny!'

His mother could not, or would not, follow the joke's banality. She sighed at the hugeness of things—children growing up and spawning more children, children being so odd you barely knew what or who they were. She noticed in a shop window how the grey in her hair was more noticeable in daylight than in her dark Victorian house. When she'd come out from the hairdresser's the week before, she'd almost believed she was defeating age; the conditioner they'd used had made her hair dark and glowing. She was wondering now whether she should gracefully age or dramatically resist (given that her new boyfriend was eight years younger).

It was then that Flinn asked her, 'So are we all on for the Christmas gig?'

She had forgotten, or perhaps pushed to the back of her mind, the plan to borrow a friend's cottage over Christmas and New Year. She and Tom were to have the children one week, and Owen and his new wife (whom she'd barely met) would take over the next. It still made her feel excited, putting her and Tom's names together. But she wished she didn't have to think of their names and then, the next minute, add Owen's.

'It seems complicated, Flinn.'

'Only emotionally,' said Flinn, drawing on a cigarette, and stopping to look in a computer shop window, full of games and ugly machines and bits of wire. Flinn had a habit of doing this, startling her with his perspicacity, and because generally he avoided—or could not even see—the emotional or psychological, she often wondered if she had heard him right.

'For you?' He gave her a look.

'If you don't want to go, Mum, that's fine. I'll take Macie and Freya on the train.'

This was doubly valiant of him since he had said, just a few days before, how hard he found it to be a dad. He said he found his weekends with her a tie. She was naughty; she didn't sleep well. Kylie no longer fought Flinn for weekend custody; she seemed bored herself with all the paraphernalia of motherhood. She was dating someone new; she was back at college. And Flinn's new girlfriend, after initially being impressed that he had a child, found it boring. When Macie threw a tantrum, Emma went home.

'We could just say we'd seen Freya from a distance.' They stopped at a bus stop. Jan's new sandals had rubbed her heel raw and she bent to touch the tender place. 'She seems happier now she's got involved with this church place.' But this was not something Jan believed, just something she hoped.

'She'll be looking out for us.' It was Flinn who turned the buggy back into the precinct.

Near the hotel, a random group of people were banging away on instruments. Although Jan was not musical, she knew something, or everything, was out of tune and rhythmically wrong. Freya was wearing a white dress that was not hers; she had gone out that morning in jeans. Jan stared at the flimsy material fluttering in the wind. Freya's mouth moved, forming the shape of words that possibly belonged to the hymn everyone else sang.

'I'm gonna jump up and down, gonna spin around, gonna praise your name forever. I'm gonna shout out loud, gonna deafen the crowd, gonna praise your name forever...' In her white frock, just a touch too big, with her white thin arms poking out, Freya seemed insubstantial and ethereal. She was standing next to a robust, plump girl, also dressed in white, who sang vigorously, drowning out the hesitancy of Freya's mouthings.

'What have they done to her, Mum? It's like they've brain-washed her or something. She's only eleven, for God's sake.' Freya did not see her family approach; her eyes were focused on the ground, her cheeks burning red. She was having difficulty drawing in enough air to breathe, let alone to sing and she seemed to be having trouble nailing herself upright. A woman was thrusting leaflets at those who hadn't the foresight to give the stall a wide berth. Moira, the woman who took Freya home for tea once a week after High School, so Jan could work late, was standing off to one side, talking intently to an elderly man and woman.

On a nearby green bench, a group of teenage girls and boys watched the guitar playing and tambourine banging. They smoked and laughed, falling off the arms of the bench into one another's laps, collapsing on and off as if it were their playground. Freya's shoulders were hunched away from them, as if the mocking glances could pierce her.

'We have to save her from them, Mum.' Flinn was watching a young man standing to one side of Freya, playing the guitar and occasionally bumping against her, touching her shoulders as he swung his guitar around. When they finished the number, he put his arm around Freya and whispered something to her. She smiled then, and her cheeks became even redder.

Flinn was struggling with Macie, who kept escaping out of the buggy. He was getting more exasperated each time he had to push her back in. Finally he rounded on Jan. 'If you don't get her out of there, I will.' Macie shot off towards a low table that had chocolate and smartie cakes on a patterned plate in the shape of a cross. Flinn let the child grab at the sponge things, while he confronted Freya.

'We've come to take you home. This is bad for you.' He towered over his sister and was taller than the man who stood next to her, who was backing off and protectively moving his guitar out of the way.

'Go away. What are you doing? I don't want to come home.'

Flinn grabbed at his sister's shoulder and started dragging her towards the buggy, which Jan still gripped. Jan had seen Moira turn at the raised voices, then start off in Flinn's direction. 'Let me go Flinn!' And then Freya's shoe caught him in the shins, and he did let go. 'Pig! Bastard!' she yelled.

As Jan rushed forward, it was to Moira Freya turned, letting the woman envelop her as Freya wept in some drama of emotion, which Jan thought manufactured. Perhaps Freya was protecting herself from the revelation of a temper that she'd kept hidden from this new, adopted family.

'Well, don't fucking ask me to save you in the future. It's your bed. You lie in it.' Flinn was rubbing at his leg, glaring at the kids on the bench, who were laughing at him now.

'I'm terribly sorry,' Jan announced, but wasn't sure whether she was directing this at Flinn or at Moira, who was asking Freya if there had been some misunderstanding, whether she didn't ought to go home after all, if that was what she and her family wanted.

141

'I don't want to go home. I don't want to go home ever again.' Freya was clinging to Moira, staring at Jan with eyes full of loathing. Her shoulders were shaking, perhaps from the cold, but when Jan tried to put her arm around her too, Freya pushed at her. 'Just leave me alone. You spoil everything. Everything you touch goes wrong.'

And Jan felt at that moment, this was possibly the truth. She stared at her Midas hands, at the flecked sunlight that played across them. Perhaps, given the circumstances, she should never have had a third child? It was then that they realised Macie had gone.

On the refreshment table, several cakes had smarties removed, leaving circular indentations of icing. Most of the cakes had been taken off the plate and some were on the floor. But Macie was not there—had gone, perhaps, in her determined way, to find fizzy drinks to go with the cakes. She was not yet two. They spread out. The teenagers on the bench went off in one direction, the church group fanned out in another. Flinn set off, back towards the library, shouting Macie's name, offering her coca cola and chocolate, shouting his bribe into the busy street. He barely noticed the people staring at him.

Jan was left with the stall, the instruments, the leaflets and the empty buggy. She felt sick. Her heel and ankle were rubbed so raw, she was aware of a dull throb under the sandal's strap, and each time she shifted her weight, her whole foot hurt. She was casting around, scanning the groups and rushing people, hoping to see Macie attached to a hand, or winding her stubborn way around the bins and flower tubs.

'Do you have a gathering every week?' A woman dressed in a sailor stripe dress, with a basket full of Marks and Spencer's vegetables, was asking the question.

'Pardon?'

'I was wondering if you could tell me when and where you meet?'

142

'I don't. I've lost my grandchild.' And Jan stared off into the crowd once more, while the woman said things that made no sense to Jan and eventually helped herself to leaflets.

Jan watched the woman walk away, then rushed away herself to look around the nearest corner. There was nothing. She went back to the stall, trying to ignore the empty buggy. She found herself entreating God, just as she knew she would if she were about to crash in a plane—I'll go to church, even pray again; let Macie live. Please don't let my grandchild die. It was when she framed the word 'my' that Jan understood something—Macie was, after all, as much hers as her own children. She had always seen the pasty-faced thing as a changeling, foisted upon Flinn, an ugly little girl, belonging in her appetite and wilfulness more to her mother's side of the family than to Jan's. She put up with Macie for Flinn's sake, but had not thought she loved her. Now she believed that she did. Jan thought of making cakes with the child, reading her bed-time stories, walking along the river and playing games. Only the night before, Macie had made them all laugh, doing funny walks and imitating Flinn. Jan began to hurt with something that was not straps rubbing or blisters. There was a sick, tight band inside her head; she found herself reading the words fluttering on the leaflets on the stall—Let Jesus into your life. Sing God's name and be reborn. Join with our Group—join with God. The words made as much sense as the huge banners in the shops: Final reductions 70% off everything. Jan walked as far from the table as possible, scouring the crowds. She glimpsed, everywhere, white socks and sandals and pink shorts, disappearing into shops and cafes and skipping up steps and down steps.

A child about Macie's age, dragged along by her mother, was banging on her mother's hand with her spare fist, wailing that she wanted to stop, she wanted a drink, she wanted a pee, she wanted a drum. Macie was like that, not like one of those cherubic children pictured in the bibles and hymn

143

books on the table. Maybe there were children as perfect and saintly, but Jan didn't know any. She was getting out her mobile to phone the police, when she saw Freya coming towards her, carrying a guitar.

'Michael's found Macie—over in the other precinct.' And just behind came the young man, carrying the struggling Macie. Jan ran across, forgetting her sore shoes and forgetting she had disliked the man for playing such facile songs. Jan was crying because she was so relieved, so happy. She did not even mind when Michael put his arm around her and whispered something reassuring; she was aware though, of his breath that smelt of cigarettes. She could not key in Flinn's mobile number because her hand was shaking too much and Freya, who had been searching with Michael, took it from her and phoned Flinn for her. Macie kept trying to wriggle free again and Jan could barely speak to her, silenced by some deity she called God or luck.

'Shall we pray?' said Michael, and it was not a question. So Jan stood there, waiting for Flinn to get back, with her hands pressed together, despite a strong desire to pull them apart, not listening to whatever it was he said, but noticing how Freya had wedged herself as far as possible from the shame of her old family. Freya's eyes were tightly closed until the man said Amen, then she opened them and smiled at him.

Macie, meanwhile, had fallen asleep in the buggy (which meant she wouldn't sleep that night). 'Let's all sing,' Michael said, and offered Jan a tambourine.

In late July it turned into an even hotter summer—a burnt up, slow time. Anna had finished the university term and was home, mostly arguing with Flinn or teasing Freya. Flinn had fixed up a hammock strung between two trees and when he came home from work Anna was usually there.

'I didn't spend a day making that thing work, for you to take it over.'

'Tough, baby brother.'

'I've been out working; I want to drink a beer out here before I go see Emma.'

'It's too hot inside; Mum's cooking.'

'Why don't you help for a change?'

'She recognises my culinary inadequacy and has sent me away.'

'I wish she would send you away.'

At the dinner table Freya barely spoke to Flinn. She was still cross about him showing her up in front of her friends. Jan knew this, and knew too, that initially Freya had tried not to talk to her, either. But this was proving harder. Freya kept forgetting, and half way through a conversation—some of them nice ones about what she wanted for her twelfth birthday—she would suddenly remember. She would taper off into awkward silence and look uncomfortable, like she wished she'd never decided on such an exacting punishment for her mother.

Freya was talking to Anna, as a way of communicating indirectly with Jan.

'They're going to give me a tea-party at church on Sunday—for my birthday, because school's broken up and my friends have forgotten me.'

'I thought I saw some cards in your bag?'

'The youngest is always forgotten. But if I'm going to have a cake at home, too, it will have to be after Church. Do you want to come to my church party, Anna?'

Anna looked bored at being the mediator again. 'Sorry, blossom. No can do. I'm playing pool with some friends. You could come with us?'

Freya shook her head, knowing she wasn't wanted.

'Anyway,' Anna went on, and Freya listened, in case it was to do with her birthday, 'perhaps I will go away; I could do an MA after I finish next year.' Jan served out extra pasta to Freya, ignoring Anna for a minute.

'Freya, you choose when you want your birthday tea. After or before. Up to you, love.' Freya pretended she was not listening.

'Or VSO? How about India. I always wanted to travel on those steam trains.'

'You could do voluntary work in this house. Like help a bit.'

'I washed up last night.' Freya tugged at her sister's arm.

'You could make me a chocolate cake, Anna. I like chocolate cake.'

'You may have washed up, but you made loads of mess later. And it's me, Freya, not Anna who makes the cakes. And yes, you can have chocolate.'

'Chill, Mum. House-work gets done.'

'By the fairies?'

Tempers erupted, perhaps because of the heat. All of them were restless, as if they sensed the changes they needed to effect, but didn't yet know how to make them. It didn't help that when Anna caught the tube or bus into the centre of town, Jan could not relax, but worried about bombs, the terrorist attack Londoners tensed themselves for, even as they pushed the thought away. The calmest times were when Anna slouched at the kitchen table, looking through travel brochures or when they all found a DVD they could watch. The Marx Brothers, Laurel and Hardy or The Simpsons were the best; it was as if the films turned them upside down and shook out all the tension. Even Macie laughed, although mostly she didn't understand what she laughed at.

One night as Freya and Macie cooked cake with Jan, neatly placing smarties in the centre of the rich chocolate circle, Anna watched, warming her hands on a mug of cocoa.

'I get withdrawal. It used to be from cider, then dope, now it's from chocolate. I need some sort of a fix each day. This will have to do. Does cocoa put on as much weight as bars of the stuff?'

'Nanna's buying fair trade now, too. She's more aware of things like that, now Gramps isn't there to mention cost.'

'Who's going to do the ashes thing with Nanna? It's been almost six months'

'I thought your dad would, but he keeps putting it off. Nanna said she wants to take the ashes up to the mill soon, so she can get off on holiday. She said it felt wrong going off and leaving the urn behind—callous somehow.'

'She could take Gramps with her!'

'I don't think he'd approve of Spain—too foreign.'

They laughed. It felt good to have the four of them sitting around together and getting on.

'You could go and help scatter the ashes, Anna! You need to do something. Use up the summer. Go and see Nanna.'

Anna didn't completely reject the idea. She scraped at the pale brown skin on the top of her drink and wiped it off on the wooden table.

'Ugh! How can such a yummy drink be so disgusting? Perhaps I will go. It would serve Gareth right. He never phones, never even comes around. So much for waiting for me to finish my term. He spends every day in the pool hall.'

'I thought he was going to Cardiff to work for his uncle.'

'He can't start in the law firm until September, but he can't be bothered to do a job in the mean-time.'

Jan took the smarties away from Macie, who had put as many in her mouth as she had on the cake. Anna came across and idly started to eat the orange ones.

'Nice for some. Perhaps you should have gone in for law, Anna.'

'So I could defend Flinn in court—or Dad?'

When Anna arrived in Somerset, she saw what her mother meant about her grandmother's house. It wasn't just that nothing had been cleaned or tidied (which Jan had thought a good thing when she'd visited at Easter—Nanna is breaking out at last, she'd said) there was also very little food. The bath was scummy, taps dripped, the garden had transformed into a jungle of weeds and a wasp's nest hung just outside the bedroom window. Perhaps it hadn't been quite so bad when Jan had seen it, Anna thought.

'Shall I help you tidy up a bit, Nanna?'

'It's not so bad, luvvy. And I'm having a bit of a sort out—going through things.'

'Do you want me just to clean the kitchen?'

'You relax; it will get done one day. The dust will still be there when we're both dead.' But Nanna looked around, as if she'd only just noticed that there were bottles with gone-off milk littering the window ledge, piles of clean and dirty washing over the chairs and a bin spilling its contents out onto the floor. 'It will get done,' she repeated, softly, sounding less convinced as she climbed the stairs to have another lie down. But by whom, thought Anna?

At first she had thought that her Nanna might be ill. But when they went out for a meal, Nanna ate more than Anna did, and Nanna walked miles every day picking wild flowers. When she came home she looked them up in the same thick books Anna could always remember being there in the back room. But something was wrong. The rank smell of bacon fat filled the kitchen—bacon had become Nanna's main meal these days—and when Anna opened the fridge, the stench of rotting broccoli made her slam the door fast, made her understand what it was she'd been smelling all morning. It felt cruel the way Anna's childhood memories were being mashed into a smelly mulch. Where was the Nanna she remembered?

For two days Anna cleaned in short bursts, hiding what she was doing. Nanna became cross if she saw her granddaughter working in the house.

'Don't you waste your time with all this, Anna, my girl. You've had an education. You don't have to be trapped.'

When her Nanna went out to discover some new flowers (they turned out to be the ones she'd collected the day

148

before), Anna knocked on neighbours' doors and talked to the people in the local shop. In the shop, they said they'd only come down from Birmingham a few months before, so couldn't really say whether Mrs Griffiths was unwell or not. Some neighbours told Anna that Nanna went out less and didn't bother with church these days—but they supposed she was grieving. It was hard to know what was normal, what wasn't. Wasn't everyone odd in their own way?

The man who lived next door, Mr Allen, explained to her, 'It's what happens when someone dies. Your world stops. It's like brambles growing up and shutting you in.' He smiled out at her as if she couldn't be expected to know about loss. 'Why does everyone grow up so fast? I remember you and your brother—playing next door, the balls flying into our garden.'

And you never threw them back, thought Anna. But she asked if he thought Nanna had been behaving oddly. He frowned slightly.

'Your Nanna can be odd, Anna. She and Molly sometimes didn't get on, but that's water under the bridge, now.' None of this helped. Anna could smell his house through the open door. It gave off the decayed smell of age, like worn talcum powder. 'Why don't you come in? It would nice if you and your Gran would come and have tea some time.' He looked surprised that he'd made this offer, was perhaps already thinking of retracting it. He stepped out onto the path, perhaps to block Anna's way. 'I did knock on your Gran's door once or twice. But it was hard. And she wasn't in.' He looked apologetic, but also slightly impatient, as if Anna had accused him of negligence. 'Molly's only just gone, you see.' He gestured back towards the kitchen as if his dead wife had only just popped out to the washing line. If they went in for tea, Anna didn't think she'd be able to swallow properly in case Mr Allen was hiding his own wife's ashes, just as Nanna was hiding Grampy's. How much dead life was there in this

149

place; how much was she ingesting as she breathed the thick summer air?

Anna didn't know where Nanna kept Gramps. It wasn't under the huge bed, nor in the big mahogany wardrobe. There seemed to be no sign of him anywhere. She was glad of this. But she knew she'd have to mention the ashes soon. Although she'd meant to stay a week or two, she was thinking that would be too long. Anyway, Nanna kept forgetting Anna was there and looked startled when she bumped into her on the landing or in the living room. Once Anna had come upon Nanna naked in the bathroom, humming to herself, and filling the sink with deep water.

On her mobile, when she went down to the shop to buy bleach and polish, Anna phoned home, but Jan was having problems with Freya again; apparently her sister wanted to be adopted. And Jan thought Anna was just not letting life evolve.

'You're hanging onto the past; it's natural. You want your childhood to stay fixed, the past to be forever in the present.'

Anna hated it when her mum sounded like a textbook. When she phoned her dad, Lois said that he'd gone camping with Ben and wouldn't be back for a week.

'Tell him I'm worried about Nanna. He should go and see her soon. She's behaving oddly.'

'Listen, honey, the whole world's crazy. The real mad ones are the people who say they're fine, the people into all this psycho stuff. You should see my crazy family. If Nanna's gone nuts, she's just joining the party.'

Anna put the phone down. Her dad's wife sounded drunk; there was lots of loud talk in the background. It was only two in the afternoon.

The next day was cooler. There'd been a storm in the night but the sky was blue again.

'Are we going to do it, Nan? Or do you want me to go alone? I know where the mill is. Dad used to take me there for walks. He told me the story of how you used to clean for his grandfather and how you met Uncle Harry and Gramps.'

'Too young,' snorted Nanna. 'I might have got away if I'd not cleaned for that man. I was going to go to secretarial college.' She was more cryptic these days and more explicit, too. There was something coming; Anna could feel it. And she sensed she didn't want to know what her grandmother intended to say. The bitterness and anger would somehow smell like the fridge and like the curdled milk in the bottles.

'If we go now, we can be back for lunch.'

'I'll get my mac, it might rain.' It was warm, but Nanna insisted on her long mac and walking boots. She got a willow basket and pushed her way through the long grass to the shed. Anna should have guessed that was where Gramps was hiding. Through the window, Anna watched the house martins dipping and diving, up into the sky, down towards the village stream, up and under the eaves of houses, a silky flash of black, then white. It had been that way forever. But in the high field that stretched up from the valley floor and from the straggle of village, towards the new road, a section had been fenced off. For the first time, someone was growing vegetables, not just grazing sheep. She'd heard that the people in the new houses, people from the city, were buying bits of stray land to root themselves in country ways, to claim territory. It felt threatening, somehow. She hoped Nanna would not sell off the small field at the back of the cottage.

They walked up the steep track that led the way to the mill. Flowers were out all along the hedge banks: toadflax, herb robert, red campion, lord and ladies. Each year, she taught herself the names and then promptly forgot them. It was a bit like being at university—memorising and forgetting, reading and forgetting, Surprised, each time, by the discovery of how much you don't know. They walked in single file most of the way, down the nettlely, overgrown paths, and then through the fields. One of the tracks led through a pine forest and here it was gloomy and quiet, with no sound of birdsong. Half way along, they saw a sudden movement, and an animal rustled down into a thicket of dense trees and shrubbery. On the path ahead lay the body of a pigeon, its head bitten clean off. There was no mess—a few grey feathers in a soft downy trail, and just a splash or two of neat blood.

'Fox!' said Nanna. She took a stick and poked at the open wound of neck, the neat circle that led down into the animal's warm body. It gave a bit and was still springy and soft, as if the pigeon had not quite noticed its head was chopped off. 'He'll be back. We could hide and wait. Watch him eat the rest.' Anna was disgusted. She looked at her Nanna who was bending to peer into the cavity, into the veins and flesh. 'That's what he did to me.' She looked up her granddaughter pointedly. 'That's what life once did to me. He did.' Her Nanna, staring with those intense grey eyes, was attempting to communicate something too painful for words. Anna would not ask, who? How? She was afraid. She pointed out a dark cloud high above the spindly pines that thrust up into the sky.

'Shall we go on, before it rains?' Her Nanna laid the stick carefully to one side, as if the dissection was a job she would come back to later, when the weather got better.

In places the tracks were quite rough, and Anna became worried. Nanna was red in the face, often stopping to dab at her skin with a torn hankie. When she stumbled, Anna put out her hand and supported her arm, but Nanna dusted her off.

'I'm not an old lady, thank you. Not yet. Quite fit—not ready for the old people's home.' She smiled grimly, as if she suspected there was some plot to get her into one. It was true Nanna was not that old, in her mid sixties, perhaps. She'd been a young mother—very young. Everyone knew her husband had been at least fifteen years older, but no-one could get out of Nanna her date of birth. A war child, perhaps, or born just after the war. Nanna's mother and father had both been old, probably hurling themselves into a desperate post-war fling. Perhaps their earlier fiancées had died, or disappeared or recklessly taken off with other people, or possibly just gone mad. Owen said that in the swirl of war, anything was possible. It was hard to think that Nanna must have been a teenager in the sixties. Probably living in a village and having old parents thickened time and made you resistant to change. Anna wondered how much this hill, the old mill beyond, the hawthorn and blackthorn knotted together had altered in Nanna's life-time—probably very little.

The sky was clouding over. They were a long way from home. Anna vaguely remembered that they had to cross another three fields, ford a stream and then make their way up a gravelly road. Even if they got to the mill before it rained, it was unlikely they'd get home dry. When she had last walked that way, people were doing up the place, changing it from a dilapidated shell into a modern home. She wondered what they would think, having ashes scattered in their millrace. Was there a law about where you could, or could not, cast the remnants of human bodies? Nanna opened the latch gate into a tilting scrubby field, full of groundsel, ragwort and dock. She stood, looking out across the span of poor grass.

Anna had remembered it wrongly. They needed to ford two streams, both in this large, sloping field. They struck off down towards the first which was muddy and wide with a bog of animal and human footprints on either bank. Further ahead, they could see the second stream. This one was deeper and faster moving, with only one place to ford. But settled across the narrow path, blocking the way, was a large white cow with horns.

'Bull!' said Nanna decisively. 'I think that's as far as we can get.' Anna was surprised by her Nanna, that such a country girl, was suddenly getting everything wrong.

'Do bulls have udders, Nanna?' But even if it wasn't a bull, it was huge. Anna couldn't imagine asking it to move, prodding it with a stick or umbrella. Over the crest of the distant hill, where two stubby trees—Rowan or Hawthorn—spiked the skyline, more cows began appearing, some of them bullocks, cantering along with a sprawling leggy stride. There was also a largish animal, bigger than the rest, swaying its bulk heavily from one side to the other.

'I think that's the bull,' Anna said.

Nanna scrutinised the beast that picked its way first left, and then right, along some secret animal route. It would eventually get near the entrance, the gate where they'd come in. There was a choice. They could rush back or force the white cow out of their way so they could cross the ford. Anna armed herself with a branch she picked from the ground; the damp, thick stick had peeling bark and moss on one side. She moved it around in her hand, assessing the weapon's strength. Against a bull, it would snap. Anna became intensely attuned to the animals in the field, to their shifts of movements, their snorts and flicks of tail. The air felt cold on her damp skin. She could hear familiar birdsong—blue-tits flitting somewhere to the left of her.

'Let's walk back.' She tried to make her voice sound casual; she didn't want to make her grandmother panic or become obdurate.

Instead of turning with her to make her way back up the bumpy path, Nanna scrambled down the muddy bank to the first stream. She flicked open the lid of her picnic basket, pulled out a small wooden box, then prised open the lid. Her shoes were covered in squelchy mud; she was having trouble keeping her balance. She bent and emptied out the contents into the brown swirl of water. Anna winced as dust blew across Nanna's coat and legs, while the rest of the ash floated for a moment in an oily slick of grey. Then, the current devoured it, breaking the dust up and tumbling it down over stones and boulders.

'There! He'll get there one way or another. Back to his roots. It was him that liked his roots, not me.' Anna was measuring the distance between the animals and the gate. She knew she could save herself but she would have to set off immediately and abandon her Gran.

'Hurry Nan! The bull's going to charge…' Anna was backing away from the stream, as if she could magnetically pull her Nanna with her. The bull had halted half way down the field and watched the women, just as they watched it. Did it think they might join his harem of cows? Bizarrely, Anna thought about gods transformed into bulls and the continual rape of women by these half-god, half animal creatures. Anna waited for the thud and tremble of the earth as the animal set off after them; she waited for her breath to become strangled inside so she would not be able to run or walk, perhaps not even move. Her Gran slithered back up the bank, but had to push her hand down into the orange, sticky mud to get some purchase. She was puffing as she grabbed Anna with this same muddy hand.

'We'll make it if I don't fall over. I think it's starting to rain, Anna.'

'Give me your arm, Nanna. I'll help. Don't look at it. Don't let it think we're afraid.' The gate was getting further away, not closer. The bull set off once more, jolting its way toward them, stopping now and again to shake its head or snort. Anna held up her stick, as if she were a farmer. But her heart wasn't in this lie. She caught her hand on nettles and could feel the pulse of pain—her head throbbed, too. The legs that had so sturdily carried her all morning, now felt frail and wobbly as if detached from the rest of her.

The bull stopped ten yards before the gate, watching them. They tried not to look it in the eye, or to look for the ring that pierced its broad nose. They fumbled with the gate, breath held, then pulled the wooden slats toward them, before rushing through and slamming it shut behind.

When they made their way back through other fields and then down the gloomy track in the pine forest, Anna kept feeling that they were being followed. Once she did hear undergrowth snap behind her. She imagined the bull charging through the rickety gate and thundering down the lanes to get them, to snap off their heads and ravage them. Further on down the path, the dead pigeon had gone. Just the drops of blood and a few feathers were left as evidence.

'Isn't that meant to be a public footpath, Nanna? Why was there a bull there? Has that ever happened before? When you've been walking?'

'I can't remember. Perhaps.'

'Did that stream lead to the mill, Nanna?'

'Probably the sea. It's downhill from the mill.'

That was as much as they said on the journey back. The wind picked up and the rain gradually got heavier. It was harder going downhill than it had been climbing up. Several times Anna slipped, and her grandmother grabbed at her to steady her.

'Do you think Gramps will mind, Nanna?'

'Mind what?'

'Being sent downstream to the sea.'

'He'd still have ended up in the same place if I'd emptied him out up there. Anyway, he didn't often ask me what I minded.'

When they arrived back at the cottage, Nanna's strength had all drained away. So had Anna's. She made hot chocolate for them both, after carefully smelling the milk. Then they went to lie down with their books. When Anna slept, she dreamt of rain and wind, a river sluicing along and a threat, just out of sight, but steadily pursuing, however hard she tried to outrun it.

The next day was W.I. day. Anna found her Nanna packing jam-jars into a large wicker basket.

'I'm going to drive these last batches of rhubarb and tomato chutney down to the girls. I won't be here to use them, and I haven't really been pulling my weight, recently. Haven't been to a meeting for ages. Do you want to come, Anna?'

'Sure! I'll just get some breakfast.' Anna unwrapped the fresh loaf she'd bought and the new slab of butter.

'I'll make you toast, Nanna.'

'I've got some of those cross things somewhere, if you'd prefer them. They're French. Grace says we could drive up to the French border when I go to stay.' At the back of the bread bin, some greening croissants were stuffed up against some hard pitta bread.

'They don't last long, Nanna. I'll make us toast. Fresh bread toast.' She pulled out the going-off stuff and put it in the bin. Anna had noticed that although her grandmother was buying all sorts of foreign food, her appetite at home seemed to have diminished; she'd always been plump before, but now her clothes were hanging off her. 'It's such a wonderful smell, Nanna—coffee and toast. Doesn't it make you hungry?'

Anna ate her fourth slice, trying to encourage the recalcitrant child to follow suit. 'It's such good bread. Much better than London.'

'Is it, dear?'

Later Anna went to be sick. She felt disgusted that she had pushed so much unwanted food inside. The toilet basin stank of wee, a sour smell, that increased in pungency the further she put her head into the bowl. She brought up lumps of undigested toast and could feel a fizzing in her nose, bitterness at the back of her throat. When she'd finished, she looked in the mirror and her watery eyes were glazed and shamed, post-fix. She had not done this since she'd been at university in London and her boyfriend had said she was overweight, that she looked pregnant. She mouthed herself—stupid—but really she felt the opposite. She was cleansed and in control again.

157

Anna felt that she'd changed over the last few years. She used to be more confident. Then there'd been the marriage break-up, bad luck with boys, the horrid time at her first university and doing badly in her exams. That had all been a bit of a shock. In the grand scale of things, it wasn't much. When she read about terrible events in the newspapers, she felt ashamed of being self-centred and pathetic and for being more cautious. She had learned, though, however much you made yourself sick, you could never bring up self-doubt and self-disgust; you'd have to find a different way of expelling that.

'Are you ready, Manna?' Nanna called out as she passed the locked door. 'I'll get the car out. We need to be there for 9.30, latest.' Anna registered her pet name, the name she'd often called herself when she'd been little.

When they arrived, they delivered the chutney and empty jam-jars to someone called Beryl. The room was full of tables covered with white cloths and women briskly laying out knitted things and gift cards, pies, cakes, vegetables, fruit, jams and chutneys. Each stall had different things for sale and each of the items had a label saying who had made it and when. Anna hoped that no-one who bought Nanna's chutney knew what her kitchen was like these days. At some time in the past, there'd been an inspection. She remembered that, the stir it had caused, Nanna saying family couldn't come and visit until it was over.

Anna moved around vaguely smiling at people, but they all seemed preoccupied. There was a fuss about floats and someone not having got enough silver to go around. Then no one could find the right chair for the woman who took the payments and had a bad back. Anna picked up a knitted doll and wondered if she should buy it for Macie. A tall woman, with grey hair seemed to be in charge and had a sheet on which she was listing things.

'They're queuing already. Someone go out and tell Jean not to let them start turning over the plants yet. They have to wait until ten. Anyone who touches won't be allowed to buy.'

'Don't let her see you picking up that teddy, dear. I'll put it under the counter for you.' The woman took the toy from Anna and stowed it safely away.

'Thank you. It's for my niece.' Anna liked the sound of that; it made her feel grown-up, even if she didn't much like Macie.

'I remember seeing you at your Gramps' funeral. How's your Gran, dear? She looks a bit peaky. We've missed her.'

The woman in charge came across to Nanna. 'Are you staying? You're not on the rota. You could have let me know.'

Nanna couldn't have heard properly.

'No I'm not staying. I'm off to Spain.'

The woman talking to Anna intervened. 'I'll just take Mart and her granddaughter out to the tea-room.' And then as she led Anna and her Nanna out to the kitchen, she said, 'You wouldn't want to be standing there when the doors open. They invade. And most of them have no manners. You sit and have a cuppa and one of my shortbreads. I always keep a batch back for the end. We need something once the hordes have trampled through. They're worse than city people. You'd think a hunt was on and they were trying to find a fox on the stalls.'

On the drive back, Anna's grandmother forgot which way to go. Anna was sitting in the back, holding a basket full of things that her Nanna's friend across in Spain had asked her to take over—mostly jars of marmalade, and plants. Anna wasn't sure how Nanna would manage these on a plane, and it was because she'd asked this question, her Gran had shot past the turning that led down to the ford and the Merry Harriers.

'I'll get petrol now I've gone wrong. I know a secret route back. I used to go there with my lover.'

'You had a lover?' Anna was not sure if she had heard properly. But it sort of made sense. She'd never noticed her grandparents kiss, or even hold hands. She saw her grandmother looking at her oddly in the driving mirror.

'Not that sort of lover, silly. We went out walking when we were girls—sometimes had a kiss with our boy. We just called them our lovers. What did you think I meant?'

In the petrol station Nanna forgot which side the tank was on, and had to ask for help pulling the heavy pump over to the right side. In the end, the man who came to help filled the tank right up. Perhaps because this flustered her, when Nanna pulled out, she stalled the car. Then she stalled again. Behind them, also waiting, the man who had helped sat in his Jaguar watching. When she stalled the car a third time, Anna knew the engine was in danger of flooding. Though she'd only had six driving lessons, she'd learnt that much.

But the car, perhaps used to this sort of treatment, eventually started and they set off again along the busy road. Every now and then they passed a village, with houses pressed close and in these sections they were meant to drive at thirty. Nanna sped up in here, but slowed in the open road. Soon they were followed by a trail of cars, and Anna tried not to turn to catch the eye of the driver in the Jag behind. She spent time rearranging the jars so they didn't make such a rattling sound, clutching the basket tight, as if it might protect her. She calculated that if she pretended everything was normal, it just might be.

When they turned off the main-road at a crossroads Nanna indicated left but turned right, almost taking out a man who'd been crossing the narrow lane. If Nanna saw, she didn't comment.

'Nearly home. I'm hungry now. Gone a bit shaky, I think.' She flicked her eyes up to the mirror again and gave a reassuring smile, as if Anna were still a child. 'What would you like for lunch today, dear?' Anna wanted to say, nothing, just concentrate. And in any case, so far, her grandmother had not managed to remember a single meal-time.

They drove around a tight bend a bit too fast and found themselves facing a tractor that lurched towards them, filling the entire track. The tractor stopped. Nanna skidded to a halt.

'Well what does he think I'm meant to do now? Reverse?' And the tractor driver, as if he'd heard her, or read her lips, did start to gesture backwards.

'I can't. I can't turn my neck. He'll have to go back.' So Nanna also gestured to go back. The man hauled himself out of his seat and clambered down onto the road. He came lumbering across, looking over at his fields to left and right, walking as if he'd been riding a horse.

'You have to go back, my dear. There's room up behind. There's no place back up my way.'

'I'm sorry, but I can't. I have a bad neck.'

'Can't she do it?' He pointed at Anna who was holding the basket and looking down at the floor.

Anna was about to say, I'm not insured and anyway, I'm not very good yet. But Nanna interjected, 'Can't you do it?' She smiled up hopefully, almost coquettishly at the farmer.

'I'm not insured for your car, Missus, and I'd make it stink. There's proper roads for cars back along. I don't know why folks have to come this way.'

'I'll do it.' They both turned to look at Anna. She felt an impatience that was almost a pleasure; it floated through her like a reminder of her younger self. She could not bear to sit there any longer, imagining more cars coming along and everyone stuck for hours, all asking each other to go backwards. In the field over to the left, flies buzzed around cow-pats and a large black and white cow drank from a metal tank. In the hedgerow was the sticky grass that Anna used to throw over her brother on long country walks, so he'd arrive home with his jumper covered. Anna got out the car and motioned for her grandmother to do likewise. Nanna

161

probably had no notion of how few lessons Anna had actually had, or perhaps she didn't care.

When Anna took the wheel, it was strange having no-one sitting next to her; it was also illegal, but the thought of her grandmother beside her, as she tried to concentrate, would have been too much. Anna took deep breaths, checked her mirror (where she saw her own grave, competent face staring back), checked her handbrake, then carefully slid the car into reverse. She pulled her foot up from the clutch, engaged the accelerator, felt its bite and then took off the handbrake. Slowly, slowly, with the engine revving too much, she backed the car, checking her mirrors and stopping sometimes to look over her shoulder. At one point she got too close to the bank and had to edge forwards. But she set off again and found the gap where a fence was set back from the road and there was a place she could pull in. She thanked God no other car had come down the road. When she finally parked, nudging up against the fence so she could feel its pressure against the side of the car, she felt amazed at herself. Jubilant. She wanted to phone her boyfriend and tell him what a brilliant driver she'd become. She wanted to immediately take her test. Instead, she put the handbrake on, got out and called to her Gran. The tractor growled past first, the man giving a curt, unimpressed nod as he went by and then Nanna came puffing along behind. Anna clambered across to the passenger side and let her grandmother take over.

'You can drive all the way if you like, Anna.'

'I'm not insured Nan.'

As they jerked down the narrowing lane, trees hanging over them, blocking their light, Anna began to wish that she had, after all, driven the car. Nanna kept getting the gears wrong and speeding up and slowing down randomly.

'Too much excitement,' Nanna muttered at one point, 'Ashes and bulls and cars.'

Anna spread her fleece over the jars so that glass would not fly up and scar her when the car hit the side of the road or went down a ditch.

'I feel a bit car sick, Nan.'

Behind them, another car had appeared and seemed like it was part of the same show-ground ride, tilting and veering in unison with their car.

'We'll stop when we get to the bottom of the hill; there's a new tea-room.' Anna's Grandmother said these words tersely, concentrating on the road ahead and gripping the wheel tight, as if it was her first lesson. Anna crossed her fingers and looked out at fields of rapeseed, sweet corn, hay and tall grass. As they ground their way up to the top of a precipitous hill, another car suddenly appeared driving towards them.

'Oh,' said Nanna and started to brake, pulling in as close as she could to the hedge, so the other person would have to squeeze past. Then she stalled. When she tried to put the handbrake on, it did not hold, and the car began to roll gently backwards. 'Oh,' said Nanna again, and looked down at the handbrake, then up at the car ahead. Anna looked over her shoulder. They were not far from the car behind. Nanna seemed to have her foot on the clutch rather than the brake, and she had given up trying to start or stop the car; she was instead trying to steer backwards, looking up into the mirror and then attempting to translate opposite movements to her hands. Anna saw her gran's concentrated face in the mirror and the scared face of the man in the car behind. He was mouthing something and his eyes were communicating resistance to what he must have felt was inevitable.

They were not going that fast when they hit the car, but it nevertheless made a loud noise. And when they got out to look, there was a big dent on the other man's bonnet. Nanna's bumper had somehow got wedged under the tyre so her car wouldn't drive, couldn't pull forward off of the car it sat on.

The man in the oncoming car, who had avoided the accident, eventually put Nanna and Anna in his car and reversed them down the lane to the tea-rooms. He said they should wait there for the recovery vehicle. On the table, Nanna placed the details of the other driver's insurance company, his address, his make of car. When Anna had told him about the funeral, the ashes and her grandmother's confusion, he suggested that perhaps she should give up driving for a while. He was terse and unfriendly, like this had come on top of a day full of other misfortune.

'I'll stay put with the cars—put out some warning signs. You'd better make sure she doesn't drop dead too.'

The man stayed with the two cars while Anna and her Gran waited in the empty café, drinking hot tea with sugar. Nanna kept telling the story of their journey home, re-telling it again and again, until, in the end, she made it sound almost normal, like it might have happened to anyone. It was then, as Anna began to wonder whether there was something really wrong with her grandmother, that Nanna started to tell another story.

'I don't hate him for what he did, in fact he was the only one who was kind, but I'm free now he's gone.'

Anna was picking at her fruitcake, taking out the sultanas, which she'd never liked and had stopped concentrating.

'It wasn't really his fault, even if he was a bit close; it was us that ran into him.'

'Gramps. I mean Gramps.'

Anna knew that she was expected to ask what Gramps had done and why it wasn't his fault, but she stayed silent. She wondered if Gramps sometimes hit her grandmother. A friend's mother had left her husband because he'd been slapping her and locking her in a room. She remembered how her grandfather had stomped on the earth and thrown his garden equipment down like an angry child.

'It always felt like a marriage of convenience. Owen and me against him. Owen and me against his family. They never

164

accepted us.' Now Anna was meant to ask, why, but all she could do was stir the sugar in the cup, around and around. 'He didn't have to blame me because his father made him marry me. When I think about it now, I should probably have married Harry; he was less bossy.'

'Didn't Gramps want the child?' Anna whispered, knowing that the pregnancy was why they had married. She felt that she was hearing a fairy-tale about characters in a far-off world; she couldn't accept it was about her own grandmother, her own father.

'Well it wasn't his.' And as she delivered these words, there was something like triumph in the woman's face, as if she'd known all along that this card she'd held all her adult life would trump anything anyone else could play. For a moment, her expression wavered, as if it was a disappointment to have finally given the secret up. Or perhaps she was concerned that the person she'd served it up to was the wrong one, was only a pawn who would probably get hurt.

The bell on the door pinged in a jolly sort of way and two people came in, shaking off rain from their jackets. Anna and her grandmother looked up, both hoping it was the recovery man.

'Unexpected,' said the woman behind the counter. 'It was forecast dry.'

'Well it's a good thing we could escape in here.' It was a mother and daughter, their faces similar. The two chose a seat in the window. Anna wondered if her Nanna would go on talking. If the couple listened, they would hear what she said.

'I don't know why I'm telling you, Anna. It's your father I need to speak to. But I'm going away next week and he's cancelled each time he was supposed to come down recently. I think he's scared I may have cracked up.'

'Have you?'

'I don't think I know.' She smiled then, as if something funny had occurred to her. 'Do any of us know?'

'But Dad has the same nose as Gramps does. Did.'

'They both have their father's features.' Anna could not, for a minute, understand. Or perhaps she did not want to comprehend. Her grandmother sighed.

'I was sixteen. A bit in love with the whole family. They were a good-looking bunch. I went to clean to make a bit of extra money. The mother had died; Bea had a job in a shop and didn't want to give it up to look after her father and brothers. I'd gone to school with the youngest girl; she died of a brain haemorrhage, but the father remembered me and asked me up to help out at weekends.'

Anna had broken the fruitcake up into separated bits of fruit and dough and moved them around her plate, squashing some under her fingers as she listened. Through the window, they could see a flock of crows chasing a larger whitish bird.

'What's it called, Anna? I've forgotten its name.' Nanna whose nails were lined with black, as if she hadn't washed recently, was pointing up at the thing that circled in easy sweeps, while crows threw themselves into its flight.

'Buzzard, Nanna, a buzzard.'

'That's right. Buzzard. It's a bird of prey.' Other people were drifting into the café, perhaps brought in by the rain, and the woman behind the counter emptied coffee grinds from the espresso machine with rhythmic clunks. When the machine started to hiss, Nanna looked up, as if it reminded her of something.

'I used to make tea for him. We sat together, drinking tea and not speaking. He was handsome, Owen's father. A bossy man. But interesting.' Anna saw her grandmother finger that past, then draw back. 'What does it matter now? What does any of it matter? And I never agreed to it. I didn't want to get pregnant. It was his fault.' She sounded petulant. Anna could not work out if her grandmother was implying she'd been raped or merely saying that she'd chosen to sleep with the man, with the man who was Owen's father, not his grandfather.

'I'll write your father a letter from Spain. Or maybe I'll phone him—tomorrow, not today.'

'Nanna this is awful. Awful for you, for Dad, too.' She wished the recovery man would come banging in and make them have their lift home; she wished she had not been force-fed this terrible story and wished she could have her childhood back and also her rose smelling, clean Nanna.

'It was a stupid accident, Anna. I should never have got pregnant. I would have had such a different life. I would have left Somerset and never come back and I would have travelled far, far away.'

Owen flicked over the postcard from his mother. She'd spent most of August in Spain, staying with an old school friend who'd bought a house there. He felt guilty he hadn't seen her enough since his father's funeral in the spring. He'd gone down two weeks running just after the funeral. In April he'd been about to go down, but then he'd got a bad cold. Another time, he'd packed the car when there was a call from nursery school: Benny had fallen and broken his wrist: Owen would need to take the child to hospital. It didn't make things any easier that his mother hadn't taken to Ben or Lois, and Lois didn't like him going alone, leaving her with the child to look after.

In June he'd finally driven all the way to Somerset (having told his mother he'd be down) only to discover she wasn't there. No-one knew for certain where she was—visiting a friend for the weekend, the man in the shop thought. Owen had climbed over the back wall and been surprised at how high the grass had grown. The contents of the garage and shed were emptied out on to the patio, and when he peered through the kitchen windows, boxes were piled high on the kitchen table. A wide crack had appeared near the back door, as if the extension was on the move, splitting itself off. Owen usually phoned his mother every week, and since she'd got e-mail, he sent her quick family up-dates or internet links he thought she'd like: gardening places, travel for the elderly, home shopping sites. He also knew that Jan was keeping in touch. Jan phoned him after she or one of the children had been to Somerset; sometimes she'd ring to warn him his mother had a scheme to go alone to Morocco or Egypt, and last time it was Bolivia. He didn't mention to Jan that this may well have been his fault; his mother's last e-mail had thanked him for the link to Saga holidays, but said she'd rather not go to South America with a load of doddery oldies.

The postcard he held now had been sent from Lisbon. It said his mother and her friend Grace were in the Stevedore quarter, having a meal of crab. They'd been given little hammers to bash the shell apart and the owner had come over to show them—holding their hands and guiding them—how to crack the legs apart. His mother wrote (knowing he liked a store of facts) that this was the oldest part of the city; it had not been destroyed by the 1755 earthquake. In Grace's writing, a tagged-on couple of lines said they hoped to find some sailors to look after them, followed by exclamation marks and then kisses. It did not say how they'd made their way to Lisbon, nor when his mother was returning. He propped the postcard next to the photograph of Freya in her baggy confirmation dress. He'd never realised his mother had wanted to travel. When Owen was a child they'd always gone to the Lake District or the Peaks or sometimes Cornwall.

Owen pushed aside his marking and did a quick Google search for flights to Spain and Portugal, but it was the summer—flights cost the earth. Anyway, he couldn't decide whether he should go to Portugal or Spain. And all he knew was that Grace's house was somewhere outside Alicante. He decided he'd go down to Somerset the following weekend and see the family doctor, or perhaps the vicar—check if they thought his mother was sounding odd. Next day he phoned Jan.

Anna picked up the phone. Ever since the funeral, or was it just after—sometime in early summer—she seemed to have been avoiding him. He wondered if she'd felt abandoned that day he drove off from the funeral with Jan. Perhaps it was some other thing that he'd said or done, or something he hadn't said or done.

'Hi Poppet. How you doing? How's the holiday job?'

'It sucks, Dad. I'm just dashing out. Shall I get Freya for you?' Owen heard her put the phone down and bellow up the stairs. Jan picked up on the other receiver.

'Hi, Owen. Freya's not home, I'm afraid; she's at Sunday School. You'll have to ring later. But make sure you remember this time.' He heard the censoriousness and ignored it.

'Actually, it's not the children I want; it's you.'

'There's a client due in a half an hour; I know it's Sunday, but I had to cancel him last Saturday.' She did not tell Owen she had cancelled because Freya had screamed at her she was a religious bigot, and then had rushed to her room, slamming the door so that one of the wooden panels cracked. Jan did not say how, when she'd heard the child crying (she was crying so much these days) and banging something on the wall (which well may have been her head) she'd decided it was wrong to be counselling a complete stranger, to be taking money instead of seeing to her own child.

'I'm worried about Mum, Jan. She's behaving oddly.'

'Do you mean she's stopped pandering to everyone?'

'I think she's going senile.'

'Oh, Owen! She's travelling, like we did when we were young. Let her be! I went down for the day not long ago and she was fine. We went shopping and had a pub lunch in Minehead. She told jokes. Made me laugh.'

'But she's forgetting things; muddling her words. Getting Dad and Granddad confused.'

'I call the children by the wrong names all the time. We all forget things. It happens more as you get older. In fact, I'm

169

looking forward to forgetting everything. I'm tired of trying to remember what I've got to do each day, and what I have to do in the future. Three children are hard work. When are you going to have Freya for a bit?'

'At half term, and at New Year—you know that.'

'Thanks a bunch! She needs to see you more, and I need you to see her more.'

'Is she okay?'

'I'm not sure she is. But she shuts herself away. I found a diary the other day. I wasn't going to look at what she'd written, and then I thought I ought to. I think she hates me. Owen.'

'What did it say?'

'That we were both selfish. She said her family was full of 'careless egos' and that none of us had any morals and we wouldn't get into the kingdom of heaven.'

'Is that all? I'm quite happy not going heaven. I sold my soul long ago. How about you?' Owen was not really concentrating and had started trying to mark student work at the same time as he talked; he was already a week past the dead-line. He realised he had written Heaven instead of Heather.

'Don't joke, Owen. There was some cryptic stuff too, initials and abbreviations and the initial M—a boy she has kissed three times.'

'She's sounding normal. She's a teenager; she hates her parents and she's about to get a boyfriend.' This was not exactly what Owen thought; he had a sense of something brewing, but could only cope with one disaster at a time.

'You know she's not as simple as that, and on one page she'd written in capitals—I wish I was dead.'

He did not know why the words came gushing out. 'Actually, it should be 'were'. I used to think about death all the time. But there's a big jump from feeling crap to actually topping yourself.'

'Like my cousin did, you mean?'

'Christ, I'm sorry, Jan. I didn't think.'

'You never do.'

'Of course you must be worried. I'm worried too. I'll come up in a fortnight. I want to see Anna too. Is she okay? Has she said anything to you about why she's cross with me?'

'Is she? I didn't know. She's had a cold, been a bit off colour, that's all. And working in a call centre is a lousy job.'

'I'd come next week, but I have to go to Somerset—gather intelligence about Mum.'

'Is she back?'

'Not yet. You know, I think it's okay to read the diary, Jan. There are times it's perhaps alright to be deceitful. Keep me posted about what it says.'

'I would, but I can't. She's changed the hiding place. She left a note where it should have been saying: stop reading my private thoughts.'

'Perhaps you should write something back—say how you're worried. You could pretend to be someone else. She might listen to us if we weren't us.'

Owen could hear other voices in the background—Flinn, he thought, a girl and a child's voice—probably Macie.

'I've got to go, Owen. Flinn needs to talk to me and the doorbell's ringing.'

'I'll call Freya; we can talk about where we'll go when I come up. Could I stay? I'm really broke at the moment.'

'Fine, I won't be here anyway. Flinn's going to look after Freya on Saturday week. A friend has booked me a night away.'

'So I won't see you? Have you decided what you're doing about Christmas?' It had already seemed a long year: his father dying; full-time work taking its toll; Lois' partner messing up the business accounts.

'We'll take the first week in the cottage—for Christmas. You can take over for the New Year, if that's okay. I promised I'd take Freya to church on Christmas Eve. I can just about bear it in that lovely old church.'

'I'll tell you what. I'll come next weekend instead—to see Freya, to see you all.'

'We're going to my other cousin's wedding—all of us— the one who said she'd never marry. Come as you arranged— the week after.'

In the end, Owen didn't have to try and find his mother; she found him. She was already back in Somerset; the postcard had taken longer than she did to cross continents. She phoned him in the middle of the night. At first he thought she must be still in Spain, having a heart attack or something. It was 3am.

'I had to tell you, Owen. I've had the time of my life. I should have been an air-hostess, like I always wanted. What you see from the planes! And it's so quick! And they all look after me; I just pretend I'm a bit confused. I got upgraded last time!'

The next weekend, Owen drove down to his mother's house. Now it was September, he could leave Ben in nursery most of Friday so Lois could get on with her design commissions; he decided Lois could manage the Saturday alone: Ben was three and a half and less of a handful. His mother was on her way out, driving up the lane, as he drove down. As they drew alongside one another, she wound the window down.

'Have you come down to see me? This is a nice surprise, Owen.'

'I phoned you last night, Mum. I asked you if there was anything you wanted and said I'd be down by midday.'

'Did you? I thought you were coming next week. I must be a bit jet-slagged still.'

'Jet-lagged, Mum. Jet-lagged.'

'That's it!'

Owen was surprised at the state of the house; the garden he'd seen a few weeks earlier, although the grass was inches higher. Even his mother seemed perplexed at the jungle she had to push through to find the shed.

'Shall I cut the grass for you, Mum?'

They were both staring out of the kitchen window at the rippling sea of green, waiting for the kettle to boil.

'I've given the lawn mower away to the summer fete. I decided I couldn't manage the lawn anymore.'

'But someone has to manage it. And you're young, Mum. You're looking younger, too.' She was tanned from her holiday, and her hair was longer and looser.

'I'll bring our mower down, the week after next. But I'll have to bring Ben with me.'

'I don't know why you think I'd don't like him. It's just that I'm busy these days. I've got over the novelty of grandchildren. But he has nice hair. I would have liked to have had dark wavy hair.'

'I'm taking him to London next week to see the other children.'

'Has Anna said anything to you yet?' His mother was plugging the kettle back in after warming the pot; she was having problems getting the plug into the socket. Owen leaned across and helped

'Anna? About what? She barely speaks these days. Jan says it's her job. I think she's having second thoughts about Gareth. He's a waste of space, that boy.'

'Welsh. Like your grandfather was.'

'My great grandfather, you mean.'

'Whatever you want to call him, Owen.'

'Jan said Anna was upset by the crash you both had. But no-one was hurt, were they?'

'Stupid man shouldn't have been driving so fast. He could see me coming backwards.'

'And you're going to sell the car, now?'

'Anna's a good girl. She's kind, you know, even if she does wear silly clothes.' The trees and borders were full of birds, but his mother was having problems naming them. She pointed out a flitting coloured movement. 'There's that lily, again,' she told him, pointing out a blue-tit. When she noticed Owen's frown, she frowned herself and quizzed him. 'What was it then? One of those buzz things?'

'It's a blue-tit, Mum. You know blue-tits. They're blue.'

'I don't know them,' she said and pulled the curtains, perhaps so she couldn't make any more mistakes.

'I've spent too much time abroad,' she told her son, 'I'm losing the language.'

'Have you picked up any Spanish?'

'At my age? Anyway, they all speak English. They all are English.'

Owen wondered through the shabby rooms, fingering the dust, trying to recapture the time, not so long ago, when his mother's world had felt brightly secure. Now, she did not seem to notice the disorder, the erratic mealtimes, food that often tasted gone off—she who had been such a brilliant cook.

When they had their evening meal in the village pub— Owen thought there was less chance of food poisoning there—he tried to find out how she was managing the business of getting to airports and paying bills. He had a sense she was spinning in some orbit separate to everyone else. His mother seemed tired and he was not sure if she was cross with him, or scared of something.

'Oh, I manage. Don from next door helps me; he's got a computer. He sorts things out. I can't depend on you. You're always too busy, too bound up in that university or with Ben. Why did the poor thing have to be an illegitimate child?'

This was something new: sudden streaks of outspokenness. His mother had always been kind, so kind that he'd often wished that she'd argue more or would stand up for herself in supermarkets and against his father.

'We're married now. Ben will be fine.'

'I hope so, but technically he'll always be a bastard. I made sure you weren't a bastard.'

Men propped at the bar with pints of beer shifted in their seats to turn and look at them both. One man raised his hand. Owen's mother nodded back, giving a terse smile. Owen wondered why he hadn't noticed his mother's oddity sooner.

'At least that wife of yours comes and sees me. And your proper child—Anna.'

'I'm not married to Jan anymore, Mum.'

'The daughter of the pub owner slid fish and chips in front of Owen, and a plate of Calamari before his mother. The girl bent down to the old lady, and touched her arm.

'Your favourite.'

'Spanish,' his mother announced with satisfaction, smiling up at the girl. To Owen, it all—the fried sea stuff, the floppy bit of lettuce and the fat chips—looked perfectly English. Owen smothered his meal in vinegar and salt, thinking it might make the food taste better. After his first mouthful, he regretted it.

'Are you thinking of moving out there, Mum?' His mother was cutting her own food into minuscule pieces in a concentrated fashion. Sometimes Owen had noticed her doing this before; he wondered if her teeth were getting bad.

'I've got to leave the house to you, so you can come back to your roots and take over the garden.'

'But I grew up in Bath; these aren't my roots. You can blow it all, if you want to Mum. Go and buy a place in Spain, if it makes you happy.'

'I am happy. I like Spain. Perhaps Grace and I might share her house; we could have one of those civil ceremonies.'

The salt caught in Owen's throat, so he suddenly could not breathe. He started coughing and had to pull out tissues to dab at his watering eyes. His mother shook her head at him, as if he could not be trusted to behave. He wiped at his mouth and looked around again quickly to see if the men at the bar had heard.

'Or I could come and live with you—only you'd have to go back to Jan. I can never understand what that other one is saying; she sounds like all those people on the TV, on *Friends*. I watched it with Anna.'

'Lois is American, Mum; she speaks the same language as us.'

'Well she twists up words and they don't sound friendly.'

It was dark when they walked home down the unlit road from the pub. Owen's mother took her son's arm, picking her way along the rough road.

'What a beautiful night.' She gestured to a pincushion of stars, flickering in the blue-black sky. 'In the country they seem to sing out brightness. You don't get that in the city. It makes me feel that anything is possible, anything. I've never felt so alive.' She halted him and he felt her turn to look up at him. 'It wasn't such a bad thing, having you when I did. Remember that.' Owen did not know what exactly to say, nor what she meant. He wanted to say something kind and gentle back, but before anything had come out, she had pulled him forward again and was humming, then singing a hymn: '*He who would valiant be, 'gainst all disaster...* 'Owen squeezed his mother's arm close, feeling her shaky voice inside him and, though the men from the bar were somewhere behind, he joined in, surprised by his own clear voice echoing hers in the darkness.

Rose stared out of the window. She'd been up half the night, staring at the moon and stars, until dark clouds had obscured them. The new day still seemed full of clotted night and the things she'd been worrying about kept spilling into this fragile morning, trailing after her whichever room she sat in. She didn't look well, and needed to lie down after lunch, especially if it was hot—and October was hot this year. She'd come to London to see all the paintings in all the galleries, and although she hadn't admitted defeat, she now said it wouldn't be worth seeing them all; she'd just check out her favourites

Rose waved away Flinn who was trying to bring her another cup of tea, attempting to be kind again. At the moment tea made her feel sick, even the special liquorice stuff she'd got from the Bristol cancer clinic. She hoped Flinn would not sit down on the couch next to her, but he did. She'd been sitting by the window so she could watch the altercation outside. A woman had reversed into a car as she'd tried to park. The rather beautiful black man, whose car she'd scraped, was gesturing at the bumper, then raising his hands in the air. It was all very dramatic. He appealed to passers-by to look at the dent on his sleek sports car and paced up and down declaiming, as if he were an actor. The blonde woman followed, holding out a scrap of paper and a pen.

'Where is it today, Aunt Rose?' Flinn always irritated her with his attentiveness; Rose preferred Anna. Anna was more like her, she thought.

'Wallace, then V&A with Freya, then Harrods for afternoon tea, then taxi back. I'll have to find a corner seat in the museum so I can doze; I told Freya to bring a book. But she doesn't bother me.'

'She seems to have come on all your trips.'

'She's borrowed your mum's art stuff; she's been drawing—mostly biblical stories. I thought we could get away from that in the V&A.' When Flinn went she pulled herself up and studied Jan's appointment book, calculating how much her sister made in a week. It wasn't much.

Rose heard the doorbell go. She studied that day in the book, wondering if she'd have to vacate the front room— James L.M 10.30 a.m., it said. She was leaving the lounge, with its sofa, cushions, coffee tables and the judiciously placed box of tissue (for sobbing, Rose presumed) when Jan rushed in looking surprised to see her there.

'You okay?'

'Fine.' But it was hard keeping up the pretence that she was managing this illness, even more exhausting than tramping around the galleries.

177

'Good.' Jan plumped up the cushions.

'You know, Jan. You should try laughter therapy. It works better than crying. I know.'

'Perhaps we could sell our phone calls to clients.'

'Do you understand anything we say? You'd lose your clients. They'd think you were madder than them'

'I suppose it's about what we don't say, what we fill in for ourselves.'

'We could make money selling silence, gaps. That would be surreal.'

'You're missing the point, Rose. It would be funny silence.' As Rose left, she saw the black man standing in the hallway, talking to Flinn.

'How you doing bro?'

'Fine, bro and you?'

'Bad day, bro. Bad day.' Rose slipped her scarf off so that her bald head was revealed.

'This is a bad day, bro.' She gestured at her pate. 'Believe me, the rest of life is a piece of cake.' That felt true as she swept towards the kitchen, aware they were staring after her. But she knew that illness had its own neat parameters. When the mess of that other life once again hit and she experienced more normal dents, she'd feel as aggrieved as this young man did. At the kitchen door, she turned. 'Would a coffee and Middle Eastern pastry help the bad day?' She hoped he would say no; the smell of coffee was another of the things that made her feel sick.

Earlier in the year, she'd thought she'd be okay in the weeks when she didn't have chemotherapy, but this was proving to be untrue. The trip to London was meant to be a rejection of illness, two fingers up to it: but Art was wearing her out. True, it had been good to look at the Impressionists again and to check out Tate Modern, but she was stuffed full of images now. She would squash in a last few and then rush back to bed in Manchester. She phoned Max in the kitchen as she made the coffee, standing as far away from the cafetière

178

as she could. He had been expecting the call. He said he'd drive down after work, or could come immediately.

The taxi to take Rose and Freya to the Wallace arrived just as Jan's client was leaving. He'd arranged for his car to be transported to the garage and so shared their taxi part of the way into the city. He said he was an ambulance driver, that it helped sometimes, when you saw things, to shrug the—and seeing Freya listening so closely—he just said that it helped to see Jan now and again.

'And there's me thinking I've got a struggle on. You do stress for a living.'

'But you should hear the crack. It's like a comedy team in the front of that cab. Bob and me have missed our true vocation.'

After he had gone, Freya said, 'I saw him driving once. The lights were flashing and everything. I was going to wave, but I thought he'd crash if I did, so I stayed very still. The other girls walked on, but I couldn't move; I just stayed by the crossing.

'I think that's what you do, Freya. Stay very still so life doesn't crash.'

The rooms in the Art gallery were fairly empty. Rose remembered how much she liked the Fragonard in the Wallace—the girl on the swing, who seemed to be taking life as Rose had always tried to. But after looking at the swing for just a while, she'd felt dizzy and needed to go and sit in the courtyard café. Rose left Freya to roam with her sketchbook, while she sat at a table, looking cautiously at the postcard of the painting, holding the edge of the table just in case she needed steadying. Someone sitting close by had been eating some sort of stew; the smell made her feel sick.

It was strange how, when you'd just seen the original of a postcard, you knew how poor the reproduction was. Yet after a while, once back in Manchester, the postcard would become the painting and be no more, no less, than the real thing. Up until now, Rose had always preferred to trust in life's surfaces. She thought that scratching away at emotions, at the duplicitous underworld was a fool's game. Now she was not so sure. This postcard, this surface, was a very thin affair. She did not feel dizzy when she looked at the reproduction. And somehow, she wished she did.

Rose sipped her water and tried to guess the nationality of the customers and staff; the waitress, she decided was Polish. Unlike the girl in the postcard, who didn't have to work, this dark haired woman was red-faced as she dashed from table to table. She was taking orders, delivering food, seeing to the growing queue (it was nearing lunch-time) and yet smiling all the time as she talked in a polite and clipped way. The girl in the postcard kicked out her legs from under a flouncy pink dress. She was swinging up through the air into a spot full of arched trees and greenness and sunlight. Pushed by one man, another man stood ready to catch the delicate pink shoe that was flying off as the girl gave herself to movement and pleasure.

Rose unbuttoned her cardigan, and slouched it off over the back of the chair, making sure her bracelet didn't catch on the cashmere. The café made her feel like she was in a painting, with its silk-fringed parasols, its camellia trees and elegance, its diners coming and going. She placed the Fragonard postcard on the table and piled a large tip on top for the over-worked foreign girl.

It had seemed possible that this day would be a difficult one, a bad day bro. But it turned out good. The museum was cooler than the Art galleries they'd dragged themselves around, and while Rose sat and read a magazine in the garden café, Freya pored over stained glass detail, trying to work out the hidden bible stories. Every now and then she came and found Rose, telling her about pot metal, silver staining and grisaille. In Freya's sketch pad was a beautiful copy of a sixteenth century window of Susanna and the Elders. She was in the second year at High School and already was saying she wanted to be a painter.

'That's like the picture Dad showed me, only Susanna was naked in that one.'

'Really?'

'I don't like being naked.'

'Why not?'

'When you undress, men look at you.'

'So when do you undress in front of men?' Freya didn't answer.

In Harrods, Anna joined them, taking them straight to the terrace café, to a corner that was shaded and not too busy. She made her aunt sit while she ordered, got a tissue out for Freya who was complaining, and then sorted out their bags and books.

'So how's things Anna? I've barely spoken to you. You've come up from Bath to spend time with me, and yet I've hardly seen you.'

'I've been doing some work on my dissertation, hiding away a bit and thinking. Could we go out somewhere and talk tomorrow—alone.' Rose scrutinised her niece. It wasn't like Anna to be evasive. Freya stopped eating her ice-cream.

'Are you pregnant?'

'Are you mad Freya? I've had enough of babies in our house.'

Rose took some money from her purse. 'Here's twenty, luvvy. When you've finished, see if you can buy that Art book you wanted. Let Anna and me have a chat, and be back by four.' When Freya eventually got up to go, Anna caught at her sister's sleeve.

'Tell you what. Go and have a look at the Dodi and Diana shrine; you'll like it—it's gross!' Rose waited until Freya had threaded her way through the tables and chairs.

'Since when has Freya been naked in front of men?'

'I don't think she has.'

'Your sister is either very odd, or just behaving oddly.'

'Aren't they the same thing?'

'That's what I used to think.'

When Rose first arrived in London, she thought the strange atmosphere in the house was embarrassment about her illness. There is an egotism in illness, she realised, that blanks out the other dramas that are playing out simultaneously.

'Is it Freya you're worried about, Anna?' Anna looked up, surprised.

'I'm more worried about you.'

'How sweet. Come and stay—up in Manchester. It was good having you visit last month. And we could talk again about the business, about you doing a bit of work.'

Anna was fiddling with the fringes on her bag, plaiting three strands together and then unplaiting them again.

'Actually, I think Freya's just being a bit of a pain. Adolescent stuff. No, it's Nanna I'm worried about—and Dad, too. I'm not sure if I should tell Mum what I know, not sure if I should tell Dad.'

'Tell me.'

Rose took Freya back to Manchester for the rest of half term, away from an overdose of church. She told her sister there were some glass-making work-shops that Freya might like—and she hoped that there would be, somewhere. She no longer felt panicked by her illness. It was as if she suddenly knew how to conduct herself, now life had got so precious. But she didn't trust herself to remember what she'd learned if she got better. So the first thing she did on her return was ask Max to marry her.

'I thought you'd never ask,' he said. 'White dress? Ely Cathedral?'

'Notre Dame! And you might be marrying a business, Max, but you're also marrying a corpse.'

'Well, it must be noisy in hell if all the corpses are like you.' He made her stretch out her legs on the sofa while he prepared cocktails to celebrate. Only hers had no alcohol, just liquidised organic fruit.

'Don't get any hopes up. I've left all my money to other people.'

'I should hope so. I wouldn't know what to do with more than I've got.'

Rose couldn't find any craft classes so Max had suggested sailing. Rose was sitting in the clubhouse on one side of the lake, trying to read, but finding that she couldn't concentrate on words: even pictures demanded the sort of attention she couldn't run to. Her mind kept sliding off onto other subjects, other thoughts. But it felt comfortable with the magazine there, anchoring her, and keeping at bay bored looking people (mostly mothers) who stared out of the window and watched the progress of that morning's lesson.

She could see Max, who had sailed in his youth, hanging around on the shoreline, chatting to staff and following with his eyes the dinghies bobbing back and forth. The coffee she'd got him must have gone cold, but he wouldn't care, would drink it in any case when he came back to her. He was a good man—and a good businessman, too. She would never have chosen someone like him when she was younger, but now, facing this thing, that might yet be death, it was good having him around. A friend who made her laugh sometimes, and who could also cook was not a bad deal. It was him, she thought, who was getting the short straw.

Out on the boat, Freya knew that her aunt was watching and waiting in the clubhouse. Aunt Rose had said Freya would have an appetite by the time she'd finished and that they'd go out for a pizza or burger. At the moment, the idea of having lunch was more appealing than being in this boat. She was not sure she liked the slop of water in the hull, nor the wetness on her trousers from the water that dripped from ropes down onto the wooden seats. But she liked the varnished tiller and the flap of the sails. She liked it that they'd come so far so fast. She could see Uncle Max, a dot of red, standing near the shore. He said his anorak would keep

183

him like toast even if the temperature dropped below zero; he could go up a mountain in that anorak and still keep snug. Her Aunt Rose, like Anna, would rather wear nice clothes and stay inside to keep warm.

The instructors had warned them that if it was too windy, they wouldn't be allowed out. But it had stayed mild and the sun was shining on the blue water and on the green banks that plunged down all around. Each time they changed direction (and she had learned to call it changing tack) the boom went over and the wet ropes trailed after. The instructor was telling the three of them (they were all beginners, but Freya was the oldest) how you had to catch the wind by tightening and slackening the ropes. When he had the wind tight in the sails, the boat arched up, the sail went taut and they sped along with a clack, clacketing noise on the side as the water tried to catch them up. The man (who was young and tanned and smiley) showed what happened when you got it all wrong (but he said it wouldn't matter if you did) and you lost the wind. Then the boat slowed and rocked from side to side and the sail went slack, but quickly started to flap, first one way, then another. If it was very windy, he said, you could even capsize.

'Shall I capsize to show you what it would be like?'

'No,' everyone chorused, looking down at the icy water and not wanting their bodies to freeze as their hands already had.

The main part of Freya's torso felt as snug as Uncle Max's must have, up the mountain. The life-jacket, like a great corset, was holding her tight and warm, and the jacket under was zipped up to her chin; it was only her bottom that was uncomfortable.

'Okay Freya. Your turn at the helm. You did well tacking yesterday. Let's see if you remember today.' Freya reddened, while shifting back along the boat, edging carefully past the boy, whose name she kept forgetting, who spent his time trying to dangle his hand in the water.

Once at the back, Freya settled comfortably with the large wooden tiller in her hand and the mainsheet threaded through. She liked furrowing the waves, liked the steadiness of being at the helm, watching the action, yet also controlling things. She felt linked to the man giving the orders, like they were a team, setting out on adventure, with the younger ones as their crew. She wondered if he went to church, too, and whether his church group would be kinder.

Moira didn't get on with Michael these days, and several of the older people didn't like him or his music, and didn't approve of the way Moira took things out onto the streets so much. There was a lot of arguing, and the sort of nastiness Freya wished would go away, so it could be like at the beginning. Michael was her friend and tried to get her on his side, but she could see that Moira, when she saw Michael and Freya talking in a huddle, thought they talked about her (and sometimes they did).

A flotilla of ducks were off to the starboard side so she guided the boat in the other direction, enjoying the fluster it caused as the boy had to dodge when the boom came over sling himself to the other side while tightening his rope.

'Communicate Freya! Tell us what you're doing. Don't go off in a dream.' But she was in a dream, thinking about home and church in a way that she hadn't been able to before. When everyone argued at home, and people argued at church, and Michael kept saying it would help him if Freya let him kiss her again—nothing else—behind the hall, she sometimes thought it would be nicer to be dead. Just her and Jesus. She hadn't liked it either, when they all undressed in the hall and Michael watched as she put on a skimpy white dress. She thought the people at school might be jealous if they knew she'd kissed a real man.

They were getting closer to one of the other boats, and suddenly the instructor had clambered along next to her, had taken the tiller and was shouting,

'Turn about.' And when he saw Freya look appalled at the other boat so close and the ducks scrabbling away, he patted her. 'Don't worry. That's what I'm here for. Let's just see if we can aim for that boathouse at the far end, nice and steady, concentrating.'

After the lesson, when they were having lunch back home (because Freya had said she felt a bit sick) and Rose was picking at hers, lying on the sofa, Freya asked her aunt whether death might be restful. She asked whether it might be easier being dead than trying to live. Rose looked up, placing her own fork on the side of the white plate. She was trying to work out if Freya was talking about Rose's illness, or about herself.

'Well I don't know about you, luvvy, but I'm going to do my best to keep living, however hard it gets. And if I have to give up on life, I'm banking on you taking over the fun. I think you're going to be a great little artist one day; you should ask your mum to give you lessons.'

'Sailing feels like life. Half the time, it's all good, all strong, so you don't even know you're doing anything to make things work. Then the next minute, everything goes bad and life is flapping at you, and the wind wants to topple you, so you don't know how to get things back the right way, or even what the skill was that kept you on track.'

'And a philosopher too! You know what your mum used to do when things went wrong?'

'No.' It was strange for Freya to imagine her mother being a child or having a life separate to hers.

'When she got worked up, she used to draw. I could show you some of her folders. She used to go and sulk by the canal, sketching barges.'

Christmas

They went through a latch gate that clicked shut behind them, then down a path with a straggle of frosted bushes and flowers spilling from either side. At the end of the path was a porch sheltering an oak door. The wood was darkened with age and Flinn dumped his bags on the flagstones and knocked, hearing the thickness of black wood, the echo of himself inside the house. The farmhouse had been there for centuries. Beyond its walls, obscured now by the thick mist, lay a ruined priory.

This was the house that belonged to an old friend of Owen and Jan. Over the years (as it had been slowly done up) they'd often stayed there together, then had continued to borrow the place separately. At first it had been shell—a summer-time camping place—and then, as it had gradually altered, they'd both felt something like pride, as if it was their own hard work that had been instrumental in the transformation. The outbuildings still lay around in a tumble, some without roofs, some with just a few bricks missing. But that was Merle's next job, that and the orchard garden that would need a tree surgeon.

The farm was perched in South Wales, different to the other place they'd rented way up North—here the landscape was hilly, even bleak in parts, but it was less scoured by poverty, by wind and sea-salt. There were pretty towns around with interesting old buildings, cafés, theatres and nice shops. And probably because this bit of Wales was close to England, other cultures had threaded through, making it a place where you could belong, even when you didn't. When they had stopped to get milk, the woman serving them had a Bristol accent and told them they should visit Hay on Wye to buy books, should take in the market and museum in Abergavenny and go see the old Norman castles dotted around. They could never work out if they liked this sort of easy welcome, or whether they liked better the exoticism of alienation.

Hearing Flinn knocking, Jan thought he'd misunderstood the plans.

'No-one's there, Flinn. Your dad takes over from us at the end of the week.'

'I wanted to hear the place—as well as see it.' Jan stared at him, then looked around at the mess of outbuildings, the wizened trees, the dry stone walls, as if they might reveal her son's meaning. Through the windows she could see a chintzy sofa, the pile of logs by the fire, the lamps and shelves of books. Outside it was inhospitable, damp and cold. In the juxtaposition of her friend's tasteful bits and the frightening landscape that sloped away from the shadowy farmhouse towards snowy hilltops, there seemed to be something significant to be grasped—but it lay beyond Jan's reach. Perhaps that had been what Flinn was groping towards: the intertwining of civilisation and savagery. Or perhaps he was just musing on the significance of his family assembled in one place.

It was not lost on Jan that this whole Christmas and New Year enterprise was going to be strange, not least because she'd now properly meet Owen's new wife. The photographs the children brought home showed a tall woman who seemed to glare at the camera and beyond it. In some of the photos Lois looked beautiful, with high cheekbones and long dark hair pulled back from her face, and in others she looked grim. No doubt the reality was some blend of the two.

Freya found the key under the bird-bath, and wiped her muddy fingers on Macie. Macie squealed and wriggled free, running over the muddy grass.

'Take your shoes off when we go in, and hurry up. It's freezing out here.' Jan was stamping from one foot to another, trying not to think about her frozen hands, holding plastic carriers and rucksacks. She stared up at the deep-set windows and then at the huge stones out of which the house was constructed. She found it hard to imagine that these great stones—some dragged from the priory—were almost a thousand years old, mined from quarries that had long ago been filled in and lost to memory. Merle had told her that parts of the house dated back to medieval times and that the upstairs rooms were where the abbot had once done his accounts, listing financial and moral outgoings against incoming cash and virtue.

When they opened the huge door, it smelt damp. Flinn dumped his bags in the hall and found the box of matches in the coal-scuttle.

'Come on girls. Who's going to help me get the fire going?'

'I am,' they both shouted and Macie started her rhyme:

Jeremiah blow the fire,
Puff, puff, puff
First you blow it gently,
Then you blow it rough.

Flinn lit the paper and Macie blew hard at the smoking mass of paper. Singed bits drifted upwards with the smoke.

'Whoa! Careful! We don't want to burn the house down.' Flinn looked tentatively up the chimney, to see if any gusts had carried paper up to settle on a ledge and smoulder slowly, waiting until they were all fast asleep. 'I'm glad we're here together.' Jan had put things on the stairs to go up and was dragging the foodstuff into the newly done kitchen. 'Hey, it looks wonderful in here. Very fancy. I'm surprised Merle wanted to go to Paris for Christmas.'

Freya pushed past her mother, to look at the new kitchen. Unimpressed, she went to help Flinn bring extra coal and wood from the outhouse. She had avoided her brother since the embarrassment in front of her church friends, but now, on neutral territory, she seemed ready to forget the past. Freya was too intense, Jan thought, but sometimes, like when she'd taken up cello, and more recently, with her drawing, being obsessed had its advantages.

'Don't run away again,' Freya called out to Macie, as the smaller child disappeared deep into undergrowth.

Upstairs, Jan made the beds. Her movements were brisk and efficient, tucking the linen under with a flick of the mattress up, so the ends made a neat fold around the corners of the bed. She copied instinctively the movements of her mother, whose method she must have studied as a child. Pulling back the cream counterpane in the big room, Jan came across a bottom sheet stained with blood and semen. The sight shocked her, as if she'd just walked in on somebody copulating. Don't be so stupid, so prurient, she told herself; the whole adult world has sex—and probably even those monks vowed to celibacy. But, as she pulled off the grubby sheet and pushed it into the wash box, she felt uncomfortable, as if it was her own shame she'd caught sight of. It might even have been her sheets. She could not remember if she was the last person who'd been staying—when she snatched a weekend with her new boyfriend, Tom. Or perhaps these were Owen's sheets; his wife had been advising Merle about kitchen design and Jan knew they'd stayed recently.

It had been strange to be here with Tom. Someone in the local shop had recognised her and had asked her to send their best wishes to Merle, who now lived in London. They had eyed Tom, who looked even younger that day, and Jan could see them wondering if he were her grown-up son. Tom appeared as if he was in his twenties. She knew that he would transform one day from boy to thickening man, probably when nearing forty, and that if she were still with him, it would surprise her more than him. She often wondered why he had chosen her, when he could go out with younger women. But someone told her that all his girlfriends had been older, some even older than herself.

Life with Tom was not the cerebral relationship she'd suggested to her sister she wanted. She found him beautiful with his olive skin and dark eyes, but it wasn't his looks that had first interested her. There was an edginess to him and a restlessness; he gave off the sense that he would not hold back from pleasure or danger. She guessed he might have been a serious drinker once, or perhaps took drugs. But now, as a youth and community worker, it was his job that gave him a fix. It was not until they'd come away to the farmhouse that she realised he might have felt their previous sex life tame. Once at Merle's, he seemed to make up for lost time; he had taken her off to bed several times a day and after lunch had drawn the curtains downstairs so they could roll over the Indian rug and shut out the stark mid-day light. She had noticed how beautiful and irregular the patterns on the hand-made carpet were, how vibrant the oranges, reds and greens. They lay together; telling each other their life stories, surprised by how much there was to tell. They had sex in the bath, against walls and even under a bush half way up Offa's dyke. At Sunday lunch, just before they went back, he told her what a relief it was to be there without her children. So perhaps she should have guessed that a family Christmas would be too much for him, and shouldn't have been too surprised when he said he'd dip in for a bit, just catch the big day.

The days before Christmas passed in a flurry of food shopping, present wrapping, cooking and snatched walks. It was almost too perfect: no arguments, muddy adventures and tea and cake when they got home. One afternoon they found a small Christmas tree in a conifer wood and hauled it back, at dusk, along the deep-set lanes.

'Isn't this stealing?' Freya asked, 'There are still rules in the country.' She jumped when a blackbird fluttered out of the hedge, giving its cry of alarm.

'It was chucked on the rubbish pile—it's too threadbare for anyone else; we're giving it a home, like you would a stray dog.' Flinn's words puffed out into the still, cold night.

Freya turned to her mother, carrying holly and mistletoe. 'It's not threadbare at all. It's perfect, as if someone had been planning to come and get it.'

'It's a bit close to Christmas for anyone else to want it now—and there were about five in the pile; they looked like the rejects.'

'Well, I call it thieving.'

The next day, Freya helped Macie make star decorations out of sticks and used foil and glitter for other baubles, but she refused to hang the things. By evening, Jan noticed everything had been carefully rearranged. She told Flinn to say nothing. They were clearing up the meal he had made and she reminded him she'd be taking Freya to the evening service.

'I promised, remember—said I'd take her religious choices seriously. Macie could come too.' Flinn frowned and then shrugged—the first hint of tension.

'Freya is your affair, but Macie's better off in bed.' He took a breath as if to launch into what he thought about churches, but then, looking across at the tree, just said, 'Forget it. Do what you want, Mum.'

'I will.'

Later, she pulled on her pink scarf and borrowed one of Freya's woollen hats. Flinn was back in front of the television. She went in and contemplated him.

'I'm surprised you aren't clamouring for religion too—being so sanctimonious.' He put up two fingers; Macie copied. In the hall, Freya was dabbing on eye shadow.

'Churches are so cold, Freya. If it didn't look rude, I'd take a blanket, too.'

'Have my gloves, Mum. The singing will warm me up.' Freya smiled and slipped her arm around her mother. Jan wanted to scoop up the moment. They stepped out into the dark night together, breathing in the crisp, cold air that made them hurry down the path and along the rough track to the brightly lit church. Half an hour earlier, they'd heard the first cars arriving, crunching up the gravel drive. Jan was surprised to see the National Trust car park so busy. When she creaked open the latched door, the church was full of people, rowed up on the benches, talking near the door, assembling near the altar, or handing out hymn books. A man wearing a black hat gave Jan the order of service and pointed to some spaces on the nearest benches. Jan squeezed in, thanking people as they moved aside. Two men and a woman were talking quietly to one another, bundled up in coats and scarves and woollen hats. A younger man and woman were turned to the pews behind them, chattering. Over in the corner, a child sat on the wooden plank that covered the font, and Jan wondered if, years before, it might have been baptised there. Freya settled into her seat and sat stiffly upright, her face fixed and serious. But really the event seemed jolly and casual to Jan, a meeting of local friends and families who had come for a seasonal get-together.

When the service started properly, there was a rustling move to turn to the front. There were readings (some given by the congregation) and carols that Jan remembered from her school days. Freya seemed surprised her mother didn't need to read the words, but stared around as she sang, watching the elderly men and women who sat, then creakily stood again, watching the children and the teenagers, the boys and girls who led the singing from the front. The lady next to Jan had a crocheted hat pulled square over her head and each time she stood, heaving herself up a second or two after everyone else, her piping voice floated out high over all the others. The candles at the altar sent out a wonderful haze of light and Jan wished their warmth could make her nose less cold. Each time anyone breathed, they puffed out a foggy cloud of cold air, so that the church seemed to be some sort of noiseless engine producing a magic gas.

It wasn't comfortable on the benches and the service was perhaps too long, especially the bit when the children were called up to bless the crib, and some older ones refused to go and no-one could hear what was being said by the youngest near the altar. But at the end of it all, Jan felt better, as if the singing had purged something. She half wished she knew people; could join the group that were planning to meet in the local pub, then have a meal together.

As she and Freya stood near an arch, waiting to slide out again, Jan saw how the stone on a column near the altar was a beautiful pink. She wondered where it had been mined, how it was carried up to this lonely valley and whether the first people to see its delicate colour must have felt blessed by such unusual beauty.

The farmhouse had three bedrooms, all elegant. There was a stylish open-plan living area and the new, very modern kitchen. No-one knew where Merle's money came from, but she'd used most of it to restore this, her first home. The rented flat in London was basic, and she constantly talked of returning to Wales—so she was careful about who she let stay in the farm. Jan guiltily noticed that over Christmas, in that stretch of days when presents and time were ripped open, bedtimes got late and laziness set in; Merle's holiday home started to look as messy as Jan's house in London.

It happened imperceptibly. The sprawl of Christmas toys, DVDs, clothes, Wellingtons and unwashed dishes gradually changed the place from show-house to home that needed work and strain to make it habitable.

Tom arrived late on Christmas day. Something urgent had come up, he'd said, and he arrived by car, just in time to eat the dinner, pull crackers, clink glasses and tell funny stories. After that, he spent most of his time in bed or out walking alone down muddy lanes. Meanwhile, Jan cooked, organised outings, played with Macie and began to feel middle-aged and dowdy. She decided her relationship with Tom could never work. Whenever Tom said she should come with him, he hadn't waited for her to finish the thing she was doing, but strode off, suggesting over his shoulder that she catch him up. In that place of winding lanes and tracks cutting across fields and hillsides, she might have wandered for months before she'd found which way he'd gone.

Now Jan's part of the holiday was over. She was scrubbing at the toilet, making ready for the hand-over to Owen and his new family. Freya was cleaning the sink and holding her nose against the stench of chemical.

'In the past, Freya, servants would have done this. I bet the abbot never cleaned his own toilet.'

'Did he have one?'

'I don't know. He might have. In that castle we visited, there were toilets—holes that emptied down into the river.'

'Macie put her head down the hole.'

'Remember how she got stuck in our cat-flap, when she tried to crawl through?'

'She got stuck in a bush yesterday when Flinn took us for a walk.'

'I think we should keep her on a lead.'

'I've finished the sink. What shall I do now?'

'It's nice having you help me. Are you happy here?'

'I don't know. I haven't really thought about it. But I'm glad I'm not in London. It feels comfortable here, like I'm me again.'

'Had you lost "me"?'

'That's a funny thing to say.'

'I felt I'd lost you a bit.'

'But I'm home all the time. The only places I go are school and church. Everyone else goes out more than me.'

Downstairs they could hear Flinn and Tom arguing about football. It was what they did—talked about football because there was nothing else they had in common.

'It's funny this cleaning business. Now that most of us don't pay cleaners, we pull on old clothes and become our own servants. Then when we've finished, we transform into lady of the manor, pretending we haven't been on our hands and knees all day, head down the loo.'

195

Jan knew that Owen's house was tidy and elegant; Lois paid for a cleaner. She piled the smelly towels in a heap, ready to be washed. She remembered how, just before she'd left London, she'd let in a market researcher, out of pity. It had been raining outside and the woman carried a drenched umbrella, laptop and pile of cumbersome files.

'It's an awful day,' the woman had said. 'Everyone's been rude to me.'

'Go on, then, you can do me—if it won't take long.' Jan hadn't taken her into the neat front room—the counselling room—because there were case-notes spread across the floor; she took the woman into the messy kitchen. Freya had left a cornflakes bowl on the table and the woman promptly put her elbow into milk splashed on the cloth. As Jan answered stupid questions about mobile phones and chocolate bars, the woman kept wiping at her sleeve with a tissue, rubbing so hard the tissue fissured into dusty fragments. When the woman began to cry, Jan thought at first it must be something to do with the spilt milk and the pale pink cardigan.

'I can't do this!' the woman said at last, snapping shut her laptop. 'I can't work today. My daughter's run away. I'm worried sick.' And she looked around Jan's kitchen, taking in the smelly hamster cage, the pile of composting peelings— that should have been taken outside by one of the children— and the open washing machine with its spill of clothes. Jan had been in the process of pushing towels and clothes in when the doorbell rang. The woman stared back down at the table, as if she was going over something that she couldn't make sense of. 'She's left her job—at the bank.' She said this slowly. 'And he's a Muslim.' The tiny, manicured woman was fidgeting with the gold bangle she wore on her tanned wrist. She took off her reading glasses and stared at them, then looked at Jan.

'Is she very young?' asked Jan. She had instinctively taken against this woman with her immaculate clothes and tight-lipped expression. Jan was cursing that she'd invited her in, letting someone slice into precious time.

'She's twenty-seven. Why doesn't she know better? How she can stand to live in that squalor? I did everything for her—cleaned her clothes, put meals on the table. But then she just ups and goes.' The woman slid the laptop into its black bag and Jan helped her collect up the sheets of paper and the clipboard.

'You could come back another day—next week?' Jan would not be there. But the woman was making no moves to go. Jan wiped the table and then went across to finish filling the washing machine.

'There's enough blacks to marry their own kind. Why does he want my daughter?' Jan stood upright. Took a breath to tell the woman not to be so racist, then noticed tears spilling down the woman's cheeks.

'Perhaps she loves him?'

'But she's been brought up a Christian, a decent Catholic.' The woman was exasperated with Jan for not understanding how impossible the situation was. If Jan had been paid to see this woman, she would have devised some method to reflect back the woman's words, to let her see her own intolerance and fear. But Jan had the day off. She was going shopping to buy something youthful and glamorous for when she met Owen and his new wife.

'To live in the student filth he lives in, with mess everywhere, and no proper curtains at the window. I bought her towels. Went out and bought her towels, so she wouldn't have to touch that filth.'

I'm glad she's not my client, thought Jan.

'I'm terribly sorry, but I have someone to see in five minutes.' Jan was lying. 'I'm sorry for your unhappiness, but perhaps you should let your daughter live her own life.'

'So she can grow up to live in the sort of mess you do? No thank you.'

For a day or two after this visitation—sent to Jan when

she'd been worrying too much about cleanliness,—she had a clear vision of the importance of mess. As she dashed around Covent Garden or Camden Lock (grabbing at presents: toys, books, jokes, games, chocolate, soap and jewellery) she instructed herself in the delights of fracture. The world was divided, she decided, not into separate religions and classes, but into the madness of control and the relative sanity of those in free-fall. She wanted to hold on to the idea that greater tolerance came from letting go, but she knew this vision would fade, as all revelations do. Yet some private god, she felt, had watched out for her, giving a sign. In Roman times, she'd have adopted this god of chaos and set it on the hearth to guide her. Already the vision was fading. She wanted to hand over a perfect house to Owen, to suggest to him, and his wife, that she was fine. Not missing him (and she wasn't). Not lonely. Strong. Perfectly happy with the new man. If someone had asked her why having a tidy and clean house could possibly suggest all these things, she would not have known how to answer.

Jan looked out of the window at the scattered medieval stones in the yard, stones that had once held together a system of beliefs and framed a monastery full of daily exaction and privation. Compared to that life, she decided, perhaps it was not so hard to clean a toilet. In the twelfth century, after three children she would have been lucky to be alive. She thought of her sister, who had just finished having chemotherapy and who she phoned every day. They talked a bit, exchanged gossip and then, by the end of the conversation, Rose would have her laughing. Jan kept thinking that they ought to be more serious, facing what could be death, but Rose had different ideas: if she only had a short time left, she wasn't going to waste it being sad.

Freya said she'd like to make cake for her dad, so although Jan didn't feel like baking, and knew they'd have to wait until Tom finished making dinner, she agreed.

'We've got Christmas cake and Italian cake. Flapjacks are

quick. I'll help you with those and clean the kitchen at the same time.'

It was only two o'clock and yet it felt like evening. Low clouds pressed out the light and the valley sides were steadily closing in. At night, they often marched right up to the house. That was one of the problems with this place; the light and the space went so quick every day. If you lived here, you'd spend most of the year feeling breathless and hemmed in. If Jan wanted to pick flowers and twigs, she'd have to do so soon—while she could still make them out from brambles. Sometimes, when she went outside at night to look at the stars—pick out Orion or the plough or the one she called the snake—she was frightened by the monastery ruins looming above. She had an icy sense of her own transience and an awareness of all those dead monks, abbots and farmers, all layered into the place. Would someone else, she wondered, in a hundred years time, stand in the frozen darkness, as she did, staring into infinity and wondering how you were meant to live?

Downstairs, Macie was watching a *Power Rangers* video. Flinn, spread along the sofa behind her, was watching it too. The curtains had been pulled shut, either because someone had forgotten to open them that morning, or because the gloom replicated the cinema.

'It used to be better than this,' Flinn was protesting to no-one in particular. Macie, lying against him with her thumb in her mouth, seemed satisfied with the tacky dialogue, the stagy gestures, the characters leaping about, fighting aliens, making America and the civilised world a better place. She was still in her pyjamas, her round tummy rising and falling with each breath, her pink toes curled in pleasure as she leaned against Flinn. When Jan came down and piled fresh logs by the open fire, she could hear the trite moralising, the luring platitudes, a world made simple.

She bent to plump up cushions and collected the children's books into a neat pile, which someone would no doubt shortly scatter. She placed her own and Tom's belongings at the bottom of the stairs, ready to be packed into their cars.

Tom had tired of nature and was in the kitchen, making an elaborate meal. Jan could hear the scraping of pots and pans, a liquidiser whirring. When Tom cooked, Flinn complained, he made so much mess you couldn't even get a drink or piece of toast without wrestling with piles of dirty dishes and having to delve under scattered knives, herbs, measuring jugs and gluey pastes to find a breadboard. Coming from Flinn, this was rich. The day before, Jan had suggested to Tom that, contrary to plan, they should escape when Owen arrived. They could linger, perhaps, to have a cup of tea and make the children feel it was all friendly and natural. But really Jan wanted to be gone—though she was annoyed that they would now have to drive in separate cars because Tom had not caught the train down.

'But we said we'd eat together—last supper and all that,' Tom said, standing behind Freya at breakfast, pulling her hair back into a pony tail as he spoke, making her squirm because it exposed her pointed ears. 'I'll make something special; we can share food—make friends over wine and Korma. Anyway, I've never met your 'ex'; I'm curious about a man who courts scandal. I'll book us into the pub in the next village. We can drive back to London on New Year's Eve— straight to Merle's party.'

Jan had pulled a face, but could not be bothered to say that scandal had taken hold of Owen, not the other way around. Then Flinn got up and left the table, leaving his toast half eaten.

'Freya, how about going to feed that fat horse some apples?' Freya pulled away from Tom, shook her hair loose then trooped out after Flinn and Macie to find bruised apples. Jan took a breath to tell him he should be more tactful when he talked about the children's father. Tom leaned over Jan and slipped his hand down her shirt.

'How about we slide upstairs? Quick, before they get back?'

Freya and Flinn hadn't spoken much to Tom over the four days. They'd thanked him for presents, argued with him over which TV channels everyone should watch, but had, on the whole, acted as if he had not been there. This was pretty much what they did in London—although there, everyone had space to escape from one another. In London when Tom visited, the children shut themselves in their rooms with TVs and computers. In this farmhouse, thrust together, Jan found herself elaborately including Tom in the conversations, as if he were an awkward school child who needed the teacher to involve him.

Now Tom put his head around the kitchen door and frowned at them in the gloom. His curly hair was growing quite long, and although there were bits of grey near the temple, he looked handsome, still boyish for thirty-five. He was wearing Merle's floral apron and had a glass of half drunk wine in his hand.

'Garlic, hon?' and he smiled at Jan. She could hear ska music coming the DVD player in the kitchen. Flinn answered.

'In the middle drawer.' But he didn't move his eyes from the screen.

Freya had started scratching away at a babyish etching given to her when she went to the Carol service. The black piece of paper revealed a blond, bearded Jesus, whose eyes gazed heavenwards. Freya seemed as obsessed with religion in Wales as she had been in the capital. She had even taken to wondering around the ruins of the monastery, dressed in one of Jan's long skirts. She said that long skirts were warmer, but Jan had come across her, hands clasped together in prayer, looking as if she were an itinerant nun, searching out grace in the bleakness of the windy ruins. Jan thought her behaviour worrying. The teacher at school had said that Freya did not mix, that her work had deteriorated; that sometimes she

201

seemed to be upset. When Jan had talked to her, Freya had said it was nothing. She was fine.

By the time Owen's white Volvo drew up the steep road to the farmhouse, it had been snowing for over an hour. There was an eerie glow over the valley, the light a mingled yellow and purple. The fields and trees were layered in white snow and the car left deep tracks as it edged into a rutted parking place. It was nice to see Anna climbing out from the back, groaning about how she'd felt car sick—some things didn't change. Jan hadn't realised how much she'd missed her until she was there. Her hair had been dyed purple again. She was wearing the same sort of baggy dungarees that Jan had worn when she was pregnant with Freya. Perhaps they were her dungarees.

Although Anna had intended to spend Christmas with Jan and Tom, she'd phoned at the last minute saying she'd stay in Cardiff. Jan had not been able to ask her, with Flinn and Tom in the room, if she'd told Owen about his real father. Jan had made it clear to Anna that she wouldn't mind speaking to Owen instead, but Anna had said it was her burden. Perhaps, though, Anna had chosen to stay in Cardiff for Christmas because she didn't like Tom.

Owen helped Ben out of the car. He'd been sleeping and looked confused to see so many people.

'Did you have a nice Christmas, Freya? We've got presents in the boot for you.' Owen kissed Freya and gave Flinn a slap on the arm. Jan knew, then, that Anna hadn't told him.

'I got an art jigsaw, clothes, earrings, books. And Father Christmas got me a whoopy cushion. That got into my stocking by mistake.'

Macie was pushing her way in, curious about the boy clinging to Owen's leg. Everyone started talking at once, exclaiming about the weather as they pulled luggage from the car. Owen heaved Anna's bags out of the car and she immediately took them, dumped them in the snow and hauled out her presents for Macie and Freya.

'You'll love these,' she said. 'I wanted them myself. And it's not dolls. When she turned to hug Flinn, she pulled back.

'You lazy slob; you need a shave. And a shower.'

Owen's wife, dressed in a red trouser suit, was taller than Jan had imagined; in her high heels, which punctured the snow with crisp indentations, she towered over Owen. She led the way to the front door, saying little, and Jan remembered that, of course, they knew the place too, had stayed there often. The woman—beautiful, with her pale skin and dark eyes—had shaken Jan by the hand, and then spoken to Tom, saying how nice it was to meet them properly after so long, but Jan thought she glimpsed indifference, boredom with this complicated trail of Owen's past. She was all surface politeness, all decorum—the interesting bits of herself hidden and private. Or perhaps she was shy. As they stood in the hallway, in front of the antique mirror that stretched over the whole wall, Jan wished that she had not worn orange.

Lois said she was going upstairs, that she needed a lie down—would Owen bring up the bags and a cup of tea in a while? The little boy—a beautiful child, so beautiful it was hard not to keep looking at him—clung on to Owen's hand and eyed the other children with suspicion. He had only once or twice met Macie, and Freya had stopped being a regular visitor to Cardiff; she was busy weekends with the church.

Owen ignored Jan, as if he was scared of her, and followed Tom into the kitchen with the bottle he clutched. They began talking about French gites, music in the eighties and good Indian places to eat in London. Ben, with his curly hair, like a picture of the infant Jesus, was fiddling with his silver Game Boy, pretending to be engrossed, but taking in the mix of people, the other children.

'Want to see my den?' Freya took Ben by the hand and, followed by Macie, opened the door onto the snow and the low stone buildings that clustered at the end of the long garden.

'Look after him, Freya. Don't let him wander away. Have

you got a torch? Hold his hand.' It was her father, looking worried.

He has absorbed motherhood, been ambushed by its fears, Jan thought.

'I can't tell him, Mum,' Anna whispered as she passed.

The meal was a disaster. Tom had forgotten to salt anything, and although Owen said how much he liked it, nearly everyone left food on their plate. They sat there being polite, Anna looking pale and every now and again glancing across at first her mother and then her father. She did not even drink her wine. Jan could feel Tom's hand on her thigh so that when she asked Lois about her business and how she had started it up, it sounded as if she was being stiff and over-formal.

'I did architecture at university, then taught art classes, then met someone who was English and wanted a partner to help design kitchens. That's about it, really. I thought I'd be in Britain for a year or two. But then I married him—fool that I was.'

Jan wanted to ask what the man was like and why she was a fool.

'Why were you a fool?' Tom was drunker than Jan.

'Let's just say that he was more interested in bedrooms than kitchens— and they were other people's, not mine.'

'You mean he was male?' No one but Tom found his joke amusing. Flinn darted a look at his father and changed the subject.

'Dad, I do like the Gombrich book you gave me; I've read bits—but you gave it to me for Christmas last year as well. Don't you remember?'

'Did I? Sorry, Flinn. Give it to Anna, then. Did you like the jeans, though?'

'Let me have it.' It was the first thing that Freya had said all evening.

Jan smiled across encouragingly. 'Freya's really good at art; we went across to the church and she drew the nave and got

204

the perspective just right.'

Lois turned to Freya and asked her about pastels and charcoal and which other media she had used.

Jan did not say how, after they had both drawn the church, she had later taken Freya to the Christmas Eve service, just as she had promised she would, months before. She did not say, because she had barely registered it herself yet, that this had made something change between them.

Jan did not tell anyone about their trip to the church, for she would have had to say that she enjoyed it, and felt more peaceful after. And she did not know what she thought about this. Freya had said she wasn't sure about the carol service; it had seemed so ordinary, so lacking in the holy.

Later, they all talked about books. Jan told Lois, as she poured more wine, that she sometimes felt like a character in Chekhov. She was always meaning go places, but somehow never got around to it.

'I can't see the point of those plays. Too depressing. Hopeless. No one gets anything done. You have to have faith. Believe in yourself. Those taps in the kitchen. Each time I use them, I know Merle couldn't have got better.'

'Well, they're better than that pump outside,' Flinn said, enigmatically. 'I tried to give the horse some water that wasn't iced over—it took me an age to pump it out.'

'I'll take that as a compliment.'

Jan couldn't think what to say. She felt like they were performing, each in turn. And Lois made her feel insubstantial. It was something, she decided, to do with being too porous, so she constantly felt emptied out. She thought it would be pleasant to hold firm to the contours of self, as Lois seemed to, squaring up to anyone who challenged her.

When the younger children had gone to bed, and Flinn had trudged up to his room, borrowing Ben's Game Boy to help him get to sleep, Owen, Tom, Lois and Jan brought out the liquors. There was something desperate in the way they poured huge amounts into the wine glasses. Anna pulled a

205

face and said she felt too tired and sick to drink—she'd go on up with Freya and read. Jan kissed her good-bye and said she'd phone the next day. She turned to Tom.

'Will you be safe to drive tonight? I'm not. And are you sure you've been checking the weather?'

'Taxi! We'll pick up the cars tomorrow.' But when they phoned for a taxi, the Abergavenny firm laughed at them.

'There's nothing on the roads, mate. It's a white-out. If you're up that valley, you'll be lucky to get out this year.' And the man laughed at his own joke.

'Could we walk to the next village?' Jan asked Tom. 'I think it's about three miles.' They went to the door and looked out. The world was pale and glassy. Deep snow lay piled on the garden. The road had a thick coating of flawless white. The sky was starless and dark. It was cold.

Behind them was the warmth of the house and a log fire; in front it was ferocious, sub-zero.

'Why didn't we notice—or think. We're so stupid.'

'I could offer you the sofa.' Owen said, 'Or you could squeeze in with us!'

Nobody laughed. Lois put her arm around Jan.

'We could squeeze in together. You share with Tom, Hon. You twist and turn too much.'

Jan and Tom tried, unsuccessfully, two other taxi firms. Then Tom said he'd take cushions up to Flinn and Macie's room—he was so drunk, he wouldn't notice the hard floor or Flinn's snores. Owen followed Lois upstairs—perhaps worried he would be ejected if he didn't lay claim to his bed—leaving his sticky glass half full. Tom turned to Jan.

'You get the sofa, babes. I'll make you tea in the morning—or perhaps Owen can, if he's up first. She's got him pretty well trained.' And he screwed up his face at the idea of being so tame. He kissed her and for a moment, as he pressed hard against her, she worried he might suggest they creep out to Freya's den. She could not say no to him, did not know how to reject the gift of his youth. But then he yawned and wobbled off towards the stairs.

Jan changed in the bathroom and was creeping around when Owen reappeared.

'I wanted to tell you. I rang your sister, to tell her how sad I was about the cancer. She gave me short shrift, but I think she was pleased I'd made contact. She's not as hard as she pretends to be.'

'I know.'

But that was not why Owen had come back downstairs.

'Your sister said you were more worried about Freya than you let on, that she's not 'growing up', and seems to be hiding something. When you were at your cousin's wedding, she said Freya was about to tell you something about the child minder or something. Why haven't you told me Freya's got this new problem? You were meant to keep me informed—about the diary and stuff.'

'A problem with the childminder? I can't remember anything about that. But, anyway, what could you do that I couldn't?'

He looked at her as if she were stupid. 'Talk to her! You're the one who's so keen on exploring what everything means. I sometimes think I would have been a better shrink than you. You seem to miss what's happening in front your nose. Anyway, I'm Freya's dad. Rose was surprised you'd kept me out of things.'

'I suppose I hoped it would all go away. I couldn't face more things going wrong.' This was the first time she had admitted as much to herself. She plumped down on the sofa, where she could still smell Flinn's stinky feet. She knew that if she did not change the subject, she would cry.

'I'm just so exhausted. Everything goes wrong—and now my sister.' She wanted that comment to end the conversation, but the tears started and it suddenly didn't seem to matter that Owen was glimpsing the vulnerability she tried so hard to hide. Perhaps it was because they were both drunk. He put his arm around her, awkwardly.

'I didn't know. I thought you were fine. I thought it was just me in a mess.'

'What sort of a mess?' She blew her nose noisily, wiping at her eyes and smudging her mascara.

'My jobs are only temporary; it doesn't look like they'll renew the contracts. Lois keeps renovating the house—attic conversion, en suite bedrooms, patio, new kitchen; we're so over-mortgaged, we'd have to sell if they don't renew. She's saying she won't go smaller; she'll go back to the States—and take Ben. She could sell our house and get a bigger one there.' Owen was sitting on the sofa beside her. When he bent forward, Jan could see how his hair was thinning and that he had a scar on his scalp, some childhood accident, a story he had never told her or possibly didn't remember himself. 'I love Ben—adore him. And Lois wouldn't know what to do with him, anyway. She says her aunt would help look after him in the States—the aunt that brought her up.'

'Are things that bad between you, then?'

'No. We get on okay. Day by day things seem okay.' Jan passed him the glass of green liquor and took one herself. 'And now this stuff about Freya. I feel so bad that I haven't seen much of her; lately she's always been doing something else when I come up.'

'I don't think I know Freya, either. She's mostly self-possessed and quiet, but I don't know what she thinks, where she is; especially when she goes wild—shouting and swearing. She sort of got trammelled in all that stuff between us.'

'By our lives falling apart.'

'I don't seem to be a very good parent to her—and I can't even use my counselling. She sort of slips away from me, as if she doesn't really exist. I sometimes think that when we were on holiday in North Wales, and all those terrible things happened, a fairy came and took our real child away. And now all this stuff about religion—and she's stopped eating properly.

'Anna didn't tell me that.'

'Anna hasn't noticed. And she's had enough to worry about.'

'I know!'

Jan flashed him a look, wondering how much Anna had hinted to him about his father.

It was strange how easy it suddenly was to talk. Jan rushed on.

'There's something else I've got to tell you, only you won't want to hear. Anna came to Cardiff especially to tell you—but got scared. She's asked me. It was what your mother told her—when they scattered the ashes.' Owen leaned back on the sofa and closed his eyes. He spoke to Jan out of his darkness.

'You were huddled together earlier—when you were clearing the table. I assumed it was Freya business, or Anna's new problems.' He opened his eyes, fixed her with his clear blue gaze. 'Well, what won't I want to hear?'

Jan was catching at meaning slowly, her drunken brain dragging words along behind, making sense of them gradually.

'I didn't know Anna had other problems,' she said.

'What did my mother tell Anna when she was there?'

Jan took another gulp of liquor and felt instantly sick. If she didn't tell him, Anna would have to.

'Your father. He wasn't your father. Your mother said he wasn't your father.'

Owen stared into the embers of the fire, gazing at the logs, ridged and perfect above, eaten away in intricate red and grey patterns below.

'Though Anna still thinks your mother may be wrong, that she may be getting muddled.' Jan was rushing the story out, with no sense of being careful about Owen's feelings. She wanted to unburden herself, unburden Anna too, even if it left Owen sinking.

'Who *was* my father?' he asked in a small voice, perhaps hoping that the man might still be alive, might be someone grand and intellectual, who could transform the mess of the past, and even that of the present. And then Jan could not speak. The words were stuck; it was all too ugly, too sad to say.

'Come outside.'

In the darkness of the ruin, in its huge space, she hoped the things she had to say might be diluted somehow, might be given perspective by the context of crumbling history and a starry universe.

They wrapped themselves in coats and pulled on Wellingtons. His unstylish stripy pyjamas (that Jan was surprised Lois allowed) were stuffed into the tops of his boots. Jan and Owen slid through the back garden, past Freya's den and opened the gate onto the huge space of the abbey. Each breath was sliced by cold. Their chests hurt with the stiffness of holding themselves taut. They stumbled along the outline of the presbytery and into the nave. To the left of them, one huge pillar remained, with a portion of arch that began, but was broken off mid-curve. They could hear the restlessness of what must have been birds in the branches of a tree that stretched over a grassy wall. The snow clouds were passing, revealing a clear sky and a bright moon.

'Even they can't sleep in this cold.' Jan was postponing the moment.

'So tell me. And how long have you all known?'

He turned to her, and his eyes, the eyes that looked so like Freya's, pleaded and accused at the same time. Perhaps he thought she had held this secret to taunt him and her telling him now was a malicious retaliation for his betrayal.

'Anna told me a few weeks ago. She's known a while— but was too upset, too scared to tell anyone. She hoped it wasn't true, that your mother would say she was wrong about it.'

'Mum's acting oddly; I told you. She's being saying lots of weird things. But you said leave her alone, she's fine. I told you I should be the shrink.'

210

He was pacing up and down to keep warm. But Jan could tell, even as he muttered, fighting the cold inside him and shivering, his hands thrust deep in his coat pocket, that he wanted to know the rest.

'You and your counselling. Couldn't you tell my mother's been acting all her life? I knew, but I couldn't work out why. And couldn't you tell something was wrong with Freya? And can't you see that Anna's pregnant?'

'Anna—pregnant?'

'She told me last week. She isn't sure what to do. She might have a termination. They thought of getting married, but guessed you wouldn't approve. She says that having a baby can't be worse than her work.'

'What? Who's she kidding? I can't bear any more babies to look after. Not her too.'

Jan strode off, half running, half falling out of the nave, with its treacherous, uneven stones. She turned when she got to the section that once was the infirmary and waited for Owen to catch her up. 'More babies!' She was appalled, imagining she would be forever chained to her offspring and her offspring's offspring.

'Why couldn't Mum tell me herself?' Owen reached for her, roughly gripping her. 'Tell me, Jan. Who is my real father?' All around the listening night was still; black shrubs crouched inside the old monastery walls, spilling over the edges, camouflaged by the pale glow of snow. Up on the steep hillsides huge trees, great clots of blackness, sat like sentries against escape. The sky—both blacker and brighter than in the city—showed, as the heavy clouds started to roll over, a peppering of stars.

'Tell me!'

'Your grandfather.' She stood beside him going limp, each intake of breath hurting her chest; she was shaking with cold and with deep, compassionate misery. All around, the walls and towers and broken arches, like some great pantomime of ancient beliefs, of sin and retribution, sent deep shadows across the lawns and dwarfed them. 'I'm sorry.' It was useless to say, but she didn't want him to think she was enjoying this.

'How?' She had thought it would end with telling him, but, of course, it was only just the beginning.

'Once she said that he forced himself on her. She didn't say rape, exactly. But Anna says that later she said something different.' Owen had gone slack.

'My grandfather? Grandfather Griffiths?'

'She told Anna, Grandpa Griffiths asked Uncle Harry to marry your mum. But he didn't want to. So John did instead; he felt sorry for her. She'd been going with the man who later married Auntie Bea and he spread rumours in the village, said she was loose. So John stepped in and married her. He was a good man, Owen.'

Owen had sunk down onto a huge slab of stone, his head bent forward,

'It might not be true, Owen. None of it might be true.'

'But it all makes sense: things people said; him leaving me that money; how Mum talked about my grandfather—how she sort of admired and hated him; Auntie Bea; how it used to be the family joke—that auntie Bea's husband always had a soft spot for Mum. So they went out together?'

When they went back inside, it was almost three in the morning. They made tea and set kindling on the grainy glowing embers and huddled in front until the wood caught. Owen was holding Jan's hand, hanging onto it as though he was a child.

When Freya came down in the morning and found her parents huddled together on the settee, with blankets wrapped over them, she crept back upstairs. When she heard Ben clambering down, and then Macie after, she followed. Owen was in the kitchen making coffee and rummaging for paracetamol, Jan was poking at the fire, exclaiming that there still seemed to be glowing embers that she might be able to get the thing going again. When Freya scrutinised her, Jan looked embarrassed.

'Look at the snow! Look at the snow!' Macie had hauled open a curtain and was pointing out at a world made silent and white. The stretch of drive was thick with snow, and only some animal prints wound a drunken pattern from left to right down to the road to the bottom of the hill. The bushes drooped with a crusting of snow and Macie pointed at the soft flakes still drifting down, covering the parked cars with an even deeper layer.

'Those boys are there again, Mum.' Freya had pulled the curtain right back, letting a slash of light into the darkened room.

'Where?' Jan came to look. They were not on their bikes this time, but were across the field, down by the big barn, that might have once been a granary or the entrance for the monastery. It had thick walls, a huge opening that was now boarded up and, through some window slits, her children had noticed piles of straw or hay. The boys—Jan supposed they were local children if they could reach the farm on foot—had clambered up the side of the building and were dropping one by one through a gap in the top. Jan was not sure if she should phone someone, to suggest they might do damage. But then, one of their fathers might be the farmer whose sheep grazed in the nearby field, who owned the barn.

'I'm scared of them. They look at me.' Did that mean, Jan wondered, that Freya meant they looked at her sexually? In the last few months, Freya's shape had changed; she had grown a bust and got taller. It was only natural at thirteen, yet she still played with her dolls and wore as many layers as she could, even in summer.

'They won't hurt you.' Jan tried to sound assured, final.

'What's that?' Owen was carrying the pot of coffee on a tray and had brought out croissants for the children.

'Some boys. They've been hanging around; I think they're local lads.'

Owen went to the window.

'Looks like they're having a smoke. It's what fifteen year olds do.' Owen pulled Freya towards him for a cuddle, but she jerked away, and Ben slipped in between his father and half sister.

'Shall I butter the croissant for you, Ben?'

'I want Freya to. I love Freya.' Ben followed Freya across to the table and sat next to her.

She smiled down at him. 'We'll go out to the den later, Ben; we can have a picnic in the straw.'

'In this weather?' Owen looked unsure; he still felt the chill from the night before deep inside. He had barely slept, had kept circling around the unpalatable words, remembering scenes from childhood, things unspoken, things hinted at. He felt a fool that he had never noticed, that he had never pushed into the thick silence between his mother and the man she had married.

'We'll have to try and get a tractor to drag us out, Owen. We can't stay. Lois won't want us here, anyway. Are you going to be all right?' Jan gave him a solicitous look. She came across and rested her hand on his arm. 'Anna knows. Flinn doesn't.' Her voice was a whisper.

'Knows what?' Usually Freya paid no attention to the nuances of the adult world. Jan looked surprised that she had been listening.

'Nothing, luvvy. Just something Nanna Griffiths said.'

'Did she go to Spain for Christmas, after all?'

'Actually, no-one knows if she went there or to her friend in Cornwall.'

'No-one knows what?' It was Tom, dressed, with his rucksack over his shoulder and his walking boots on. 'You look lousy, hon.'

The tractor belonging to a nearby framer would haul their cars to the end of the lane, where the road was gritted and fairly clear. This would happen after lunch. Since there was space in her car, Jan had offered to take Freya and Macie home with her rather than leave them with Owen. But he had said that he thought he needed to make up lost time; Freya, especially, should stay.

'I've got to spread myself around my children, Jan. I can't just be a dad to Ben and not Freya.'

It was about mid-day and Macie had come in from the den; she always got tired first and wanted to watch the *Power Rangers* video again. Everyone else was in the huge kitchen that Lois had helped design for Merle. Jan had been complimenting her, hoping she could build on their friendliness from the night before.

'I love the way you've used lighting—and the shelves look brilliant. And I'd have never thought of using that corner so well.'

'Thanks, but it's my job, you know.' Lois smiled across at her, cautiously. 'It always seems to me that each job opens a door to a new vocabulary, a different perception of an area's possibilities. Anyone could do what I do, once they start to spend all their time thinking about it, reading about it. It's just that we don't have time to be everything.' Jan nodded her agreement back. Whatever she thought, she wouldn't have risked contradiction, wouldn't have risked wobbling this fragile friendship.

Jan and Owen stood side-by-side, chopping vegetables to make soup for lunch. From the window, they could see the outbuilding that Freya had turned into her den; it had a small window, low door, two rooms and another window at the rear. Freya had got Flinn and Macie to help her use straw bales to make beds, tables and chairs; she had already taken down cups and plates, blankets and crisps. Ben was running in and out of the door while Freya (who should have been too old for this game) was playing mummy, called him in to have his mid-day nap. This part, perhaps resembled Ben's reality too closely and he was hiding from her, peeping out of windows, then diving out of sight.

When Anna came into the room, looking grey and tired,

Jan saw that Anna could tell she knew about the pregnancy and that her father knew about Nanna.

'So are you going to offer me champagne or poison today, Mum?' She flopped down beside her father, who put his arm around her. He spoke for Jan.

'We could always poison our champagne? Or is alcohol poison for you these days?' Everyone else stared, apart from Jan, who concentrated on making the nubs of carrot and courgette neat and small.

'Mum?'

'It's okay love, it's okay.' And Jan hoped that the onion she had just chopped would explain the tears that started to trickle down the side of her nose. She thought it was strange that you could make courgette bits so tiny.

'Onions,' she announced, to make sure everyone else read the situation correctly, and then sniffed.

'It's those boys again,' said Flinn, and Lois put down the paper she had been reading to look curiously at the handsome sandy-haired boy whose mouth, when he smiled, reminded her of her own son's.

'They're climbing over the garden wall.' Flinn was fumbling with the back door, which Macie must have locked when she came in. She had a thing about keys and locks. From outside there was a scream. No game. Everyone jumped; Jan's knife skittered across the surface and onto the floor, Lois threw her paper aside and it scattered, pages separating.

'Where's the fucking key?' Flinn was sweeping his hand over surfaces, feeling desperately on ledges and on the side of the sink. They all pressed to the window, staring out at the bent, bare apple trees, and the white lawn with its pattering of footprints back and forth. Lois was pulling at the door, with the heavy lock that she had sourced herself to keep burglars at bay. 'Macie! Where's the fucking key?' It was the first time Flinn had sworn at her. Macie, standing in the hallway, near the entrance to the kitchen looked scared. When Flinn shouted again, she burst into tears and ran away.

Jan started to bang on the kitchen window. Freya was standing in the entrance of the den, her hair wild around her face, bits of straw sticking out of it, screaming in sharp yelps, like she was a wounded animal. Jan was signalling for her to run up to the kitchen, to come to them.

'Where's Ben. Where's Ben?' Lois was still holding the door handle, as she stared out through the toughened glass panels. She turned to Owen.

'Do something.'

'Is that mist or smoke?' Anna was pointing to the tiny window, out of which curled tendrils of white. In the next second there was flame, red licking flames out the window, and smoke billowing through the door. They watched Freya turn, amazed by what was happening in the den. Then she plunged back in through the doorway, into the enveloping dirty smoke.

By the time Owen, and then the rest had run out of the front door, around to the side and climbed over the snowy wall, the heat of the flames could be felt yards away. Everyone was half shouting, half sobbing, trying to get past the burn of heat to get inside, to get at the children. They could see through the open doorway the intense red of straw burning, could hear the crackling sounds of bales eaten by fire, could feel the thicker wood —the reserve wood pile— snapping in the heat. Owen had spread his jacket in the snow and was wrapping the wetness around his head so he could charge into the flames. Flinn had meanwhile wrestled the backdoor key from Macie and was running down the path with two buckets of sloshing water that everyone knew would make no impact. The flames were licking up the outside, blackening the doorframe and the beams above.

Behind their backs, the towers of the monastery reared up out of the whiteness of snow into the grey sky; rooks, flapping from arch to arch cawed in the quiet of the winter's day. Suddenly, from over the stone wall, that the outbuilding

217

abutted, a head poked up, then fell back again. The next time, the fair curls stayed there a moment longer, swaying above the six-foot wall before they disappeared. Lois was screaming her son's name, and everyone was running around, slipping in the snow, skirting the snapping and hideous burning den to get to the wall that stretched around the garden. Someone shouted, 'Keep clear of the glass in case it blows.' Jan scrambled up an apple tree, climbing as she had never dared to climb in her childhood, leaning right out so she could see over the other side of the wall. Her words came out in rasps so that no-one could hear her clearly.

'Both. Both. Okay. Both.'

In the snowy field below her, Freya was hoisting Ben up so he could scramble up the wall and back into the garden. Later, when they asked her why she had not gone straight around to the garden gate when she had first pushed Ben and herself out of the den window, she'd said she was afraid of the boys, afraid that they would touch her again. They had pushed her onto a straw bale and had pulled up her skirt. They had laughed when she had cried.

'Freya, go away from the fire. We'll come around for you. Get away from the den. Something may explode.' Jan scrambled back down the tree and everyone followed her out of the back gate, into the priory and then around into the field. They stumbled across the rutted earth, their feet drenched by the deep snow. Jan noticed that Lois had no shoes on and was just wearing socks; the bottoms of her black trousers were heavy and saturated. She and Lois rushed at the two children, scooping them up into their arms.

The fire brigade, called by Flinn, arrived when it was too late to do anything but douse water over the charcoaled building. Freya was not sure if the boys had set fire to the place on purpose or accidentally. They had been smoking, teasing her for making a house out of the place they used as their own den. One had asked if she had a boyfriend and had put his arm around her waist. She was not sure if he was teasing or serious. She was not sure exactly what they said or did. All she knew was that she started screaming. The boys had looked scared because she would not stop—she kept screaming and screaming. She remembered one saying 'We're out of here, she's crazy' and then they had pushed past to the back window and Ben had fallen off the straw and hurt his arm, and she had gone outside, until she saw the smoke.

Tom made the firemen tea. They filled up the kitchen in their heavy fireman clothes; their boots had come tramping in straw and snow and the smell of burning. Out in the garden, water was drenching the den and melting the snow in the garden. The stench of burnt wood filled the air. Freya and Ben were wrapped in blankets on the sofa, with Macie between them. They were watching *Power Rangers* and eating the chocolates that Jan had given Lois for Christmas. The grown-ups moved from the living room—checking continually that the two children were okay—to the kitchen where the firemen tried to establish what had happened.

'So some local boys were smoking you think?' Jan felt limp and shaky; she could see that Owen was breathing in a shallow tight way, that Lois' face was drawn, that Flinn was continually flicking off the lid of his zippo and clicking it back on. One of the fireman looked across, as if Flinn might have started the fire.

'We've seen them around. I don't know if they're local — but they have bikes.' Jan was sure she had already explained this once. The fireman had very blue eyes and his breath smelt of alcohol. He seemed restless, like he wanted to get away from them. Jan didn't know whether he, or one of the others, was in charge. Only Tom, childless Tom, seemed to be enjoying the excitement and the strange end to his holiday.

Owen said that he wanted to show Jan the place where he'd seen badgers the first time that he'd stayed with Lois. They set off across the field towards the stream and high banks. When they got out of sight of the house, he turned. The sun

219

was so bright, and the snow so sharply glinting, he had to squint.

'Do you forgive me?'

'For what?'

'Any number of things: breaking up the marriage, sleeping with my student, not being a good enough dad, marrying Lois. All the things I hear in your voice every time I phone up or drop in to pick up Freya.'

'Why do you want my forgiveness? What does it mean, anyway? I could mean it when I say it and then change my mind next time I got irritated with you.'

'Sometimes I feel like we're still married. I know what you're going to say. I hear your voice when Lois and I have rows; it's often about the same things.'

'Rows?'

'It's a real marriage. We have rows like everyone else. She's been good for me. I know you won't believe it, but she's very funny. She makes me laugh.'

'And I didn't?'

'Stop making me hurt you. There's no comparison. It's just different.' He stood there glumly. Perhaps he wanted to clear the ground, leave space for friendship. 'Are you serious about Tom? He seems a nice enough chap. Young.'

She laughed. 'Too young?'

'I suppose we all go through a phase of trying to get them young—and then realise that it creates complications. I didn't think I'd end up needing to be a father again, but Lois wanted children. Then I think she found out she didn't actually want them.'

'Is she really going back to the States?'

'Today she said she wasn't. She thought she would set up a web-site, get clients that way. She knew I didn't come to bed last night. Perhaps she's jealous.'

'Are you making her jealous now? I hope you're not going to try and kiss me again?'

'I'm sorry; I was drunk. And you'd just told me about my

220

father. Perhaps I wanted someone to love me. It was pathetic, I know.'

Jan turned and wandered toward the stream, breaking off a stick from a low hanging tree. She stirred the water, crossly.

'I don't want you dabbling in my life, making me unhappy for nothing.'

'What about if it amounted to something?'

'What are you saying?'

'I'm not quite sure.' Then he grabbed and shushed her— pointed downstream. A heron stood like a statue in the shallow water. Tall and grey, its ludicrous legs, like awkward stilts, stuck out of the rushing water.

'What do you want from me?' She was hissing at him, ignoring his attempts to make her be quiet. He gave up watching the stream and turned to look at the brown eyes fixed on him. He sighed. If he had told her that he wanted them back together, she knew it would have been true and not true.

'I want a simple life.'

'Ha!'

'You see. As soon as we're together, we row. It's impossible.'

'I forgive you. If that's what you want, you can have it. Simple. Have my forgiveness.'

If he had not heard clearly what she was saying to him, the heron had. It took off, flapping its great heavy wings up and down. Slowly, and with painful effort, it rose past overhanging bushes and trees and up into the open sky.

'Free, but hungry.' Owen stared regretfully as the huge bird flapped away from him.

'It will just go and fish somewhere else. Have another go in another place.' She took him by the arm and squeezed it. She would not believe anything he said right now. If she were in the counselling room, she would call it transference. He had lost a father and needed a mother.

'Like us?'

'Like us.'

They walked along the path a bit further. He showed her, without enthusiasm, the badger set he had brought her there to see.

'So you're going to come to London after New Year to take Freya back more often?'

'I will.' And as they realised what he'd said, they both laughed for a moment, embarrassed. She turned from him, listening to the rush of water, the cawing of crows. She was getting better at expecting less, at learning to live moment by moment.

'When I was a child I was always embarrassed by those dinners my dad cooked. All that ludicrous effort should have produced something great—or at the very least, something edible. Now I understand why he did it. You give and you take pleasure in the simple things: the seasons, making cakes, picking flowers, reading, dancing along to a CD. That's all there is, really.'

'Ben and I garden, press our faces up close to seedlings. It's what we do on Sundays—our religion. And there's the other stuff, too: music, art, books; they make a difference. More now I'm older. They stretch things, make life bigger.'

'You know Owen, I like my job, and I'm good at it, too, whatever you think. . I once thought I wanted to be a great painter, but that was kid's stuff—for me, anyway.'

'You're really good. You are an artist.' They both waited for the joke he and she used to make—piss artist, more like. But that time was past.

'I'm going to train to do art therapy. It's been helping Freya. We talk more—as we draw together.'

'She was talking yesterday—after the fire. Said she wasn't going back to the church anymore.'

'I'm glad. But there's still stuff she hasn't told me. I can't rush her, though.'

'We're so lucky that Freya and Ben are still alive. I keep getting flashbacks, and I can smell burning everywhere.'

222

'If my life stopped now, Owen, I'd say I'd been lucky, really. That it had been full of sweetness. Although I might say something different tomorrow.'

Owen had taken a stick and was idly poking at the snowy bank that was perhaps a mole-hill. Jan was standing with her back to him, staring up the mountain to where some greyish birds circled. She talked more to herself, than to him.

'Perhaps I'll do a better job with my grandchild. Flinn's going to do an Access course next year—see if he can get into Agricultural College; I said I'd help him with Macie. I'll make things fun for her.'

Owen was dragging the stick across the ground as if he were drawing on a white canvass.

'When you stand back from your life, imagine it as someone else sees it, it looks okay—'

'I like Lois.'

'Cheese!' Jan and Owen turned. Anna and Lois were watching them, camera poised. When they came up, Jan felt awkward, as if Lois must guess her husband had been courting his first wife. 'We've been talking about Freya.'

'She needs to spend more time with me. I just brought Jan up to see that badger set, and we were talking about Freya.'

'Sure.'

When Lois sent Jan the photo and she peered at herself, bundled up in Tom's thick coat, her nose all red from the cold and Owen, standing yards away, shoulders hunched over, it looked like a photo of two people estranged, awkward in each other's company. She wondered if that was what Lois had read, when she'd seen them standing together, or if she'd seen that other thing, vague and insubstantial, hanging by a thread between them, that Owen should brush away. When Anna and Jan looked at the photo more closely, at the birds circling overhead, that might have been gulls, and at the strange light that enveloped the valley, they saw in the muddy and grey river, just behind the two people on the

223

bank, a heron.

'I wonder if it was the same one?' said Jan. It was a smudged presence, hiding by the bushes, quietly fishing while the people in the photo looked away, unable to see what lay ahead of them or even what lay behind.